PRESCOTT PIONEERS BOOK 5

HIDDEN

PROSPECTS

Karen Baney

desert life
media

Prescott Pioneers Book 5: Hidden Prospects
By Karen Baney

Publisher:
Desert Life Media, LLC
Gilbert, AZ 85295

www.karenbaney.com

Printed in the United States of America

ISBN-978-0-9855862-7-0

To our home group,
thanks for being
a hidden treasure
and great blessing
in our lives.

———

I will give you hidden treasures,
riches stored in secret places,
so that you may know that I am the Lord,
the God of Israel, who summons you by name.
Isaiah 45:3

CHAPTER I

Near Prescott, Arizona Territory
April 17, 1869

Paul Lancaster closed the gate behind him and paused to take in the quiet morning air. A chorus of pine-scented breeze and the burble of Granite Creek greeted him like an old friend. He hadn't been out this way in weeks. Too many repairs at the boardinghouse, too many decisions about furniture and rugs for the new lodging house. Now, with the housekeeper handling breakfast and the boarders set to their routines, he finally had a day to himself.

Sunlight filtered through the towering pines and danced on the water. The placer mine sat just beyond the bend, tucked between jagged granite and patches of sage. He'd missed this—digging, sifting, and the promise of discovery. There was something honest about coaxing a living from the land with his own hands.

He adjusted the satchel slung across his shoulder and began the descent toward the mine. The trail curved down steeply. Birds chirped overhead. A squirrel darted across the path. Paul smiled. Prescott was growing, changing. So was he. For once, he allowed himself to feel proud.

Down at the creek bed, he rolled up his sleeves and shoveled a scoop of gravel and silt into the top of his shifters. The weight of it hit his shoulders as he bent low, gripping the frame in both hands. Back and forth. Slow and steady. He rocked the box over the water, letting the current rinse away debris. The mud and stones lingered in the upper screens. Tiny golden flecks slipped through into the catch basin below.

He leaned closer. Not much there today. Just a glimmer or two. No surprise. This mine never made him rich. Never would. It was more of a hobby, something to pass the time and enjoy the peace of nature. A man needed that, especially when the days ran long with bookkeeping, small talk, and cranky boarders.

The rhythm of the work settled his thoughts. His mind drifted—to the new furnishings, to the way Prescott shifted with each passing year. To the silence of the creek.

Then came the snap.

His body froze, his pulse racing.

A second later, the sharp crack of gunfire shattered the morning stillness. Paul dove behind a pine tree just as bark exploded beside him. The crack of gunfire ricocheted through the canyon, shattering the serene babble of Granite Creek below. Splinters burst from the trunk, needling his cheek and jaw. The sting made him flinch, and he tasted iron—either blood or adrenaline, he couldn't tell.

His lungs burned. Every breath was a battle. His ribs ached from the constant flexing.

Why didn't I stay at the boardinghouse? Instead, he'd chosen the mine. The worst mistake of his life.

He gritted his teeth and sprinted toward the next tree, the forest a blur of green and shadow. Heat lanced through his side— a burning sensation that stopped him midstride. His hand instinctively pressed the wound, and when he pulled it away, crimson glistened on his fingertips like fresh paint on raw wood.

A growl escaped his throat. He yanked the revolver from his belt and twisted around, half-blinded by the sting of sweat and the haze of pain. The figure behind him moved—an Apache warrior, fierce and fast, emerging from the trees. Paul aimed. His hand trembled, but the bullet hit true. The man dropped like a felled sapling.

Paul didn't linger. He holstered his gun and pushed forward, stumbling through underbrush. Whoosh. *Thwack.* An arrow embedded itself into the tree mere inches from his temple, vibrating with malice.

The sound of another shot split the air. He froze, bracing for the strike, but nothing came. The bullet must've missed—again. He didn't wait for a third chance. He tore off, his boots sliding over pine needles and loose rock. His breathing turned ragged, each gasp a desperate plea for survival.

The wound in his side pulsed with every movement. His vision blurred, curling at the edges like burnt paper. But up ahead—buildings. Prescott. Civilization. Safety.

"Come on, Paul." The voice echoed in his head, rough and familiar. His father's voice. *"Dig deep. You can make it. Give it everything you've got."*

He pushed harder. His legs felt like sandbags. His boots pounded against the dry, dusty path. Another tree exploded beside him. He barely registered the bark peppering his arm. He couldn't stop—not now.

Then, a sharp sting sliced through his calf. He grunted, stumbled, then dropped—face-first into the forest floor. Pine needles scratched his skin, and the earthy tang of moss and loam filled his nose. He lay motionless, dirt caking his lips, fire coursing through his limbs.

"Get up, Paul."

He couldn't. His legs refused. They were dead weight beneath him. Blackness crept in from the corners of his eyes, whispering surrender.

An arrow zipped past, grazing his shoulder.

He gasped. Eyes open. Chest heaving. *Keep going.*

Prescott. He had to reach it. Just a few more feet.

With a groan, he dug his fingers into the soil and shoved himself upright. His entire body screamed in protest, but he dragged one foot, then the other. The trees parted. A dusty street appeared.

"Paul!"

His name pierced the haze. Someone ran toward him. Relief

surged, cracking through the wall of pain. He tried to speak, lips dry and clumsy.

"Need…" he gasped. "Doctor."

His knees buckled. The world tilted. He hit the ground hard. The last sound he heard was his own voice, low and hoarse.

"I… killed him."

CHAPTER 2

Wickenburg, Arizona Territory
April 18, 1869

"Miss Pritchett, that was a lovely song," Mrs. Ritter said, reaching for Millie's hand on her way out of the meeting tent following Sunday services. "You have an angelic voice."

"Thank you," Millie replied as heat rose to her cheeks. Why had she let Dad talk her into singing the solo?

An awkward grin spread across the face of Stanley, Mrs. Ritter's youngest son, as he craned his head up to make eye contact with Millie. "Can't wait for your next solo, Miss Pritchett. Your voice is beautiful."

Millie's stomach turned over as she looked down at the much shorter man. She understood the look of interest sparking in his eyes. It brought forward memories of the past she wished would stop haunting her. She quickly turned to the person behind Stanley, feeling a little remorse for snubbing him.

There wasn't anything particularly wrong with Stanley. He was a nice enough young man. But his twenty-three years felt entirely too young compared to her thirty-seven. He had a sweetness about him that would endear him to the right young woman whenever he met her. *She* was not that woman.

Her mind fought against those old memories, the ones that would likely see her die an old maid. If she ever did find a man with whom she could share her heart, and if he was closer to her own age, he was sure to run when the day came to tell him her secret. All the others had.

A frown threatened to scrunch her forehead, but she managed to stop it in time. It wouldn't do to make the next parishioner think her sour expression was intended for him. She kept her feelings buried as the last member of her father's congregation exited the makeshift church.

As far as she was concerned, her first solo would also be her last. After today, her singing would be relegated to the front pew. She felt too uncomfortable with all those eyes staring at her—hanging on the flowing lyrics. To finish the song, she had closed her eyes and let her soul speak the words directly to her Heavenly Father. Perhaps that honest expression of worship had drawn the congregation in even more.

It didn't matter. There was no way she would allow Dad to talk her into it again.

"Millicent," he was saying to her, "They're right. You delivered the song so perfectly and sweetly. It was as if we stood before the throne of glory and listened to all of heaven praising Him."

Now she let her frown show.

"You'll have to plan another song in a few weeks. Especially if you're trying to catch yourself a husband." He winked at her.

"Dad, I'm not trying to catch a husband. And certainly not with a song of praise to the Lord."

His face sobered. "Sweetheart, I was just teasing. But perhaps it is time for you to think about finding a mate."

She fought the urge to roll her eyes. He knew better than anyone that she would never marry.

Dad took one last look around the meeting tent and then offered her his arm. They stepped out into the bright noon sun. She squinted until her eyes adjusted to the intense light.

The meeting tent wasn't far from home.

"I see Mason's new saloon is open." She gestured toward the clapboard building across the dusty street. She hoped Dad would take the bait.

Dad frowned. "On Sunday, too. We now have one church

for every four saloons."

They fell into silence during the walk. The warm sun beat down on the back of Millie's lavender dress. With little touches of lace near the collar and running down the row of decorative buttons in the front, it was her favorite. Even with no mirror in sight, she knew how the color of this dress made the violet in her eyes more prominent. Perhaps if she had worn her dull gray work dress, Stanley Ritter would not have been so mesmerized.

As they walked past Mason's original saloon, the sound of the tinny keyboard and off-pitch singers assaulted her ears, nearly undoing the glorious feeling of worship from that morning.

Dad had been adamant when they first arrived in Wickenburg that the church should be centrally located. Little did either of them know that seemed to be the same plan the saloon owners had. It seemed strange to walk by so many saloons to get to and from church on Sunday morning.

Soon enough they passed the last saloon on the main street of town. Dad led them down another street, and they walked by several businesses including a tailor, the Ritter's stage stop, and Bradburn's Mercantile. Thankfully, most of the saloons were built further away from the respectable businesses.

They finally arrived at the small house Dad built. The house faced east, with a modest porch shading two rocking chairs from the heat of the day.

As her father held the door open for her, the savory smell of roast drew them in.

"Smells good," Dad said.

She stepped into the small parlor that doubled as her father's study. On the days he spent at home he could usually be found sitting at the desk in front of the window working on his sermon. Two wingback chairs faced the fireplace.

Off to the left was the entryway to their bedrooms. Off to the right, was the entry to the kitchen. She set her reticule on the mantle.

She noticed her dad's serious expression and quickened her pace to the kitchen.

"I'm serious, Millicent." She heard the muted sound of him setting his things on his desk. The soft thud of his footsteps stopped just inside of the kitchen.

"It's time for you to stop taking care of your old dad and start taking care of a husband."

So much for hoping he would forget about their earlier conversation. What had gotten into him?

"You're a strong woman—"

She snorted as she secured her apron to the front of her dress. If only he knew her heart.

"—but you can't shy away from love forever."

Using the edge of her apron, she lifted the roast from the oven. She set it down on top of the stove with a clunk and turned to face him.

"Who said I'm running away from love? Who do you think I'm in love with?"

Her father sighed heavily. "I don't suspect anyone at present. You cut them off before giving them a chance. Like you did with Stanley Ritter this morning."

"Dad, you can't be serious. He's young enough to be my son!" The words came out before their full meaning hit her heart, slamming it fiercely against her chest. Her eyes and soul burned.

Her father reached for her hand. "I know he's the same age as—"

"Don't." Millie fought back tears.

Dad cleared his throat several times before releasing her hand. He paced back and forth across the length of the kitchen, stopping in front of the small window above the washbasin.

She turned her attention back to finishing supper, filling a serving platter with the roast and the vegetables, and carrying everything to the table.

The light from the window highlighted the gray in Dad's hair, making him look older than he was. His hands were stuffed in his pockets and a frown etched deep lines in his forehead.

She sprinkled a spoonful of flour into the pan and began whisking. The mixture bubbled, thickening into gravy.

"Millie, I've been meaning to talk to you for a few days now."

She stopped whisking and glanced over her shoulder to see in his eyes an intensity matched by the edge in his voice. She was sure she would not like what was coming next.

"Do you remember Mabel?"

"Widow Cleary?"

"Yes."

She nodded.

"You know that she and I have corresponded for some time now."

He cleared his throat at her second nod.

"Mabel and I... That is, we've decided..."

"To get married." Millie's throat constricted as she finished his sentence.

Somehow, she knew this day was coming. Every time Dad received a letter from Widow Cleary, his eyes lit up with unrestrained excitement. He would retreat to his desk and pour over the letter several times before he shared the highlights with Millie. She supposed it was only a matter of time before Widow Cleary completely won his heart.

Was he ready to let go of Mother after all these years? She had been gone so long now that Millie stopped counting the holidays and special events that went on without her. Perhaps time had finally done the same for Dad.

"I know it's hard to understand. I loved Nia with all my heart for every second that I had with her. Your mother has been gone almost twenty years. I miss her so much." Her father's voice thickened with emotion. "Mabel is different. So very different from her. She could never replace your mother, but I do love her."

She stood on the opposite side of the table from him, crossing her arms over her chest.

His eyes begged her to understand. She did but she didn't. She had lost the man she loved through the worst betrayal of her life, and it had shaped her into the taciturn woman she was now. She understood love—and losing it—and so to some extent, she could understand Dad's desire to find it again. But she had long since given up on that dream for herself.

She dropped her arms to her side, stuffing her emotions away. "When is she coming?"

"Soon. She's waiting for a letter from me, and then she'll board the next stage."

"And what of me?"

Dad looked away.

Ah. That's what this was all about.

"You're a brave woman, Millicent. I've seen you aim a rifle at a criminal's chest. You sang before the congregation this morning. You are stronger and more independent than you credit yourself."

Her stomach knotted. He didn't want her to be alone because of his moving on. But didn't he know that no one would have her? She had accepted it; why couldn't he? She sat down at the table as Dad took the seat across from her, doubting that she would be able to enjoy Sunday supper.

"I know Caroline Anderson has asked you up to Prescott several times. Perhaps now would be a good time for a visit—or even a move. The town is bigger than Wickenburg. There are more opportunities…"

"You want me to move to Prescott?" Millie failed to keep the hurt from her voice.

"Sweetheart, I've thought long and hard about what might be best for you at this stage of your life. There really are more opportunities for you there than in Wickenburg. There's a boardinghouse that is safe for women boarders, should you decide to stay. All I'm asking is that you consider a visit to your friend. Go and see for yourself what the town is like."

She dished up a helping of the roast and vegetables onto her plate, and then she held out her hand for Dad's plate. "When were you planning I leave?"

"On next Wednesday's stage."

She thrust the full plate towards him and closed her eyes. Ten days. He was sending her away in ten short days.

There were all sorts of reasons why she should stay longer. He would need her to cook and clean for him for several weeks or even a month before Widow Cleary arrived. Wouldn't he want the house to look perfect for her? As soon as the argument came it left. She'd disobeyed her father in her youth, and it had cost her so much—too much. She vowed from then on to be obedient, and so she had moved from Santa Fe so her father could start his mission to save the lost souls of the miners in Wickenburg. Now she would leave.

Millie gathered up more enthusiasm than she felt. "I'll begin packing my things tomorrow."

CHAPTER 3

A few days later, Millie left the house and headed down toward the Hassayampa River, more restless than ever.

She heard the stamp mills long before she could see the river itself. More than once, she had walked down to the river's edge. The first time after moving to Wickenburg, it had been quiet. Then she learned that the stamp mills rarely stopped their rhythmic clanging as they pulverized gold ore into dust. At first, she hated the sound, but over time it grew on her. There was something about the *clang-clang-chug* of the large metal pistons beating against the round metal bases that became a source of comfort.

Clang-clang-chug. Clang-clang-chug.

Millie looked around for the dead and dried out carcass of a saguaro cactus. It reminded her of her favorite dead log back in the forest near her childhood home, only the dead cactus had gaps between the long spines that had once helped it stand tall and proud near the river shore. She sat down on it, rubbing her hand along the smooth surface.

Clang-clang-chug.

She watched as water sprayed a light mist over the men standing near the basin beneath the stamp mill. Each one lifted a shovel full of silt and carried it to a large spinning wheel, meant to further refine the silt until only gold remained.

Her life wasn't so different from the gold ore. Her heart had been a tangled mess, far from pure, intertwined with guilt and false hope. Then, little by little, God had refined parts of it. He had even crushed her a few times to do so.

She felt the weight of that now. What could God possibly have in store for her this time? Dad was sending her away.

The sting of his decision was still raw on her heart. She was going to a new town to live a new life. Except he hadn't even asked her if that was what she wanted. He never did. She hadn't wanted to move from Santa Fe to Wickenburg in the first place. But she had maintained her role as an obedient daughter.

Now that same obedience was leading her away from the only family she had left.

A tear slid down her cheek. Did all their time together mean nothing to him?

She sniffed. Mom would say Millie was being unfair. That meant a lot to him, but her well-being meant more. It was for her own good that he was sending her away.

Whom would she rely on? No one would know her like Dad did. No one would comfort her in sadness or laugh with her in joy.

Please, Lord, don't make me face the next stage of my life alone. I cannot bear it.

What had Dad called her? Courageous. Hardly.

Millie remained by the river for a few more minutes, until the sound of the stamp mills seemed to match the frantic pace of her worries. Today, they hadn't helped. Instead, they fed her anxious thoughts until she could stand it no more.

Clang-clang-chug.

She stood and trudged back home, still searching for peace for her pending move.

———

Millie retrieved her wooden stationary desk from her room and set it on the kitchen table. She had the house to herself, and she could delay no longer. It would only be right to let Caroline know she was planning a visit.

She slid a sheet of paper from the stationary, dabbed the pen in the inkwell and started to write. "Dear Caroline. My father is getting married and sending me away…"

She crumpled the paper before the ink dried then she stood and tossed the paper into the stove's fire. A bird sat on the clothesline outside the kitchen window, chirping a light melody.

Her thoughts drifted to her mother. If she had lived to Millie's thirty-seventh birthday, would she have pushed her out? Probably. Maybe even long before now. Mother had always encouraged her to be more independent.

Had her heart broken with Millie's when suitors fled?

She wiped away a tear from her cheek. No matter how much time passed, she never looked back on her journey to adulthood with anything other than sorrow. So much had been taken. So much of it, through her own fault.

Slowly the tune of her mother's favorite hymn rolled around in her mind. She allowed the music to fill her heart and rise from her lips.

Blest is the man whose softening heart
Feels all another's pain;
To whom the supplicating eye
Was never raised in vain:

Whose breast expands with generous warmth
A stranger's woes to feel;
And bleeds in pity o'er the wound
He wants the power to heal.

He spreads his kind supporting arms
To every child of grief:
His secret bounty largely flows,
And brings unasked relief.

To gentle offices of love
His feet are never slow:

He views, through mercy's melting eye,
A brother in a foe.

He, from the bosom of his God,
Shall present peace receive—
And when he kneels before the throne,
His trembling soul shall live.

Millie closed her eyes, slowly breathing in and out. Her lungs emptied, as did her heart, and she sat down to write the letter. She kept it short and to the point. She would be arriving on the stage next Wednesday and wished to stay with Caroline for a week. She resolved to find her own place by the end of that week.

Somehow, she would find a way to make Prescott her home.

She sighed and looked out the window, remembering how she'd met Caroline several years ago. As Millie and her dad got ready for the move to Wickenburg, Millie had spied an advertisement at one of the shops in Santa Fe. A young lady from Texas was looking for a chaperone to the Arizona Territory.

Millie had discussed the advertisement with her dad and responded, offering to escort the young lady if she was headed toward Wickenburg.

Caroline had arrived in Santa Fe with her eldest brother a few weeks later and explained the reason for her move. Her best friend and other brother had both moved to a ranch outside of Prescott, and she had managed to convince her overly cautious parents to let her join them.

Once Dad had established his new church in Wickenburg, he planned to escort Caroline the rest of the way to Prescott by stage. Caroline had never been a patient woman and snuck off on her own only a week after they had arrived. The choice had almost cost her life when the stage was robbed and she was stranded in the desert, left to fend for herself. In the end, she made it to Prescott.

Millie recalled the journey from Santa Fe, smiling at the memory of her friend's enthusiasm.

"Look at all the glorious colors of the sunset, Millie!" Caroline had exclaimed. She even gushed over the fact that there was an outhouse available at one stop along the way. For nearly an hour Caroline talked about her hopes that the Arizona Territory would be more civilized.

She had admired Caroline's friendliness. Despite her chatty nature, she had listened with interest when Millie spoke. She had even been responsible for shortening Millie's full name.

"It just suits you better." Caroline's voice echoed teasingly in her memory. "Millicent's too formal for you."

She had been right.

There had been a time when Millie allowed herself the same freedom Caroline exhibited—but no more. The only thing she did with exuberance now was sing.

She stood and looked around the room. The faded coffee pot sat in its place on the back of the stove. The ceramic bowl adorned with turquoise paint, a gift from Dad after Mom's passing, sat in the middle of the table with a loaf of bread she baked that morning. Should she take it with her? It didn't seem right to separate it from all the other dishes it had complimented over the years.

A tear rolled down her cheek as she fingered the handmade checkered towel hanging over the back of one of the chairs.

Soon she would leave all of it behind. She would start a new life—one without her dad—on her own, whether she wanted to or not.

CHAPTER 4

Stinging. Burning. *Ouch!* Paul woke up to the pain.

"Lie still."

"Ma?" Paul's eyes flew open. His mother's face blurred in his vision. He blinked a few times, and her face came into focus.

He looked around the small room. Glass-front cabinets lined one wall. A wooden chair sat next to a small table beside the bed. The odor of carbolic acid caused his eyes to water and his head to spin. Light spilled through a window behind Ma, giving her an almost angelic appearance.

"Where—"

More liquid bit into his side. He moaned.

"Go easy on him, Doc." Ma's voice sounded far away as he closed his eyes.

A warm hand patted his.

"Ma?"

"I'm right here."

He opened his eyes again. This time Doc Hank smiled down at him.

"You're one lucky man. Bullet went clear through the fleshy part of your side. One in your leg came out with no problems."

He started to sit up, but Doc held him down. "Don't think you should move just yet."

"When can I take him home?" Ma's voice was strained—a tone he hadn't heard since his early twenties.

"I'd like to keep him here for another day. Let's see how he fares now that he's awake."

"Are you sure?"

"Betty, he'll be just fine. I'll be back to check on him later."

When Doc closed the door, Ma sat down.

"You nearly took a decade off my life!"

Paul's head started to swim again. He closed his eyes.

"Oh no you don't." Ma swatted his arm. "You stay with me, Paul."

Typical Ma. He forced his eyes open. "What happened?"

Fear creased her forehead. Hints of red edged her eyes. Wisps of disheveled gray hair framed her face. She looked older than he remembered.

She pulled her handkerchief from her sleeve and dabbed at her eyes.

"Ben and I came in for Sunday service only to learn you were at Doc Hank's nearly dead."

"Nearly dead?"

"Well, unconscious at least. I didn't know how bad it was at first." She reached for his hand and squeezed it. "I was afraid I lost you."

Paul gave her a weak smile. "Takes more'n a few bullets to get rid of me."

The return smile he was hoping for never came.

"Ben stayed with me the first night, but he had to get back to the ranch. I've barely left your side. I was so worried you might really go to glory this time."

"You make it sound like I get shot on a regular basis."

She withdrew her hand. "You know what I mean."

Paul stared down at the wrinkles in her blue dress.

"Ma, I'm not the same man."

"I know that." Her arms crossed defensively. "It's just that... I never did like you working that placer mine. It's too dangerous."

Paul frowned and shifted his position. The movement sent pain shooting up his leg. He gritted his teeth.

Ma jumped up from the chair and hovered over him. "Are

you alright? What hurts? Should I get Doc?"

The pain subsided. He let out a slow breath. "I'm fine. Sit down."

Ma did as he asked. Silence settled over the room.

Paul glanced at his bandaged leg. Mining did have its risks. But for him, the rewards far outweighed them.

When he'd first moved West with Ma and staked his claim along Granite Creek, it had been a lot more dangerous. None of the miners could work their placers alone without fear of being killed by Apache. As Prescott expanded and grew closer to the mines, it had become much safer.

Except for recently. He frowned. He wasn't the first miner to be attacked in the past few months.

"I really wish you'd just sell the darn thing." Ma's soft voice broke through his thoughts.

"Ma—"

"Just hear me out."

He closed his mouth.

"I'm really worried about you, Paul. I'm not here to take care of you anymore. And you don't have a wife—"

"Don't start on that again, Ma. You've been at it for months."

"It is not good for man to be alone."

"Now you're quoting scripture." He thought about quoting the verse where the Apostle Paul advocated staying single. It wouldn't help.

"You're not getting any younger. I want grandchildren."

"Your grandchildren live in Missouri. Maybe you should go back."

The shock on Ma's face instantly made him regret the words. She looked down at her hands for several minutes.

"I couldn't ask Ben to leave the ranch. All I really want is for you to be happy."

He wasn't unhappy. He liked his life. Running the boarding-house. Mining. They were both fulfilling.

A pang of loneliness shot through him, and he sighed.

"I would love to find a wife, Ma. I really would."

"But?"

He looked away. No one wanted him. He was too old for the single young ladies, like Grace Talbert and her peers. His only other option were widows, but it didn't seem right somehow to pursue one—if there even were any close to his age. Anytime he got up the courage to court a lady, some other man swooped in and took her away. Not surprising; men in town still outnumbered the women four to one.

Ma reached out and rubbed his arm. "Look at me, Paul."

He did.

"God has the right woman for you. I've always prayed for her and for you. You'll meet her one day." She smiled. "Who knows, maybe she'll arrive on the next stage?"

Paul laughed. A mail order bride did not appeal to him. He wanted to get to know the woman face to face and not through a bunch of letters.

A knock sounded at the door. Ma stood and let Sheriff Smith into the small clinic room.

"Glad to see you're awake. Heard you had some trouble." Sheriff Smith stepped closer to the bed, working his hat in his hands. The badge on his brown vest glistened in the light from the window. He wore a white button-down shirt beneath it. His brown trousers looked like they might slip off his wiry frame if not held up by the double gun belt. At thirty-eight, Paul had a few years on the sheriff. But Smith's age had not hindered the respect of the citizens of Prescott.

"You feeling up to talking about what happened?"

"Sure. Ma, can you help me?"

Ma stood and propped several more pillows behind Paul as he leaned against the headboard. His leg throbbed, though with less intensity than when he had tried to shift his position earlier.

"I left Mrs. Feldman in charge at the boardinghouse this morning—er, a few days ago—and headed out to my placer. I hadn't been out there in almost two weeks. Things were fine at first. A lot of the other miners around my claim seemed to be taking the day off, so it was quieter than normal."

He closed his eyes to conjure the scene in his mind.

"Heard a twig crack behind me, like someone was sneaking up on me. When I turned around, there were three Apache braves pointing their weapons at me. One had a gun. The other two had bows and arrows."

"I ran toward the closest tree I could find, and they opened fire. I hid, but they kept getting closer, so I knew I had to defend myself. I killed one of them."

"You sure you shot him dead? We didn't find any bodies when we went out to your placer that afternoon."

Paul nodded. "Shot him in the chest. Don't see how he could have survived." A shiver ran down his back. No matter the man's race, he still felt terrible about taking a life.

Lord, forgive me.

"Hmm." The sheriff rubbed his chin. "Maybe they took the body back with them. We did find three sets of tracks. But that seemed odd, too. Most of the time, the Apache are more careful. It's almost like they wanted us to know they were there."

"Yeah. Something else bothers me. Never seen an Apache with a gun before."

"Me either. They don't usually have any ammunition for 'em if they come across one."

Paul frowned. "You don't think someone from town is supplying them with weapons, do you?"

"Not sure. Did hear that Simon Talbert's been buying up quite a few of the placers around you."

Paul narrowed his eyes. Talbert's approach last week was still stuck in his craw. What was Talbert up to? Didn't he have enough money already?

"Yeah. Guess he's buying 'em up, then hiring the former owners to work the claims." No point in mentioning that the claims had barely even been worked since then.

Sheriff Smith nodded. "Heard that too. You sure it was Apache?"

"I didn't really get a good look." Paul shook his head. There *was* something, but…

"Let me know if you think of anything else," Sheriff Smith said as he opened the door.

"Will do."

As the door closed behind the sheriff, Ma wagged a finger at him. "I told you it isn't safe to be out there."

Paul frowned as his energy faded. He was tempted to agree with Ma after this attack. Tempted to give up on his dreams.

CHAPTER 5

Doc Hank had good news the next morning. "You're cleared to go home. Just take it easy for a few days. Might be best to stay around town."

Paul held back a snort as he pushed himself up from the bed. Now Ma had the doctor hounding him about mining.

"Betty is waiting for you at the boardinghouse. Said she would send someone to help you home."

"I'm fine." Paul took a few steps to prove it. Pain burnt a fiery path from his side and wrapped around his middle, squeezing the breath from his lungs. He forced a smile to his face. "See?"

Doc Hank's eyebrow arched on his forehead. "I see very well."

"At least you're still breathing." Thomas Anderson limped into the room.

Relief flooded Paul, quickly followed by guilt. His closest friend was not the right man for the job. His other friend, Jake Waters, would have been a better choice.

A few years ago, Thomas had badly injured his leg. He had been caught in a snowstorm while riding the mail from Prescott to Wickenburg. A stranger had found him and taken him to the nearest shelter, a ranch between Prescott and Wickenburg.

After months of rest, he finally returned to Prescott, everything healed except for the bowed leg. He had never been able to walk normally since then.

Thomas offered his shoulders as support.

Paul lightly looped one arm over them, careful not to put much weight on him and both shuffled out of the clinic.

"How are you feeling?"

Paul gritted his teeth as they stepped off the boardwalk. "Fine."

"Hmm. Well, your mother gave me strict instructions to send you right to bed."

"I'm sure she'll be waiting at the door."

Thomas laughed and his gait slowed. "If you squint, I think you can see her sitting on the porch."

Paul shifted, lightening the weight he placed on his friend. They stopped and waited for a wagon to roll down the wide dusty road before continuing toward the town square. It was his favorite feature of the town. Only a few trees had been cleared from the area, leaving handfuls of cottonwoods and junipers to provide shade during events. Saloons and houses of ill repute lined one side of the square, along with the water well. On the opposite side stood several clapboard buildings. His boardinghouse, dining hall, and bunkhouses were among them. Numerous other businesses lined the remaining two sides.

The smell of pine lifted his spirits. A low layer of clouds crowded the sky, and a cool breeze rustled the leaves of the branches overhead. A perfect day to work at the mine.

"Heard it was Indians that shot at you," said Thomas.

"I think so. It was hard to tell."

"Well, Caroline and I have been praying for you."

"Thank you." A wave of pain pulsated from his thigh. He needed to think about something else. "How's the livery?"

"Doing well. I wasn't sure I'd be able to handle the competition when the fourth one in town opened. Hasn't hurt my business at all."

"Town's growing fast."

"Yeah. Surprised a lot of people that the town didn't shrivel up when the capital moved to Tucson two years ago. Guess the perfect weather appeals to the masses."

Paul smiled. Most of their rain came during the winter, and even then, it only lasted an hour or two. The summer rains were just as mild.

Thomas stopped in front of the boardinghouse porch. "Here we are."

Ma descended the stairs, arms eagerly outstretched to receive him.

"Come on. Let's get you to bed."

Paul rolled his eyes. Surely, he could manage the task by himself.

Thomas ducked out from under Paul's arm. "Can you make it?"

"Yup. Thanks."

"Anytime. Stay out of trouble."

Paul laughed as Ma put her arm around his waist. "I'm sure this lady will keep me in check."

Thomas waved and started his awkward shuffle-walk towards his livery.

"Are you feeling okay? You look a bit piqued."

"I'm fine, Ma."

She held the door open. As soon as he crossed the threshold scents of home filled his lungs. Apple pie. Beef stew. A hint of pine.

"Mr. Lancaster." Mrs. Feldman greeted him in her lilting Irish accent. "Glad to have you home, sir."

"Do I smell pie?"

"That ye do, sir. Your ma insisted I have your favorites ready."

"Would you like something to eat before resting?" Ma asked. "Wait, no. We should probably get you to bed first. Then I can bring a tray."

Paul cracked an unseen smile, warmed by his ma's care.

"I'll get it ready for ye, Mrs. Shepherd." Mrs. Feldman hurried down the hall toward the kitchen as Ma helped him to his bedroom on the first floor.

Paul lay on his back and stretched one arm over his head, staring at the ceiling of his small room. Everything looked as it always did. Near the door and opposite his feather bed—a gift from Ma—a pitcher of water and a small bowl for washing sat on the dresser. His handcrafted desk still stood next to the window. On the nightstand next to him laid his Bible.

Home.

A flash of a memory from the forest knotted his stomach, sobering his joy.

Lord, that was too close.

Ma knocked on the door and entered with the promised tray of food. He scooted up the bed and leaned against the hard wooden frame. Ma set the tray on his lap then stood by his side as he ate.

The savory beef stew melted in his mouth. In no time he finished it off and started on the apple pie.

"Ben is in town for deliveries. He wants me to come home with him. Will you be fine without me?"

Paul winked at Ma. "I think so."

"Good." She placed a kiss on his forehead and finger combed his hair—something she hadn't done since he was a little boy. Then she rested her hand on his shoulder, letting out a long sigh.

"Don't you dare scare me like that again, Paul."

He reached up and took her hand from his shoulder. He squeezed it and then released it. "Don't worry. Remember, God is watching out for me."

She swatted at his arm. "You don't have to make His job so difficult." A smile graced her lips.

"Sure, I do. I didn't go easy on you, did I?"

"No, you didn't."

She took the tray from his lap and walked towards the door, glancing over her shoulder. "I love you, Paul."

"I love you, too."

He scooted down in the bed, thanking God that she had come West with him after all.

———

Friday arrived, and Paul knew it was time to return to his normal routine. He had restlessly wandered from room to room yesterday, frustrating poor Mrs. Feldman. His housekeeper was close to his mother's age, though her hair had only recently started losing its copper sheen. She had come to work for him a few months after his ma moved out to the ranch, after losing her husband of nearly thirty years. Her children were spread out all over the country. Some were working on the railroad. Others were trying their luck at mining. None of them had the funds to care for their mum, she'd said.

The calluses on her hands proved she was no stranger to hard work. His instincts had been right.

Today was wash day. Both Mrs. Feldman and Mrs. Peng could use his help hauling water. He grabbed two buckets from the kitchen and headed toward the well.

Mr. and Mrs. Peng, a sweet Chinese couple, had arrived in Prescott several years ago. They were the first of their kind in the town. Ma had convinced them to work for her instead of opening a laundry down the street. She desperately needed extra hands in the dining hall and bunkhouses. Paul had done his fair share to help but was relieved as the couple took to their roles.

Paul carried the full bucket across the plaza looking over the cluster of buildings that comprised Lancaster's Boardinghouse.

The two bunkhouses, Mother Lode and Gold Rush, stood on the far edge of his property. Those two plus the dining hall were the first he'd built when he and Ma arrived. All the boarders in the bunkhouses were men. Some worked at the sawmill in town, others ran their own placer mines, and a few worked at other establishments elsewhere in town.

Ma's pride and joy had been the dining hall. In the early days she had insisted on serving three meals a day, even though most of their boarders worked through the noon hour. It had been a wise decision; several of Prescott's government officials and business owners chose to eat their midday meal at Lancaster's—a tradition that lived on to that day.

As Paul neared where Mrs. Feldman and Mrs. Peng set up the

wash basin between the two bunkhouses, a sharp pain in his side caused him to wince.

"You look tired," Mrs. Feldman said. "Go sit on the porch, and I'll bring you some lemonade."

He dumped the cool water into the steaming basin and took a seat on the boardinghouse porch in his favorite rocking chair. Mr. Peng dumped out the dishwater from the morning into his garden, and then disappeared back into the dining hall.

In the early days, two rooms in the back of the dining hall had served as living quarters for Paul and his ma. After he gave up his room for women boarders on several occasions, he finally decided to build a more traditional home-style place to welcome them. It had a private room for his mother downstairs, now occupied by the widowed Mrs. Feldman, and another for himself. The rest of the downstairs included a large parlor, dining room, and kitchen. Upstairs were five guest rooms, with four of the five currently occupied, and a washroom.

Paul rocked back and forth, his eyes growing droopy.

Sometime later, he wasn't sure how long, Mrs. Feldman woke him.

"I have your lemonade."

He smiled and took the glass from his housekeeper. "Thank you."

As Mrs. Feldman started to enter the boardinghouse, Mr. Lowrey exited the building while frantically waving a shirt in Mrs. Feldman's face.

"Woman! You call this starched? It is flimsy and barely free of wrinkles."

"Free of wrinkles it was when I hung it in your closet. What do ya expect to happen with ya waving it like a flag?"

"I am not waving it like a flag. I am trying to show you how poorly you have cared for my shirt."

Mr. Lowrey growled and stormed back into the boardinghouse.

Mrs. Feldman whirled around with hands on her hips. "That man!"

"Complainin' he was about breakfast this mornin'. Now tis the way I launder his clothes."

"The shirt looked fine to me."

She ignored Paul's affirmation and rambled on. "Always finding fault, he is, with the way I do things."

"I'll talk to him," Paul said trying to reassure Mrs. Feldman, though her assessment of Mr. Lowrey's nature was pretty accurate. He was a cantankerous man that valued his privacy. Probably wouldn't do any good to talk to him, but he'd try again.

Some of the fire left Mrs. Feldman. As she turned to go back inside, she thanked him.

Those two would make an interesting couple, if they ever got past their differences. Paul grunted. Maybe he had spent too much time with his ma over the last few days. Now she had him looking for matches between his boarders.

———

Wednesday morning, Paul felt well enough to tackle some repairs. There was that leak in the barn—Ma would scold him if he got up on the roof so soon after being shot. Perhaps he should stick with some of the easier tasks for now.

He grabbed his toolbox from the barn and walked the grounds. He neared the Mother Lode and stopped to examine the door. Still hanging crooked.

He inspected the hinges. Sure enough, a couple nails were missing. He dug around in the toolbox for the right size nails, hammered the hinge back in place, and swung the door open and shut a few times to test it.

That'll do nicely.

"Lancaster!" a voice called from behind him.

Paul turned to face Levi Brooks. "Levi, what brings you by?"

Levi wasn't smiling. It wasn't like the tax collector to stop by, except for an occasional meal at the dining hall. But it was too early for lunch.

"I need to talk to you."

Paul leaned down and picked up his toolbox, careful not to bump it against his injured leg. "It's a nice day out. Let's go sit on the porch."

As soon as Paul took a seat, Levi paced frantically across the length of the porch, the floorboards creaking underfoot.

"I hate to bring bad news but seems that's all I got today."

Paul frowned. "Out with it, Brooks. Stop beating around the bush."

"I don't have any record of tax payments from Lancaster's Boardinghouse for '64 or '65."

"What? Ma and I have been paying taxes every month since we started the place in February of '64. What do you mean you don't have record?"

"Sorry, Paul. I started audits on the older businesses in town this week. And, well, record of your payments start in '66."

He narrowed his eyes. "Are you sure your predecessor didn't file them wrong?"

Levi stopped pacing and looked directly at him. "I checked everywhere. Didn't find any record for those two years."

Paul swallowed hard.

"If you can't provide receipts, then I'm afraid you'll have to pay the back taxes plus a penalty."

"Wait just a minute. We already paid those taxes. What do you mean we'd have to pay again?"

"No record usually means no taxes were paid. So, you either must show receipts or pay up three-thousand—"

"Three-thousand!" Paul stood to his feet and took a step closer to Levi.

Levi cleared his throat. "Three-thousand four-hundred and thirty-seven dollars to be precise."

"How do you figure that? It's more than double what I've paid over the last two years combined."

"I'm sorry, but the territorial laws are clear. There's a steep fine for late tax payments."

Levi moved toward the stairs. "Stop by my office when you have the receipts or the cash."

Paul shook his head. He didn't have that kind of money lying around. Most of what he did have was tied up in the boardinghouse.

He watched as Levi walked across the town square and down the street towards his office.

How could he not have a record of payments for those early years?

Paul stalked through the house until he came to his room. He swung the door open so hard it slammed against the wall. He had to find those receipts and prove that Levi was wrong.

CHAPTER 6

Millie watched her father's form as the stagecoach pulled away from Wickenburg. First his face went out of focus, then the details of his suit, then all of him morphed into a distant shadow until she could see him no more.

When would she see him again? He promised that he and Mabel would visit soon after their wedding.

Millie's eyes burned, and not from the dust billowing up from the desert floor.

She shifted her gaze to the interior of the stage. Only three other passengers were bound for Prescott today.

Hour after hour blurred together. Thundering of horse hooves. Jingling harnesses. After ten minutes, she had stopped trying to keep herself from bumping into the passenger next to her. Her jaw grew sore from clenching it as they bounced over another rough patch in the road. Even though it was April, the inside of the coach warmed, especially once the others suggested covering the windows to cut down on the thick dust filling the stage.

What would Prescott be like? Caroline had described the town briefly in one letter, though most of her words were reserved for talk of her husband and son. Or for the excitement of another child on the way. Those letters had been too closely followed by tear-stained ones describing the loss. There had been no mention of expanding their family since.

She understood Caroline's hurt—at thirty-seven, her dream of having a family of her own seemed increasingly impossible with each passing year. And her desire to be not only a wife but a mother…

Again, her eyes burned. Those things were like a fairy tale now—one with no happy ending for her. There was no point in dwelling on them further.

What would she do to support herself once in town? Perhaps she could work as a clerk at the mercantile. From what Caroline had mentioned, Prescott had many stores. Some offered a variety of goods, while others were more specialized. Two sold only boots.

Santa Fe had been the same way, but Wickenburg had not. It might be nice to live in a large town again.

If not at a mercantile, she could cook or clean or work at the front desk at a hotel. She wasn't qualified to teach children, so even if there was an opening, she couldn't take it. Had Caroline mentioned a library? Or maybe that was her aunt back east.

Perhaps Prescott wasn't the right place for her. It had been her dad's wish—probably because he desired to keep her within traveling distance. But should she write to her aunt and ask if she could stay with her? Surely the demons of Millie's childhood in Ohio would be long forgotten by now.

No. Dad had made it clear that he wished for Millie to become independent. Living with her aunt wasn't what he had in mind, and she knew it.

In a matter of hours, she would arrive at Prescott. Her new life would begin, even if it wasn't what she wanted. An unknown future in an unknown town with an unknown job. Terrifying.

I will provide.

A feather-light peace wrapped her heart. God was right. He would provide. She would do her part and work without complaining, no matter where she found herself.

Thank goodness she already had a friend there to make things easier.

CHAPTER 7

Jake Waters stepped out of his tiny one room log cabin, stretching his sore muscles. A dull ache in his side reminded him of his mission. He rubbed his hand over the spot. *Was this really the right thing to do?* The doubt crept in again, but he pushed it away. It was worth it if it kept his friend from losing his life.

You shot him. A voice in his head accused.

I had to make it look real. It was the only way to scare him off. It was for his own good.

The voice did not answer.

Good.

Jake had been sure of his plan. Too bad Kilgore took one to the chest. Better Kilgore than him. It would have ruined everything if he had died. Kilgore was a fair sacrifice. The town was better off without the drunk.

No, he *had* done the right thing.

Jake grabbed a bucket and headed to the creek for some water. He needed to get into town soon. He had to check on his friend. Make sure he would decide to give up that stupid placer before it got him killed.

He splashed some water on his face before rubbing it dry with his shirt. Then he took a long drink of the cool water. When he finished, he returned the bucket to its usual spot on the front porch leaving the extra for Mother. That way she would not have to leave Sissy.

Glancing up at the sky, Jake realized it was later than he expected. He had to hurry if he was going to complete his mission without being caught. He jogged towards town, not slowing his pace until he reached the outskirts.

There was his destination. For a moment he considered how he would be able to complete his mission. If his friend was too injured to leave, there would be no way to...

Levi Brooks hurried down the boardwalk. Jake smiled and stepped into the shadows as Levi passed by. The first part of his plan was complete.

Jake forced himself to walk at a casual pace the rest of the way to Lancaster's Boardinghouse. He scanned the property looking for his friend but did not find him, so he entered the main building.

"Paul!" he called out his friend's name.

"Back here."

Jake found his way back to Paul's room. Papers were scattered over Paul's bed and desk. Jake's stomach tightened. Hopefully he wasn't too late.

He calmed his nerves. "What's going on?"

"Jake, I'm so glad you're here."

"I'm sorry I didn't come sooner. I heard what happened but couldn't get away from the farm."

"It's alright. Ma made sure I was pampered."

Jake laughed. "I'll bet. How are you feeling?" A twinge of guilt tried to push its way through, but he forced it to the recesses of his mind. He had done what was necessary.

"Fine. Still a little sore, but none the worse for wear."

"Glad to hear it."

Paul's smile faded to concern. "How are you doing... since...?"

Since what?

"Fine," Jake said as he shook off his confusion. Then he extended his hand palm side up, motioning towards the scattered papers. "What's going on here?"

"Levi Brooks stopped by."

"Oh?"

"He's saying I owe back taxes for '64 and '65."

Jake frowned again. "That doesn't sound like you, Paul."

Paul shook his head. "It's not like me. I know Ma and I paid those taxes, but if I don't find the receipts, I'm going to owe a lot of money."

"Let me help." Jake held his breath hoping Paul would not object.

"Really?" Paul's face brightened.

"Sure. I'll start over here."

The room grew silent, except for the rustling of papers. *Stay calm. Don't let him see your anxiety.*

I won't.

Jake flipped through the nearest stack of papers. The date caught his eye. 1864. Flipping through the next fifteen pieces of paper, he was certain this is what he'd been looking for.

He glanced over his shoulder. Paul skimmed through papers on the other side of the room. *I'm betraying my best friend.* The thought made his stomach lurch, but he forced himself to continue. Jake shifted his position so his back would hide his hands from Paul's line of sight. Then he folded the fifteen or so sheets of paper and stuffed them in his vest pocket, his hands trembling.

You're stealing from him. The voice nudged him.

It is for his own good. He doesn't know the danger he is in.

"Hey," Jake said. "I found some over here." He handed Paul the papers that had rested under the ones he took.

Paul came and looked over his shoulder. "July 1865. That's part of what Brooks said I was missing."

Jake continued to flip through the papers. "Looks like it goes as far back as July '65. Nothing older than that."

Paul reached for the papers. "Thanks for finding these." He set them on the small desk.

"Mr. Lancaster," Mrs. Feldman called from the entryway. "Lunch is served."

Paul jerked his head towards the doorway. "You want to eat with us, or do you need to head back to the farm?"

On any other day, Jake would have taken Paul up on his offer. But the papers in his pocket seared a hole through his chest. He needed to get out of here before he lost his nerve.

"Thanks, but I need to get back." Mother would be waiting for him.

"Alright. Thank you for helping me find some of those papers."

Jake shook Paul's hand. "Any time."

"I'll see you for Sunday supper?"

Jake held back a frown. "Maybe."

With that, he took his leave. He needed to get back to check on Mother. He had already left her and Sissy alone for too long.

When he got back to the farm, he paused before opening the cabin door. Mother had not touched the bucket of water again. He flung the door open.

"Mother. You must drink some water. Both you and Sissy need it."

His mother's fragile form sat in the rocking chair near the fireplace. She had let the fire go out again.

"Mother, Sissy won't get well if we don't keep a fire burning."

His mother did not move.

Jake looked around the room until his eyes landed on the bed. It was empty!

"Mother! Where is Sissy?"

He rushed to the chair where Mother sat. She would not turn to look at him. She did not answer him.

"Mother!"

She's dead. Remember?

A sharp pain ran like fire through his head. He closed his eyes. "No!"

They are both dead. Killed and mutilated by the Apache. Remember?

"No! It's not true. Mother is in her chair."

He opened his eyes and stared at his mother's empty rocking chair. It was true.

Jake sank to the floor and sobbed. He had forgotten again. Two months of this torture. Two months, Mother and Sissy had been gone. The pain was driving him mad.

His hand patted the papers in his pocket. *I'm sorry, Paul. But I can't lose you too.* He would save Paul. His plan had to work. He couldn't survive losing anyone else.

CHAPTER 8

Paul hurried through lunch and excused himself before Mrs. Feldman could object. He had to find the rest of those papers. What a relief that Jake had found part of them already. Surely the rest were nearby.

After another hour, Paul's hope began to fade. There were no more receipts in his room. Where could they be?

He remembered the crates of papers he had transferred to the storage room when Ma moved to the ranch. Perhaps the rest of the receipts were there.

The storage room had served as living quarters for him and Ma in the early days. It had an entrance from the dining hall's kitchen, so it became the place where he stuffed anything he wanted to hold on to but didn't need quick access to.

As he opened the door to the storage room, he realized it had been more than a year since he had been in the room. A layer of dust covered everything. His nose twitched, then he sneezed, blowing dust off a nearby crate.

Paul sniffed, waiting for another sneeze. When it didn't come, he grabbed the first crate and unloaded it. Miscellaneous junk. Scraps of metal from broken things around the property. A door hinge. A tin cup.

He dropped the crate on an empty spot on the floor and reached for the next one, repeating the pattern again.

When he finally came to the last crate, the smell of the dinner wafted to his nose. He rubbed a dirty hand across his forehead.

How could he forget? He'd promised to help Thomas.

The Andersons were expecting a visitor from Wickenburg on today's stage—some friend of Caroline's. He was supposed to be there to carry their visitor's bags.

He was going to be late. He looked at the dust, dirt, and cobwebs coating his hands, arms, and shirt. The thundering of the stage horses as they entered town confirmed that he had no time to change.

Quickly, Paul brushed his shirt and hands. Then he locked up the storage room and hurried towards the stage stop.

He skidded to a halt when he neared the stage, short of breath—half from the run and half from the sight in front of him. Wow! He'd never seen brighter violet eyes in his life. Suddenly all the worries of the day faded from his mind as he studied the woman. His tongue felt heavy in his mouth as she stepped down from the stage. When she straightened to her full height, he swallowed hard. Caroline's visitor was nearly as tall as him!

She smiled as the Andersons greeted her. Her raven hair was pulled back in into two long braids that rested just below her shoulder blades. His eyes traveled down her neck to the lace collar of the lavender dress which hugged her feminine curves in the most pleasing way.

He stepped forward with a grin plastered on his face.

What was the chance that this beauty was single?

———

Millie stepped down from the stage and arched her back to work some of the soreness from her muscles. Her eyes scanned the area around the stage stop and landed on a short woman with blonde hair and green eyes that lit with instant recognition as Millie stepped closer.

"I'm so glad you finally came," Caroline said. "I've been dying for you to visit for such a long time."

Millie wrapped her arms around her friend. "You look well."

"I am. Please come meet my family."

She followed her friend a few more paces to where a man searched the growing crowd.

"This is my husband, Thomas."

The man turned a pleasant smile towards her. "Pleased to meet you, Miss Pritchett. My wife hasn't stopped talking about you since we received your letter."

Caroline placed her hand on a young boy's shoulder. "This is our son, Drew."

The boy's head dropped back as he stared up at Millie with wide eyes. "You're tall!" It wasn't the first time someone had pointed out her unusual height.

She smiled and crouched in front of him. "Hello, Drew. My name is Miss Pritchett, but you may call me Miss Millie if you'd like."

The little boy's blonde hair flopped in his eyes as he nodded. Then he gave her a dashing grin, reminding her of his mother.

"Which are your things, ma'am?" a deep voice questioned behind her.

She turned, and when she had to look up—a rare occurrence—she found herself thinking the same thing as little Drew. *Tall.*

Broad, strong shoulders. Thick neck. Squared jawline. His nose was narrow and out of proportion to the rest of his face. His eyes were… Mesmerizing. Deep blue like the lake near her childhood home. Her pulse quickened. What a smile.

The more she stared—it was bold and improper, but she couldn't tear her eyes away—she noticed other things. A streak of dirt across his forehead. Disheveled sandy hair stood at odd ends on the top of his head. His shirt was filthy.

He lifted a hand to take hers then quickly pulled it back to his side but not before she noticed the dirt coating it.

"I was… um…"

"Millie, this is Paul Lancaster, a good friend," Thomas said.

"Paul." His given name slipped from her lips before she could stop it. It was the same as Dad's. Heat rushed to her cheeks. Apparently, she had left her manners in Wickenburg.

"Millie." He greeted her with the same lack of formality.

Gracious, was it unusually warm today?

Remember what happened the last time you acted this way.

She tore her eyes from his. She wouldn't make that mistake again—no matter how captivating a man was or how lonely she became.

The light in his eyes dimmed as she stiffened her posture. She refocused her attention on her friend, pointing out her items as they were taken down from the baggage area on top of the stage.

"Oh," Caroline said. "I hadn't thought you would be bringing a trunk."

"I'm sorry. I... If Dad has his way, I won't be going back."

Caroline's brow arched. "Sounds like we need to catch up."

Millie smiled and whispered in her friend's ear, "Seems like I'm not the only one keeping secrets. You didn't mention another baby on the way."

Caroline's cheeks turned pink as she smiled and looked down at her rounded belly. "Can you manage her things, Paul?"

He reached down and lifted the heavy trunk, balancing it on his shoulder as he grabbed the two overly full carpet bags with his other hand. Just one of those bags seemed heavy to Millie, but he treated them like they were empty.

Caroline led the way home with Millie walking beside her. She should have been clearer about the length of her intended stay. It was not fair to impose for too long. Tomorrow, she would investigate staying at the boardinghouse.

Her gaze flitted to Paul's back again. My, what a fine looking back it was. She tried to force the thought from her mind, but it lingered despite her best efforts as she and Caroline passed him.

CHAPTER 9

More than once, Paul caught himself staring at the sway of Millie's hips as he followed behind her. The heavy trunk dug into his shoulder and the carpet bags pulled on his muscles, but he was glad for it. Not just because he could lift this heavy burden for Thomas.

Miss Pritchett. He smiled.

She had to be in her thirties. Those crinkled lines next to her eyes reminded him of his mother at thirty-five. The first ten minutes of meeting her had told him a lot. He liked it when she stared at him, no matter how bold it may have appeared to others. There was a rebellious streak that she couldn't always hide.

Then some thought had crossed her mind and completely changed her demeanor. She went from approving of his appearance to erecting walls. He frowned. Maybe she was embarrassed.

As Caroline monopolized the conversation on the way to the Andersons' house, Millie said little. Was she shy? Or just quiet? A woman of few words. He had never heard of such a thing.

It didn't fit with her bold stare. She seemed a woman at odds with herself.

He shook his head. He'd just met her. Why was he so concerned with figuring her out? He didn't devote that much thought to building his sifters or planning his days at the boardinghouse.

Caroline held the front door open for him. "You can put her

things in Drew's room."

Paul walked in and dropped the carpet bags to the floor. He slid the trunk from his shoulder and lowered it gently, suspecting that there could be fragile items contained within. He sat on the edge of the bed and reached down to rub the sore spot on his leg where the bullet wound was still healing. Probably should have taken it easier today.

He stood and returned to the main room.

"I thought we could dine at Lancaster's this evening," Caroline said. "Do you suppose Mrs. Feldman has supper ready?"

"I'm sure she does."

"Good. Give us a few minutes. I'm sure Millie would like a chance to freshen up."

The ladies left the room, and Thomas waved his hand in front of his face. "Whew! Maybe you should have freshened up before meeting us at the stage."

"Pee-yew!" Little Drew pinched his fingers over his nose and broke out in a fit of giggles.

"Hey, I lost track of time, uh, working on some repairs." Should he tell Thomas about the tax debt? Naw. If he did, Thomas would probably try to help, and he didn't need any. If he couldn't find those receipts, he would just make the money at his mine.

"I did mention you were helping us with Caroline's *lady* friend's bags. You didn't think she'd be worth a change of shirt?"

Paul felt heat rise to his face.

"*Single* lady friend." Thomas grinned and slapped him on the back.

He didn't remember Thomas mentioning that part. If he had, he probably assumed she was too young to fuss over. No matter. It was too late now.

Thomas held Drew's hand in his, following behind his wife as the five of them made their way to the boardinghouse. Paul walked next to him—behind Millie again.

"You like her?" Thomas whispered.

Paul's eyes widened at him.

"You do. I wasn't sure until just now."

Heat burned his cheeks. So, what if he did?

Thomas smiled and said nothing more. He seemed to be enjoying Paul's discomfort.

Thankfully, they arrived a moment later.

As Paul held the door for the ladies, an angry Mrs. Feldman pushed her way out of the building with carpet bag in hand. His stomach tightened. Her face was beat red, and her eyes darkened when she saw him. "I quit, Mr. Lancaster. I will not work with that—that mule of a man!"

She stomped onto the porch and down the front steps with chin jutted in the air.

It didn't appear she'd be returning. Hopefully she had completed supper before storming off. Caroline and Millie warily stepped into the parlor, still staring at the back of Mrs. Feldman. Paul and Thomas followed behind.

"Please take a seat in the dining room while I check on things," Paul muttered.

He entered the dining room, unprepared for the sight that awaited him. Mr. Lowrey sat at the table. His face was crimson, and his eyes were lowered.

"What did you do?" Paul asked.

"Nothing." Mr. Lowrey kept his voice low.

Paul stared at the man, determined to wait him out.

"Okay. I might have said something about the roast being a little dry. It was. Terribly dry."

Paul looked around the table in confusion. There was no roast. No potatoes. Not even a stray fork. He flexed his hand open and closed at his side.

"She came and grabbed the plate right out from under me. And I wasn't finished. Woman's loony. Then she grabbed the rest of the meal and took it back into the kitchen."

His stomach knotted tighter. Not only did he have debts to settle, a new housekeeper to find, but now he had to get supper on the table for his boarders. Whatever the Lord might be trying to teach him, he didn't have time to learn it.

Paul left the dining room and headed for the kitchen.

Oh, no!

A nicely carved roast complete with potatoes and carrots sat untouched in the waste pail, covered in brown gravy, and topped by a smashed apple pie.

Flinging open pantry doors, he tried to figure out what to cook, and quick. Not only did he have hungry boarders waiting, but also the Andersons and their lovely guest. He'd hoped for a much better first impression.

He reached for a heavy iron skillet and slammed it down onto the top of the stove, fortunately still plenty warm enough to prepare a meal. He dropped a spoonful of lard into the skillet, followed by a few roughly cut potatoes. They sizzled and popped. What else? There had to be more he could cook.

Paul stopped short, staring blankly at a spot just left of the washbasin.

He ran a quick hand through his hair. He had to get something on the table. He snatched a slab of bacon from the counter and sliced some off. An odd combination, but the boarders wouldn't care. He made his way back to the stove, and pain shot through his injured leg, throwing him off balance. The handful of bacon slices plopped to the floor as he reached out to steady himself, and his hand shot to the hot edge of the stove. He cursed as his flesh made contact.

Rubbing his hand, he remembered the potatoes—black on one side and raw on the other. Anger burned a fiery path through his veins. He grabbed the handle of the skillet and flung it, cast iron smashing into the wall.

"Paul!" a woman's voice shouted.

CHAPTER 10

Millie tried to take in the scene as she stood outside the kitchen with Caroline. The bitter smell of burnt potatoes hung in the air. Uncooked rashers were scattered on the floor. The counter was strewn with vegetables and the remnants of a slab of bacon. A small table with chairs sat in the far corner of the room. Atop it, crumbs littered serving platters and an empty breadbasket, all that was left of supper.

She'd stepped forward to lend aid just as Paul grabbed the handle of the skillet and threw it towards the wall, barely missing the table and chairs. Millie held back a gasp as the iron skillet clattered to the ground. Hot lard and potatoes slid down the wall.

Caroline had called his name, but Paul hadn't moved.

Millie approached him, gently laying a hand on his forearm. Muscles twitched at her touch but relaxed after a few seconds. She drew her hand back to her side and bent down to pick up the skillet.

Wordlessly, she cut up the rest of the potatoes and dropped them in a pot of water on the back of the stove.

"He's not normally like this," Caroline whispered in her ear. "I'm going to see if the Peng's have any leftover meat from supper service at the dining hall."

Millie nodded and set the slab of bacon to one side. She wiped out the iron skillet and plopped a dollop of lard in it. Then she peeled the carrots and tossed them in.

She could still sense the tension emanating from Paul. She glanced over her shoulder and saw him sitting in one of the chairs at the small table, head in his hands.

Lord, please be with this man.

In the years of working with her father, she'd witnessed many strange things. Grown men broke down and sobbed at the loss of a child. Many turned to the bottle when crops failed. Others, like Paul, struggled with self-control when pressed into a corner.

Still, she hadn't needed Caroline's confirmation to know this wasn't normal for him. He didn't seem the type to become violent against others. She had seen the eyes of a kind and gentle man at the stage stop. But even the gentlest of men could make mistakes.

As her hands moved fluidly through the motions of mixing gravy, she looked around for serving dishes and cautiously approached the table. Paul didn't look up, so she retrieved the stack of serving dishes and set them in the wash basin to wipe clean. She filled a bowl with the cooked carrots and poured the gravy into a boat.

Caroline returned with a platter of roast beef. "What do you need help with?"

Millie tested the potatoes. They were soft enough. "Can you mash these while I look around for some bread?"

"Sure."

On the back corner of the counter, she spotted a loaf. Mrs. Feldman had probably set it aside for the morning, but given the circumstances, Millie chose to slice it for supper. She found some butter that looked like it had been intended for the original meal. Looked like they would be using it after all.

"All done," Caroline said.

Millie smiled. "Me, too. Let's get this meal on the table."

As she headed towards the door with the bowl of carrots and mashed potatoes, she chanced another glance at Paul. Thomas sat in the chair opposite him, furrowing his brow. Paul caught her eye and quickly looked away.

Her heart burdened for him. How many times had she done or said something she wished she could take back?

Lord, thank you for letting me be here to help.

———

Paul heaved a deep sigh, nearly coughing at the burnt odor that still hung in the air. What kind of crazy person had just taken control of his body?

He had turned away when Millie and Caroline entered the kitchen. What must they have thought of him? How could he lose control like that?

Then Millie touched him. Just a light touch. One second, he was raging mad, the next, repentant. She'd disarmed him in two seconds without a single word. Even Ma had never been that quick before.

He dropped his head into his hands. He hadn't lost control like that in years. Sure, he hadn't expected all that he'd come home to. But even all that and the bad news from Levi Brooks shouldn't have been enough to send him over the edge.

Shaking his head, he stole a glance at Millie. She didn't seem the least bit affected by his outburst. Nor did she seem to notice the enormous mess he'd made. Instead, she took calm command of the kitchen as though it was her own.

"You okay?" Thomas muttered as he took a seat across from him.

Paul looked away as he nodded. He understood Thomas's concern. He'd let his friend in on many dark stories from the past, when he still let his anger control him.

Why, today of all days, did that come back to haunt him? When he'd finally found someone that he might be interested in.

He shrugged off the questions. He wasn't that man anymore. Jesus had changed his heart and his life. Yet why did he feel as if someone had a firm grip on his ankle and was ready to pull him back any minute? He hadn't struggled with those demons for years. Not once since coming to Prescott.

Thomas patted him on the shoulder. "If you need to talk…"

Paul shook his head. He wouldn't know what to say.

As Caroline and Millie took over his kitchen, he felt completely out of his element.

"Can I help, ladies?"

Millie smiled at him. She held a gravy boat in one hand and a breadbasket in the other. "Go wash up while we set the table."

He looked down, flushing at his filthy shirt and dirty hands. He smelled awful from the day's work. Again, he wished he had paid more attention to the time. She was right. He needed to clean himself up before sitting at the table with his friends and boarders.

Mrs. Feldman had already tidied his room and placed a pitcher of water on the dresser. After washing up and changing his shirt, he returned to the dining room refreshed. Millie and Caroline had finished setting out the meal.

Millie smiled at him as he entered the room, but he could not bring himself to return it.

———

"Amen," Millie whispered when Thomas finished saying grace.

"This is really good," Thomas said after his first bite. "I can't believe you ladies threw this together so quickly."

Millie's cheeks warmed. All she did was step in to help when there was a need.

Paul's gaze darted to the food on his plate, then back to her. "It's delicious. Thank you for all your help."

She nodded. Surely her face must be a deep scarlet, as hot as it felt.

Caroline lifted a finger to her temple and began tapping. "You know…"

Millie had spent enough time with Caroline on the trip from Santa Fe to know that gesture. She was cooking up a scheme, and it would mean trouble.

"Paul, you're looking for a replacement for Mrs. Feldman, right?"

"I'd have to say so."

Caroline turned and looked at her. "And you'll be looking for work as soon as you get settled?"

Millie nodded as her stomach clenched, and her hands grew moist.

"Maybe the two of you could strike an agreement."

Paul leaned an elbow on the table and stroked his chin. "That's not a bad idea."

Millie dropped her gaze to her plate. She couldn't work with Paul. He was too handsome. And those eyes... Even now, her heart jumped between her stomach and her throat. She couldn't trust herself. She had to say no.

"What do you think?" His voice drew her eyes upward.

When a soft, repentant smile stretched across his lips, her heart changed pace. The only word that came to mind was "yes".

Millie cleared her throat, snapping her brain into focus. "I... I would like to pray about it." It was a half-truth. If she took a job this soon—well, she wouldn't be able to pretend that she was here for just a visit. It all seemed so permanent.

"Certainly," Paul replied. The crestfallen look that settled on his face made her regret her hesitation.

"Well, that's settled," Caroline said. "We'll come back and help with breakfast in the morning if Millie hasn't decided before then."

Millie frowned. From the sound of it, her friend already thought she'd accepted Paul's offer.

CHAPTER II

Throughout the meal, Millie avoided eye contact with Paul. Was she going to refuse? Was it because of his outburst? Caroline was right. The arrangement would be perfect—and not just because he needed a housekeeper.

Millie glanced at him, and his stomach flipped. Something in those violet eyes held the answer already. She really was going to turn him down.

Maybe she was afraid of him. After the destruction he'd caused in the kitchen earlier, he wouldn't blame her. An idea took shape. He needed to get her alone after supper. Convince her that he wasn't what he'd seemed.

"That was a fine meal. Caroline, Millie, thank you again."

Caroline jumped to her feet. "It was our pleasure." She began clearing away dishes. Millie followed her.

Now was his chance. He stood and carried a large stack of dishes into the kitchen, frowning when he noticed just how much of a mess he had made earlier. He set the dishes in the wash basin.

"Paul, we'll take care of this," Caroline said.

"Why don't you head on home with your family?" he asked. "I'll help Millie. It will give us a chance to discuss things."

Paul's smile faltered when he noticed Millie's eyes widened in fear.

"I'll walk her home as soon as we're finished." There. That

should reassure her.

"Are you sure?" Caroline looked from one to the other.

Millie nodded.

Paul smiled and grabbed a bucket. Then he limped from the kitchen to fetch more water. By the time he returned, Millie had swept the floor clean.

They both stood in silence beside the stove, waiting for the water to heat.

"What happened to your leg?" Millie asked.

For a few seconds, Paul considered how much he should tell her. After all, she had only arrived in town just a few hours ago. He didn't want her to scare her. "Ah… got hurt at my placer mine."

She glanced down at his leg. When her gaze returned to his face, he felt it warm. She was so pretty.

Millie quickly looked away, as if she were suddenly uncomfortable in his presence.

Paul cleared his throat. "About earlier. I'm not hot-tempered. I know it looked that way, but that is not who I am."

She turned her back and shaved some soap into the wash basin. "I know."

Her answer threw him off, but he said nothing further.

As she washed dishes, he dried them. Her slender fingers were so delicate compared to his stubby ones.

"I'll do it."

The statement came so suddenly that it took Paul a minute to decipher what Millie had meant.

"Really?" He tried to keep the excitement from his voice. "Are you sure?"

Millie nodded. "I'm sure."

"The job comes with room and board. There's Mrs. Feldman's old room downstairs."

"That's fine."

"We serve three meals a day here and over in the dining hall, though the midday crowd is fairly light."

She handed him another plate. This time her fingers brushed

his and heat traveled up his arm, settling somewhere around his heart. He lost his train of thought entirely.

"Will I cook for the dining hall, too?"

"What? Oh, no. The Pengs manage the dining hall and most of the work at the bunkhouses. Your job is to clean and cook here."

"How much does it pay?"

He named the same figure he paid Mrs. Feldman.

"That's fair." She ducked her head. "I will need help moving my things from the Andersons. Thomas can't—"

Her concern for his friend endeared her even more to him. "I'll take care of it. Would you like a few days with them?"

Millie shook her head. "No need for me to impose, if I have a place to stay."

His heart beat faster. "If you'd like, I can fetch your things tonight."

She nodded and looked away. Was that what she really wanted?

———

Millie hoped Caroline wouldn't be upset. Since she was staying in Prescott, they would have plenty of opportunities to catch up.

She just hoped she wasn't making a mistake. Part of her mind told her to say no—to run far away from the handsome Paul Lancaster. And part of her wanted to stay. A little glimmer of hope grew in her soul. Maybe things could be different this time. After all, she wasn't rebelling like she had at fourteen. She was obeying her father's wishes by getting a job and exploring her independence. This was nothing like when she'd been swayed by a charming smile and smooth words.

Tears stung her eyes. Old memories clawed at her heart. So long ago, yet the wounds were still raw. Would she ever be able to move beyond those sins?

She had to. Things were different now. She had to start trusting her judgment. Dad was in Wickenburg, and she couldn't rely on his approval to bolster her confidence. This had to be the right decision.

But what if it wasn't?

She dabbed her eyes with her handkerchief. *Lord, please let my choice be a good one.*

With the kitchen set to rights, she explored the lower floor of the boardinghouse, retracing her steps back to the front door. The stairs to the rooms started on the far-left side of the parlor. Right next to them was the entryway to the dining room. The parlor itself was rather quaint. Several armchairs were arranged in small seating areas throughout the room. Opposite the front door, a fireplace took up the center of the parlor wall. A lovely, ornate wood clock graced its mantle, surrounded by porcelain vases. Had Paul picked out the items, or had Mrs. Feldman?

In front of the fireplace, a couch faced two armchairs, comprising the largest of the seating areas. On either side of the front door, curtained windows let in the last bit of fading sunlight. She lit a few lamps on the side tables throughout the room in case any of the boarders decided to return to the parlor for the evening.

She entered the dining room, caught by the beauty of the wood furniture. The table was made of solid pine. A matching buffet lined the far wall. Another fireplace took up most of the space on the wall shared by the parlor, revealing that they both stood back-to-back. A good design idea. The mantle in this room was adorned with crystal goblets, fancy china, and serving plates—though not the same as the ones used tonight. She opened the buffet cupboards and found the rest of the daily plates and silverware. Here, she stowed the dishes she had washed after supper.

Millie sighed, comforted by the homey familiarity of her surroundings. The decor was much the same as she would have picked.

She ventured down the hallway between the kitchen and what must've been the two private rooms. Mrs. Feldman had occupied one. The other was probably Paul's. She stared at the doors, unable to figure out which would now be hers.

"It's the one on the left."

She jumped, startled by Paul's voice behind her. She turned to face him, heart still racing, and remembered that he had her heavy trunk balanced on his ever-so-masculine shoulder. She quickly opened the door to let him through, scolding her thoughts.

"Thank you for bringing my things."

"Twice in one day." He set the trunk at the foot of the bed, then dropped the two carpet bags on top of it. "Glad to be of service." He winked at her, and her face warmed.

Then he turned and left the room, pulling the door closed behind him. "Good night."

Millie waved her hands near her face, trying to cool herself down. Maybe this was a mistake.

Shoving her self-doubt aside, she began unpacking her things. The room was bigger than she expected. Besides a bed and nightstand, there was also a dresser and a small desk.

Opening the trunk, she carefully lifted out the quilt she had sewn for her long-anticipated and never-arriving wedding day. Within its folds hid the turquoise painted ceramic bowl. Dad had insisted she take it since it held too many old memories. She supposed there was little place in his new life for things from the past, including her.

A tear threatened to form in the corner of her eye. She determined not to let it fall. Instead, she set the turquoise bowl on the dresser. It would work just fine for washing, even if it didn't match the pitcher already residing there.

Millie slowly folded the quilt and, with a heavy sigh, laid it to rest in the trunk. Someday…

She turned her attention to her carpet bags. When she came to her Bible, she smiled as she set it on the desk. It was the perfect place for her morning devotions.

Morning. She hadn't asked what time she was expected to have breakfast ready.

CHAPTER 12

At least the day seemed to be ending on a positive note. Millie had said yes.

As excited as Paul was, he needed to focus on looking through his records. What good was a new housekeeper without a boardinghouse?

He entered his room and felt a breeze from the open window. Odd. Perhaps Mrs. Feldman had aired out the room before she left, and he just hadn't noticed earlier.

He sat down at his desk and picked up the stack of papers Jake found earlier. He frowned. Jake seemed even more on edge today than he had in the past few months. Paul knew the loss of his mother and sister hit him hard. Jake had never been much of a churchgoer, but he had often brought his mother and sister to town on Sunday and joined the large gathering of people for Sunday supper afterward.

That all stopped after the brutal murder of Jake's mother and sister. Paul swallowed hard, still remembering the gruesome sight. He had been with Jake when he found them. Jake had not handled it well. That day he did what was necessary, but in the weeks following, he became more of a recluse, often claiming there was too much work to do at the farm.

Paul sent up a prayer for his friend. Jake had lost more weight since the last time Paul had seen him—what was it—two weeks ago? He had been rather lean before losing his family, but now he looked almost sickly. Paul really hoped Jake would come for Sunday supper. If he didn't, then perhaps Paul would make some time to stop by the farm next week.

He returned his attention to the receipts in his hand. Heaviness pressed down on him. Certainly, he had paid taxes in '64. He would never have skipped payment intentionally.

Flipping through the receipts one by one, he found everything for the current year, then '68 and so on, until he came to '65. Sure enough, he had receipts for half of '65. But that was where they ended. Where could the missing receipts be?

A knock sounded on his door. He set aside the papers.

When Millie greeted him on the other side, he smiled. In the dimming light, she had an exotic look. Her eyes were more almond shaped, and her skin was a little darker than he remembered. Earlier in the day, he'd assumed she spent a great deal of time out of doors. But now in the soft light from the lamp on his desk, he wondered if she might be part Mexican or even part Indian.

If it were the latter... It could cause trouble.

"I was wondering," she said. "What time do your boarders take breakfast?"

"Seven-thirty. Some as late as nine."

"And you?"

"I'm with the early group."

She nodded and started to walk away.

"Millie."

"Yes?"

"I plan on going out to my placer tomorrow. Caroline said she would stop by and help you. She's filled in from time to time."

She remained there, silently looking up at him.

"Is there anything else?" he asked.

"No. Good night."

Was she just shy by nature? Hopefully she would feel comfortable with the boarders tomorrow.

Millie returned to her room, and Paul returned to his paperwork. After another hour, he still couldn't locate the missing receipts. Yawning, he cleaned up his desk. He still had a few other places to look, but it would have to wait for tomorrow evening. It was getting late, and he needed some sleep.

———

Jake woke up stiff and sore. He felt around in the darkness. Where was he?

On the floor. In the cabin.

His head pounded leaving a deafening echo reverberating through his ears. He knew he had something important to do.

He sat up and then crawled toward the rocking chair by the fireplace. The fire had gone out long ago. He pulled himself up using the rocking chair to steady him. When he felt like his legs were stable, he moved toward the kitchen table and lit a lantern.

Slowly the day came back to him. He had gone to see Paul. He stole the tax papers. Then he came home. Jake shook his head. He must have blacked out again sometime after coming home.

The papers! He had a meeting with Simon Talbert.

Normally, Jake would keep his distance from Talbert. Or perhaps it was the other way around. Talbert was one of the wealthiest men in Prescott. Much of his wealth came from his English roots. Jake heard rumors that Talbert doubled his wealth during the years he managed his own store in San Francisco.

When Talbert came to Prescott, the town welcomed him with open arms, unaware of his greedy and seedy nature. Only a few, like Jake, knew the truth about Simon Talbert and his plans for a consolidated mine where all the old placer mines were.

Ironically, Kilgore was the one that told Jake about Talbert's plan. Seems Kilgore had been hired to dress up like the Apache and scare off the miners. When Jake learned of this, he knew it was his opportunity to save Paul, so he joined up with Kilgore and his cohort, Gentry.

As Jake rounded the corner of Simon Talbert's house, he hoped he wasn't too late. He headed for the back of the house.

The Englishman waited for him in the unlit yard, the scent of pipe smoke hanging in the air.

"Got 'em," he whispered.

Talbert jumped. "Didn't see you, old chap. Nearly took a year off my life."

Jake's patience wore thin. He dug the papers from his pocket and thrust them out. "Here."

Talbert held his hands up and took a step backwards. "I told you to dispose of them, not bring them here."

Snooty jerk.

Jake stuffed the papers back in his pocket. "How's I supposed to know if you'd pay me for my word."

"Good point." Talbert clamped the pipe between his teeth and reached into his pocket. He handed Jake several bills.

As he reached for them, Talbert kept a firm grip on the other end.

"Just make sure you get rid of those. Wouldn't want to report you to the authorities for theft."

Jake gave a firm tug on the bills. "Got it." They loosened from Talbert's grip.

"That will be all, for now." Talbert took the pipe from his mouth and pointed the other end at Jake. "I will contact you if I need further assistance."

Jake bit back a sharp retort with clenched teeth. He turned on his heels and walked back the way he came.

Once inside the nearest saloon, he tossed the papers into the fireplace and headed up to the bar, his end of the bargain complete.

CHAPTER 13

Waking before dawn, Millie slid her feet and legs over the edge of the bed. Though she slept well, she felt out of sorts in the unfamiliar room in the new town. Nothing was as she thought it should be.

She stretched her arms above her head, locking her fingers together. Then she slowly released them and returned her arms to her side, deciding to make the best of her situation.

As she lit a lamp, the warm glow brightened her mood some. This was her room. Her chance to be independent.

She stood and walked to the small desk by the window. Setting the lamp on the desk, she reached for her Bible and took a seat. Her morning devotion was a source of comfort no matter where she lived.

Turning to her marker, she began reading in Psalm 101. "I will sing of your love and justice; to you, Lord, I will sing praise. I will be careful to lead a blameless life — when will you come to me? I will conduct the affairs of my house with a blameless heart. I will not look with approval on anything that is vile."

She slammed the book shut. Her heart quickened and the tears began to flow. This was not her song. She had not led a blameless life. She had not been careful. She had not conducted the affairs of her house with a blameless heart. No matter how much she tried, she could never atone for the mistakes she made.

But she had been only fourteen. Young. Naive.

It didn't matter. It set her life on a course that hurt her family. Because of her, they had to leave her childhood home in Ohio. It was where Dad ministered to the Shawnee. Where he had met Mom. Where Mom had been born and raised. Where Mom's large family—brothers, sisters, aunts, uncles, grandparents—lived for generations. It was Millie's fault they had to leave. She had brought shame to them all. And there was one she had hurt above all the others. Her penance? She could never see him again.

Millie wiped her fingers under her eyes to dry the flow of tears. How long would her sins chase her? Why couldn't she have landed on a happier Psalm? One that prompted her to sing instead of cry.

Perhaps singing would be the cure. She reached for her brush—the one Mom had given her when she was twelve. As she brushed her long raven locks, she searched her mind for the right hymn. She softly sang one of her favorites and let the words wash over her until she started the second verse.

Just as I am, and waiting not
To rid my soul of one dark blot,
To Thee whose blood can cleanse each spot,
O Lamb of God, I come, I come.

She finished the verse with choppy croaks as her tears returned. Resting her head on the edge of the desk, she closed her eyes and prayed. *Lord, why does it feel as if my one dark blot can never be cleansed? I sing these words, yet I do not feel them. They are not true.*

She felt filthy, like a pig rolling around in the mud coating layer upon layer of muck over her heart until it formed a crusted shell.

Yet, how many times had she asked Jesus to cleanse her? Hadn't He done so time and again? If so, why did the sins of her past continue to torment her?

Taking a deep breath, she let it out slowly and lifted her head. She ignored the nagging voice begging her to stay still for another moment to pursue her heart's hurt to a peaceful conclusion. Instead, she braided her hair, washed up, and donned her gray work dress.

She did not have time for such emotional pondering this morning. She had a new job, and it was time to begin her day.

———

Paul woke to the light sound of a woman's voice singing. He strained his ears to hear the words, but they faded too soon. He lay still for a moment or two, hoping the melody would start again. When nothing came, he shook his head. Perhaps he had dreamed the lovely sound.

He left the warmth of his bed and began readying himself for the day. He didn't have time to worry about the sweet music. Instead, he needed to get out the door and down to his mine as soon as possible if he was going to maximize how much gold he could pull from the creek. Since he hadn't been able to find the receipts for the first year, he was going to have to pay the tax debt. There was no way around it. Whatever gold dust he could pull from the mine in the next few days—well, he hoped it would cover the debt. It was doubtful, but he still hoped anyway.

As he neared the kitchen to grab the buckets, he paused just outside the doorway. The same sweet, light voice sang another hymn. He closed his eyes and listened to the music. Her voice was beautiful, and he felt his spirit rise in worship.

At the beginning of the last verse, he opened his eyes and entered the room. Millie stopped singing and jumped back.

"I didn't mean to startle you."

"I… I didn't hear you," she whispered.

Paul smiled, hoping it would set her mind at ease. "I came to get the buckets to haul water."

"Oh." She twisted her hands together nervously. "I already brought in what I needed."

He should have risen earlier. "Tomorrow, I will take care of that for you."

She nodded, though her eyes held a glint of defiance. "Breakfast will be ready in fifteen minutes."

Paul turned and walked through the house, out the front door towards the barn. He grabbed the milking stool and sat next to Gerdie, his milk goat. As he worked steady streams of milk into the pail, he smiled. Millie wasn't what he expected. Quiet agreement mixed with strength. In some ways, she reminded him of his mother. Hard working—he saw that much last night. Though she didn't talk as much as Ma, she seemed to be comfortable taking charge and getting things done.

Her voice. When she sang—it was the first moment of true peace he felt in weeks. Never had he heard a more beautiful sound. As he closed his eyes, he could almost hear her voice singing again.

Gerdie nudged him, bringing him back to reality.

"Sorry, girl."

He patted the goat on the rump and then put away the stool before seeing to the rest of his chores. When he finished, he picked up the full milk pail and headed back to the house.

Paul walked through the house with the pail. He passed Millie in the hallway between the dining room and the kitchen. She held a platter of bacon in one hand and toast in the other. He continued into the kitchen to set the pail on the table.

"Goat's milk." He pointed to the pail as Millie returned to the kitchen.

"Thank you." She poured some of the milk into a pitcher and put it into the dining room. Paul followed behind her.

"Hmm." Mr. Lowrey warily eyed the bacon and eggs on the plate in front of him.

Millie smiled at the older gentleman. "Please let me know if you prefer something else."

Mr. Lowrey glared at her and took a bite of the eggs.

Paul took his usual seat, holding back a smile. It was the first time he'd seen Mr. Lowrey speechless.

"Needs more salt," Mr. Lowrey grumbled.

Another boarder disagreed. "Tastes perfect to me."

Mr. Lowrey glowered at the man, then he hunched over the plate as he shoveled the food in his mouth.

Paul closed his eyes and said a silent grace this morning. When he opened them, Millie stood across from him.

"Can I get you anything else?" she asked.

He shook his head. As she started to walk away, he asked, "Have you eaten?"

"No. I was going to take my meal in the kitchen."

"Please join us."

"Thank you, but I have a few things that need my attention." She turned and headed back down the hall towards the kitchen.

He held back a sigh. She was a perplexing woman to say the least. Ma would have sat with them and talked with each of the boarders.

As soon as he finished, he took his empty plate into the kitchen. He set it in the wash basin and turned towards Millie. "I'll be out at the mine most of the day. If you need something, have Thomas send someone to get me."

She nodded.

"Breakfast was good."

"Thank you."

Suddenly he felt nervous around her as her deep bluish violet eyes studied him. It felt like she could see through his tough exterior straight to his soul.

He cleared his throat. "I'll see you around supper time."

"Until then."

Paul turned and headed out the door. He grabbed his mining gear from the barn and walked the mile to his mine. The sky darkened as gray clouds moved in overhead. If it rained, he hoped it would be light that way he could still work.

He rubbed the sore spot on his leg, a reminder of what had happened the last time he had worked his mine. No matter how much his leg was bothering him, he had to pull as much gold dust from the mine as he could over the next few days if he had any hope of making that payment.

Sweat beaded on his back as he dumped another shovel-full of the dried silt from the creek bed into the large sifters. Placer mining demanded a physical toll on his broad shoulders and thick legs that he didn't get working at the boardinghouse. The burn of his muscles exerting force reminded him of what it was like to truly labor—like on the farm in Missouri as a young man. There was something about sweating that made the work seem so much more important.

He began rocking dirt back and forth in the sifter. Some of the miners used a series of levers and pulleys rigged up to a big wheel and had their mules harnessed to it. They would walk around in circles for hours powering the sifters. Paul preferred using his own strength. It left him tired at the end of the day but also satisfied.

Some days he wondered why any man would be fool enough to mine. It took a lot of work to get just a little gold dust from the creek. It wasn't like the early days when he could plunge his hand into the icy waters and pick up a pan clear full. Still, his mine yielded a decent amount.

Some of the men were starting to consider digging into the ground. They figured if there had been five years' worth of dust readily available on the surface, surely there were nuggets hidden deeper. They could be right. For now, he stuck with his methods, especially since he was under a deadline.

He waited for the rockers to stop and gathered the smallest grains from the bottom sifter. It wasn't as much as he'd hoped. He brushed everything to the edge and gathered it into a pouch. Then he started the process over again.

He frowned. How could he have misplaced those receipts? Everything else had been in the folder. It wasn't like him or Ma to lose something so important. As he worked, he wracked his mind for where else he could have put those receipts.

What would happen if he lost the boardinghouse?

The thought hit him square in the chest. He didn't want to lose it. Even though it had been Ma's idea, he wanted to keep it going. He liked running the place. And now that Millie was here...

His mind shifted to her. Could she be the wife he hoped for?

So shocked by the bold thought, he dropped his shovel to the ground. He waited a very long time for a wife. Had pretty much given up on the idea. But, to think of her in such a way after having just met her a day ago—what was wrong with him? Sure, she was pretty. Downright pleasant to look at.

But to think of her as a potential mate—it was far too soon for such thoughts. He knew nothing about her and, if she didn't open up and start talking more, he wasn't sure he'd ever learn anything more. Looks were no reason to get hitched.

He reached down and picked up the shovel with a shaky hand. How had she managed to stay single for so long? Wasn't normal for a woman her age to have never married. Maybe there was something wrong with her. Maybe the whole "Miss" title was to hide that she had been divorced or widowed. Women in the West did all sorts of things to hide their pasts.

What was Miss Millie Pritchett hiding?

He shook his head. Focus, Paul. He needed to get to work and not dwell on some female. He had to save his boardinghouse.

———

Mid-afternoon, the skies broke forth in a torrent of rain. Paul had just enough time to gather the gold dust into a pouch before the worst of it hit.

As he walked home through the pouring rain, he held back curses. The pitiful amount of dust he gathered after five hours of labor wouldn't even make a dent in his tax debt.

When he approached the porch, a paper sat in his favorite rocking chair, held down by a small rock. He wiped his wet hands on his soaked trousers as he stood under the shelter of the porch. It was the weekly newspaper. He picked it up by the corner, careful to keep it from touching his drenched clothing.

Paul entered the boardinghouse and headed straight for his room. As he closed his door, he noticed the path of water he left behind. He set the newspaper and the gold dust on his desk before changing out of his wet clothes. Grabbing the towel on his dresser, he rubbed it over his hair until it stopped dripping down his back.

As he changed out of his soaked clothes, his eyes stayed glued to the newspaper. He was certain his name would be in it. Why else would someone have made sure he saw it?

The moment he finished dressing, he yanked the paper from his desk and scanned the contents. "Debts Owed" the title read. "Paul Lancaster, owner of Lancaster's Boardinghouse is hereby notified that he has twenty-one days to pay his back taxes or risk his property being auctioned off. Brooks announced today that he has held off seizing Lancaster's property since the debt is from several years ago and that Lancaster has remained current for the past few years. This news might be good for Lancaster's competition. Apparently the upright and honest man is not quite as righteous as he appears."

Paul crumpled the paper and tossed it to the floor then fisted his hand at his side. He should have expected such comments from the editor. After all, he had a reputation for speaking more opinion than fact.

Regardless, now the whole town knew. It was only a matter of time before Ma found out. She'd be disappointed and hers was the only opinion that meant anything to him.

He uncurled the fist at his side. Anger wouldn't help him now. It never had before. What he needed was more time. Hopefully twenty-one days would be enough.

CHAPTER 14

Millie smiled as she set a breakfast plate in front of Paul.

"Oh. Thank you," he said, appearing just as distracted as he had for days now.

When she met him for the first time a few days ago, he had a light in his eyes. That light faded on Friday and had yet to return. She found herself praying for him as she returned to the kitchen. Something was bothering him, but he hadn't said what. If her dad had reacted in a similar fashion, she would have pried into it. But Paul was her employer, so she felt it was safer not to.

Since she had eaten earlier, she began cleaning the breakfast dishes.

"Can I help?" Paul asked as he brought her a stack of dishes from the dining room.

Though she refused his help on other occasions, she accepted this time, especially since Sunday services would be starting soon. She handed him a towel.

"Caroline mentioned Sunday services are held in the dining hall," she said as she handed him a plate.

"Yes. Ma offered our place a few years ago and we continue to meet there. Our hope was to move into the courthouse last year, but another congregation received permission first. We hope to have our own building soon."

As she handed him the last dish, her fingers accidentally brushed his as he took it. Even though the contact was for a few seconds, she couldn't ignore the tingling sensation running up her arm. When she looked up at him, he smiled, seemingly unaffected.

"That it?" he asked pointing at the empty wash basin.

She nodded.

"Good. It's just about time we headed over." Paul dried his hands on the towel and set it aside. "Shall we?" he asked, angling his elbow toward her.

Millie's stomach fluttered as she quickly dried her hands and placed one in the crook of his arm. As he escorted her through the house and out the front door, she noticed again that he stood only a few inches taller than her. A smile twitched at the corner of her mouth. It was nice that she wasn't the taller one for a change.

As they entered the dining hall, Caroline called her name.

"Come," she said, pulling Millie alongside her. "I'll introduce you to everyone."

Before Caroline whisked her away, she caught part of Paul's conversation with Thomas.

"Is what the paper said true?" Thomas asked.

"We'll talk later," Paul answered. He said something else, but Millie's attention diverted to the introductions.

In a matter of minutes, she met Reverend and Mrs. Page, Caroline's brother and his wife, as well as several others from the ranch he worked on. "There will be plenty of time to get to know all of them after services," Caroline said before she joined her husband.

As Millie followed her to her seat, she sensed Paul slide into the spot next to her.

The dining hall tables lined one wall. All the benches faced the front door in two neat little columns, several rows deep. Each held four people or so. The Reverend stood at the front of the room behind a small stand that held his papers, much like the one her dad used.

The aroma of a cooking roast wafted in from the kitchen behind them.

Services started and her stomach knotted. This was the first time in her life she had worshiped in something other than the Presbyterian Church. What would Dad think?

Would she know any of the hymns? What songs did this congregation like? What about their beliefs? Were they the same as hers? What if they believed something entirely different? What if Reverend Page preached untruths?

Millie wrung her hands together. She wasn't ready to explore a new church. She hadn't given a thought to what it would mean. Perhaps she should leave and find the Presbyterian Church in town.

No, it was too late. Mrs. Page stood near the front of the room. She began to lead the congregation in singing. Millie no longer had time to escape unnoticed.

As the familiar melody and words filled the room, Millie's nerves settled. She closed her eyes and joined in, letting the music carry her heart before the throne of God.

In heaven above, the angelic throng
Around the throne rejoice;
But sinners saved should swell the song
With loudest--sweetest voice.

An image formed in her mind. Her mother's beautiful face was framed by thick, long black hair. Her mother sang the words with Millie, a scene so normal she almost forgot she knew none of the parishioners around her. How many times had the memories of worshiping God with her mother melded into an uplifting vision of her mother worshiping from the other side of heaven?

Silently, Millie thanked God for the vision today. She needed something familiar, and He had granted her that one request during the very first song.

A light touch on her arm drew her from the peaceful images of her mind as the song concluded. When she opened her eyes, she realized she was the only one still standing. She quickly took her seat and focused on what the pastor was saying.

Still, it was strange to hear a message preached by someone other than her father. She shifted in her chair. How many days or weeks would it take for her to feel comfortable here?

——

The emotion swelled in his chest as Paul listened to Millie sing the last strains of the final hymn with abandon. Every time he heard her sing, he felt as if he was listening to the heavenly host. He would never tire of it.

Paul glanced around discreetly. No Jake. He had hoped his friend would come for service and not just supper. Jake so badly needed the comfort only God could provide. Though Jake would not admit it, Paul could tell his friend was not dealing well with the loss of his mother and sister.

Pastor Page began the benediction, and Paul closed his eyes and bowed his head, silently lifting a prayer heavenward for Jake.

When Paul opened his eyes, Ma turned toward him.

"Who is she?"

He steered Ma away from Millie and towards the kitchen as the other men started moving the tables and benches back to their normal configuration. "Millie. Um… Miss Pritchett. She's my new housekeeper."

One of Ma's eyebrows arched high toward her gray hairline. "What happened to Mrs. Feldman?"

"She left after she had enough of Mr. Lowrey."

Ma turned her piercing brown eyes on him. "What's this business about owing taxes?"

Paul held back a groan. He felt like he was ten years old again and he had been caught pushing his brother. He shook his head, mystified that his ma still had that affect.

"Oh, I'm sorry," Millie said, hovering in the doorway of the kitchen. "I thought I should check on the roast."

As Paul inwardly cringed, hoping she hadn't heard his mother's question about the tax debt, Ma shooed Millie from the kitchen. "Nonsense, dear. I'll see to dinner."

"Now," Ma said, turning back on him. "Why is your name appearing in the paper?"

She pulled the roast from the oven and began mixing up gravy. He took a deep breath and let it out slowly.

"Levi Brooks says he has no records of our tax payments from '64 or '65. I found some of the receipts for '65."

"What about '64? I know we paid from the first month we were here."

Paul shook his head. "Can't find 'em."

Betty frowned. "Did you check the desk? I'm sure I've seen them in there."

"Ma, I've checked everywhere. Dug through the whole desk, my closet, under the bed, in the supply room. Nothing."

"Oh dear, how much do we owe?"

"*We* don't owe anything. I owe roughly three-thousand four hundred dollars."

Ma gasped. "That's more than what we paid in all of '65 and '66! How'd they figure that?"

"He said they take five times the value of the property and halve it to come up with the taxes due plus the penalty. I think they'll waive the part for '65 since I have those receipts. Still, it's more than I have."

"Ben and I will help. I've got some saved up from the baked goods I've been selling to the stores in town. He has some savings. We'll help." She patted his hand as if that ended the conversation.

Paul's gut knotted. He was thirty-eight years old. He wasn't about to take Ma's charity or her husband's savings to pay a debt he owed. "I'll figure it out, Ma. I have some money saved up for improvements to the property. Plus, there's the money I'm bringing in from the mine." He wouldn't tell her that it had been less than a few dollars a day lately—not even close to making a dent in the thousands he owed. "I'll make it," he lied.

She narrowed her eyes and studied him. He held her gaze using the poker face he perfected in his youth.

"Hmm. I'll be praying you do." Then she waved her hand at

him. "Go get our guests seated."

As he stepped from the kitchen, Millie approached him. "How can I help?"

Ma would be upset at him for sending Millie into the kitchen to get plates and utensils. She had this idea in her head that even though she was no longer living at the boardinghouse, she was here to serve her guests on Sundays. He sighed. He'd rather suffer Ma's wrath for putting an eager soul to work than listen to any more of her questions about his debt. It weighed heavily enough on him without her nagging.

Once Millie set the plates on the table, Paul helped Ma carry the food out to the table. Besides Ma and Ben, the entire Colter and Larson clans gathered around the table. Reverend and Mrs. Page were there. So were Thomas and Caroline and their family. As he took his seat, he noticed the empty spot across from him. Millie quickly slid into it. He offered a warm smile before he bowed his head for grace.

As soon as the blessing finished, the room filled with noise. Paul scanned the faces around the table. Still no Jake.

"What is it?" Ma asked.

"Worried about Jake."

"When is the last time he's been out?"

"He came to see me a few days ago. He was gaunt."

"Hmm. Maybe I should send Ben out to check on him."

"Wouldn't hurt. I was hoping to get out there soon myself, but I've been busy."

Ma nodded before shifting the topic to the boardinghouse. He patiently answered every question, wondering when she would finally let go of the place. Then Paul asked Ben how Colter Meat Company was doing. It seemed like any normal Sunday supper.

Except he couldn't stop glancing at Millie. She made eye contact with each person who was speaking, though she didn't join in the conversation. Her reserved behavior seemed a stark contrast to her vivacity when singing during service. Why such the difference, he wondered.

Ma asked him a question, but he missed it. Heat warmed his face.

"Pie?" she asked again.

Millie jumped to her feet. "I'll get it."

Before Ma could object, Millie was already gone. He stood. "I'll help."

The surprise on Ma's face brought a smile to his. He could almost tell what she was thinking.

When he entered the kitchen, Millie had several pieces of pie dished onto small dessert plates. Wordlessly he loaded his arms with four plates, balancing some on his forearms. Then he served their guests. He repeated the action until only six plates remained. He took four and Millie carried the last two, placing one in front of his ma and the other in front of Ben.

"Looks delicious, Mrs. Shepherd," Millie said.

"Dear, just call me Betty. Everyone does."

Paul laughed. "Except me."

Betty swatted at his arm. "Of course, silly."

————

Millie observed the playful interaction between Paul and his mother. They were obviously close. She thought back to the snippet of conversation she caught earlier in the kitchen. Something about tax debt. Paul hadn't seemed pleased by his mother's questions then, but he still humored her with answers.

Her eyes burned with unexpected emotion. The love between mother and son reminded her of her parents. She quickly swallowed her last bite of pie and gathered her dish and utensils. She stood and hurried to the kitchen before any tears could fall.

Nothing seemed right today. Everything was new and foreign. She missed Dad. They had been close, more so after Mom passed than before. Had it only been a few weeks ago that she stood in the kitchen of their small house, and he urged her to move to Prescott? That day seemed so long ago.

A longing for home—the one she shared with her parents in

Santa Fe—filled her heart. She retrieved the handkerchief from her sleeve.

A hand on her shoulder caused her to suck in the air rapidly. She turned toward Paul.

"Millie?" Concern furrowed thin lines on his forehead.

"I'm sorry."

"Are you alright?"

She forced a smile on her lips. "Just a little homesick is all. It will pass."

He removed his hand from her shoulder, leaving warmth behind. She noticed the stack of dishes he balanced in his other hand and took those from him, setting them in the wash basin.

"There you are, dear," Betty's voice came from behind her. "I'll get those."

"It's fine. I'm happy to see to them."

"Paul, can you fetch us some more water?" Betty asked.

He grabbed the bucket and took it with him out the back door of the dining hall's kitchen.

Earlier Millie had put some water on to heat while she dished up the dessert. She poured it into the wash basin and shaved a few curls of soap into the water.

"Tell me about your background, dear."

Paul entered through the back door and poured some of the water from the bucket into the wash basin to cool it to a more manageable temperature. Then his mother motioned for him to leave.

"Well, I grew up in Ohio. My father was a missionary to the Shawnee Indians. It was there he met my mother."

"Ah."

Millie hid her reaction. She figured Betty understood what that meant about her mother, but she didn't elaborate further. It was one of her secrets and she preferred not to let others know.

"After I was born, Dad built a small house near the town so I would be able to walk to school when I was old enough. It was the only home I ever knew. We left when I was fourteen so Dad could start a mission in Santa Fe."

She chose not to mention that she was the reason for the move. Her hand almost moved to her abdomen, but she reached for another dish in the water instead. Even after twenty-four years, she could still feel the looks of hatred directed her way. Cade could have protected her from all of that if he had truly loved her as much as he said. She had been far too trusting then.

Millie cleared her throat and continued. "We lived in Santa Fe for almost four years before my mother passed. She became very ill and weak from malaria. After that time, I stayed with Dad to care for him. A few years ago, we moved to Wickenburg. He felt it was time to minister to the miners there."

"How did you meet Caroline?"

Millie smiled. "She needed a chaperone to take her from Santa Fe to Prescott. My father and I brought her with us."

"Ah. And you kept in touch since then?"

"Yes."

"Paul said you are his new housekeeper. At first, I thought you might just be visiting, but it sounds like you are planning to stay?"

"Yes."

The two fell into silence as they worked through the large stack of dishes. At last, Betty broke the silence. "Well, I'm glad you're here, dear. I hope Paul is treating you well."

Millie looked at Betty, catching a suspicious glint in her eyes. "He is."

"Good." Betty smiled. "You be sure to tell me otherwise."

She nodded, wondering again what that look meant. Betty seemed rather pleased.

A loud crash came from the back kitchen door, startling both women.

CHAPTER 15

Paul heard the sound from the dining hall and rushed towards the kitchen.

"I'mmmm here for supper."

Jake Waters stumbled over the threshold of the dining room. Paul stepped forward and caught him before he hurt himself. The harsh scent of alcohol hung heavily over his friend.

"We missed you at supper."

"Misssssed me? Am here."

"We finished a while ago, Jake."

"Naw. Ammmm on time. Came hungry."

"Here, have a seat." Paul led his friend to the closest table and helped him sit on the bench.

"Wait here while I fix you a plate."

Paul turned and almost ran into Millie who held a full plate of leftovers in her hand.

"Here you go, Mr.—"

"Waters," Paul whispered.

"Mr. Waters."

Jake stared at the food before him for a few seconds before looking up at Millie. When he did, his face went pale, then flushed red. His eyes widened in terror as if he was seeing a ghost.

"Sissy?" he whispered, then shook his head violently. "No... no, you're not..."

Then he lunged from the bench, grabbing Millie by the

throat.

"You damn Apache! Trying to poison me? I am the last Waters!"

Millie's eyes went wide as she struggled to free her neck from Jake's grip.

Paul was at her side in one step. He seized Jake's wrists and twisted them away from Millie. She hurried into the kitchen. Despite the strong urge to run to her, Paul stood his ground.

"What are you doing!"

"You see that Apache squaw. She's trying to kill me!"

Paul's heart sank as understanding hit him. Jake wasn't seeing Millie at all—he was seeing the Apache who'd killed his family. His friend was completely lost in his grief and trauma.

Jake threw his body toward Paul, forcing him to let go of his hold. Then he picked up the plate of food and hurled it at the wall.

"You can't kill me! I won't let you!"

Paul grabbed Jake by the shirt collar and hauled him out the front door towards the barn. He kept going until he reached the water trough for his stock. Then he dunked Jake's head in the cool water for a few seconds before lifting it up again.

"What has gotten into you?"

"Paul?"

"Yeah."

Jake's shoulders slumped as the fight left him. He crumpled to the ground in a heap. A whimper came from the depths of his soul.

"They're gone, Paul. Apache killed 'em."

Paul crouched down next to his hurting friend.

Jake let loose a terrible wail and covered his face with his hands. "They're gone."

"I know." Paul squeezed Jake's shoulder. "I know."

He closed his eyes as his friend truly grieved, perhaps for the first time. *Lord, comfort him. Help him to see there are many that care for him. We're here, ready to help.*

Jake's sobs subsided. "I want them back." His voice was soft.

"I'm sorry."

"Paul, I need them back."

Paul's throat constricted. "They can't come back."

"But I miss them. They were all I had."

"I know."

Silence settled over the two men. A few minutes ticked by before Paul stood. "Let me take you home."

Jake nodded.

Paul left him by the trough and readied a wagon. He spotted Ma approaching from the dining hall.

"Is he alright?" Ma asked.

"Just grieving."

She handed him a bundle of food. "Take this with you."

"Thanks." He glanced around hoping to find Millie.

"She's in the kitchen."

"Is she…"

"She'll be fine. Might be best for you to talk to her when you get back."

"I will."

Paul leaned down and kissed Ma's forehead. "I love you, Ma."

She reached up and patted his cheek. "I love you, too, son."

He walked towards the barn, food in hand, and helped Jake up to the wagon seat.

The drive out to Jake's place passed in silence. After the first mile, Jake's head bobbed up and down with the sway of the wagon.

What had come over Jake when he had seen Millie? He didn't know, but one thing was certain, Jake had not been himself. He had never seen his friend so drunk he could barely stand. He knew Jake imbibed from time to time, but not to the point of being out of his mind.

The small farm cabin came into view. The area where crops once stood was overgrown with wild grass. The door to the barn sat next to the entrance, propped against the wall. On the porch of the cabin, a pail of water sat untouched near the front door.

Paul's mouth went dry as he stopped the wagon. He should

have come out sooner.

Jake groaned. Paul jumped down from the wagon and hurried to the other side to help him.

"Come on." He nudged Jake.

"Where…"

"Let's get you inside."

Paul looped Jake's arm around his shoulder, and he led his friend inside, depositing him on the bed. As soon as Jake's head hit the pillow, he was out cold.

Paul surveyed the room. The sickening churning of his stomach grew worse. Two months' worth of dust coated everything in the room, except one of the chairs at the table. The stench of spoiled food hung heavily in the air. The stove was cold, but a pot sat on top. Sure enough, that was the offender.

He grabbed the pot and dumped it outside, away from the cabin to keep wild animals from getting too close.

Shaking his head, he entered the barn. It hadn't been mucked in a while. No matter, as all the stock were gone.

He rubbed his forehead. Things were much worse than he imagined. How was Jake getting by with no food in the house, no stock in the barn, and no crops in the field?

Lord, I don't know what to do.

Paul squinted against the sunlight, cocking his head to one side hoping to hear an answer. The wind rustled the shin-high grass then silence settled over the farm. It was time to head home.

But he couldn't leave Jake, could he?

Paul checked on his friend who remained fast asleep. He shifted from one foot to the other. Surely Jake had been eating something. Though he was skinnier, he did not appear to be starving. Perhaps he sold his livestock and was buying food from town. From the state of the farm, it didn't appear he was spending much time there.

Let him rest.

Was that the answer he was looking for?

Paul frowned and shook his head. He had to get back. He would check on Jake tomorrow.

———

Millie put a hand to her throat and sank into the nearest chair, swallowing several times. Her breathing sounded loud and rapid to her own ears. She closed her eyes, still trying to make sense of the attack.

"You alright, dear?"

At the sound of Betty's voice, she opened her eyes.

"Jake isn't normally like that."

Shock forced staccato words from her lips. "I. Hope. Not."

Betty laid a hand on her shoulder. "Not that I'm making excuses for him, but he's been going through a rough patch the last few months."

Millie snorted. Rough patch! The man choked her for pity's sake!

"There, there. Paul will explain everything when he gets back. Let's get you back to the boardinghouse. Then Ben and I will clean up here and be on our way."

Millie stood. "I can manage."

"Nonsense. Ben! Can you escort Miss Pritchett home?"

"Yes ma'am."

"Really, I'm fine."

"I know y'are." Ben nodded in his wife's direction. "But would ya help me stay outta trouble with the missus?"

"Alright."

Ben winked and offered his arm and walked her the short distance to the boardinghouse.

"Was nice meeting ya, ma'am. I'm sure our next Sunday dinner won't be as exciting."

Millie rewarded Ben's kindness with a smile. "Nice meeting you as well."

"Now, get on inside. I'm sure the missus is watching from the kitchen."

"Thank you, Ben."

As soon as she entered the parlor, Millie plopped down on one of the wingback chairs facing the fireplace. Her head throbbed and her throat still hurt when she swallowed.

Apache.

That's what Jake had called her.

She rubbed her hands up and down on her long ebony braids and closed her eyes. She could remember her mother unraveling the long braids as a young girl and brushing out her hair.

"Your hair is your crown of glory," Mom had said.

"Is that why you braid your hair?"

Mom laughed. "No, Millicent. My mother—"

"Nokomtha?"

"Yes, your grandmother. She always said it was too hard to grind wheat or chase after little ones otherwise."

Oh, how she missed her grandmother and aunts and uncles! So many of her mother's people that she had left behind so long ago.

"I am not Apache," she whispered to the empty room.

It had been a long time since her heritage posed a threat. In Santa Fe, no one cared that her skin wasn't ivory and pale like her dad's. No one ever asked why she was so tan, not even after her mother passed away. Same with Wickenburg. Both towns had a large Mexican population. People probably assumed her mother had been Mexican.

Only she wasn't.

Millie stared at the clock on the mantle, not really seeing the time. It had been a mistake to move to Prescott. She should never have left Dad. He was the only one who loved her just as she was. With him, there was no pretending.

A tear slid from her eyes. She wanted to go back so badly. She wanted the safety of her dad's love. But she couldn't go back. He had started a new life without her.

She squared her shoulders and stood. She would make the best of her new life even if it meant pretending to be something she wasn't.

CHAPTER 16

By the time Paul arrived back at the boardinghouse, the sun was low in the sky. He hurried through caring for the horse.

Hopefully Millie hadn't left. He had enough to worry about with the looming tax debt payment and Jake. He needed her to stay, if for no other reason than he didn't have time to look for another housekeeper.

Yet, there were other reasons he wanted her to stay. She was a good cook and did a fine job caring for the boarders. And oh, that soft smile. In a very short time, she had made herself a pleasant part of his life.

He shook his head. How could he ask her to forgive Jake? She knew nothing about this man, save that he assaulted her the first time they met.

Paul opened the front door and stepped into the parlor. Millie sat in a chair facing the fireplace. The book in her lap started to slide and he caught it before it fell to the floor. She didn't stir.

He studied her face. Tan. Dark hair. So beautiful.

"What?" Millie slowly straightened in the chair. Her eyelids fluttered open, revealing the brilliant violet eyes he loved so much.

"Oh, Paul."

She glanced away and smoothed the wrinkles from her dress.

He gave her a minute to compose herself as he took a seat across from her.

"Listen…"

Millie met his gaze.

"I'm sorry about what happened."

Though she looked at the floor, he saw the emotions march across her face. Fear. Worry. Regret.

"Jake's been through terrible losses lately. He lost his pa several years ago and has been caring for his ma and sister since. Then a few months ago, while he was in town for supplies, Apache raiders attacked his farm. His mother and sister… they didn't survive."

"For a time, it looked as if his mother would pull through. She had even gained enough strength back to help care for his sister."

"It was only a few days after the attack when his sister passed away. The next day his ma joined her. Doctor said she gave up."

Millie twisted her hands together in her lap.

"Millie."

She stopped fidgeting but did not look up.

"I'm sorry. I've never seen Jake act like that before. I don't know what got into him or why he did it. All I know, he wasn't in his right mind."

Silence seemed to speak so loudly. Why didn't she say something? Anything!

———

Millie's eyes burned as Paul recounted the tragedy Jake Waters had faced. She knew what it was like to lose someone, for she had lost not only her mother, but another who had been so dear to her. She could imagine Jake's grief.

Still, he had attacked her. Accused her of being an Indian. Oh, she could not bear that thought being implanted in the parishioners' minds. In Paul's mind.

Maybe she should go back to Caroline's house for a while. Stay with her until she could find other work. If it wasn't safe for her to stay here…

"Millie."

She lifted her gaze and met Paul's handsome eyes. She couldn't leave.

"Please don't leave. You are a fine cook and housekeeper. The boarders love you already. I know it's been only a few short days, but I need you to stay."

Her breath stopped. She was needed. In that moment, some of her hurt lifted.

Paul scooted to the edge of his seat and reached for her hand. She let him take it and savored the warmth created by his thumb rubbing the back of it.

"Jake won't do something like that again. You'll be safe here. I promise."

She slowly let out a long breath.

"Does he come here often?"

Paul released her hand. "Um… He visits from time to time. Mostly in the evening or on Sunday afternoon."

"And you'll be here when he is?"

"Yes."

She closed her eyes, fighting against the desire to flee. It would be easier to find another job than to stay and risk another encounter with Jake. Yet, she had stood her ground and defended herself well against all manner of ruffians in Santa Fe and Wickenburg. She did not need to rely on Paul to protect her.

A niggling fear whispered in her ear. What if the town learned of her heritage? What if Paul did?

Millie opened her eyes and squared her shoulders. "I'll stay."

Paul stood and pulled her up and into his arms with a *whoop*. "Thank you."

Then he quickly released her, as if he realized what he had done.

"Thank you. Please don't worry about Jake. You have nothing to fear from him. He will treat you well. I'll make sure of it."

She nodded, even though she wasn't sure Paul would be able to keep that promise.

CHAPTER 17

May 21, 1869

Paul absentmindedly filled his pouch with the small yield from a long day at the placer. The sun hung low in the sky—a good indication that he would be late for supper. Millie would save a plate for him just as she had each of the last few days. She was so sweet to take care of him.

He frowned as he thought back to the conversation with Ma when she came to town with Ben yesterday to deliver beef from the ranch.

She had caught him watching Millie again.

"You like her?"

He nodded, knowing there was no use hiding the truth from Ma.

Ma smiled and said nothing more. She didn't have to. His brain chewed over all the reasons he should not fall in love with Millie. She was too quiet. He always thought he'd end up with someone more like Ma.

He suspected Millie was part Indian after Ma told him that Millie's dad worked as a missionary among the Shawnee. If the townsfolk learned of her parentage, he would have no chance of a relationship with her. In the Arizona Territory it was illegal to marry an Indian. He doubted if the law would care that she hadn't come from the Apache tribe.

But he didn't really know if she was Indian or not. She didn't dress like one. She didn't act like one. From all appearances, she dressed, talked, and acted like a white woman. Never mind her tanned skin.

Regardless, she had many redeeming qualities. Her cooking rivaled Ma's. That alone earned his respect. She worked hard, often refusing his help on the rare days that he stayed at the boardinghouse instead of trying to squeeze another ounce of gold dust from his mine. Her voice—it was mesmerizing, especially when she sang, which she did often.

Those violet eyes. Her full welcoming lips. He closed his eyes to conjure her image. So beautiful in so many ways.

He opened his eyes and shook his head. He didn't have time to pine over a woman. He only had a week left before his tax debt was due and he was still at least one thousand short.

Maybe it was time to talk to Thomas. Perhaps he could borrow some from the profits at the livery then pay him back over time.

No. Not with another baby on the way. Thomas was nervous enough as it was. Paul wouldn't place his burden on his friend.

"Ben and I will help." His mother's voice followed him as he headed back towards the boardinghouse from the mine.

He sighed. There had to be another way. He ran through the possibilities again and came up short.

By the time he made it back to the boardinghouse, the sun had set. A soft glow illuminated the front window. He paused on the porch for a few minutes, savoring the silence of the evening. When his stomach growled, he pushed the door open.

Silence greeted him as he stepped into the dining room. The table had been cleared of all dishes. He looked at the clock on the mantle. It was even later than he thought.

He walked through the dining room, down the hall towards the kitchen. Humming drew him into the room, and it stopped as soon as Millie noticed him.

"I was beginning to fear something happened to you." Her soft smile hinted she had not been too afraid.

"Long day." He ran a hand over his hair and started to take a seat at the small kitchen table.

"I can see that. I saved you a plate, but it is probably cold. I'll warm it over the stove while you go and wash up."

Heat flushed his cheeks. He was so hungry he hadn't stopped by his room first. "Thank you," he said over his shoulder as he walked down the hall to his room.

Rushing to clean up, he stopped long enough to hide the pouch of gold dust from the day. Tomorrow, he would weigh it to see how much more he really needed.

When he made his way back to the kitchen, his warmed plate sat on the small table. He took a seat as Millie brought him some coffee.

"You look tired."

"I am," he said around a mouth full of food.

When she took a seat across from him, he hid his surprise. She had never sat with him as he ate.

Taking a sip of his coffee, he grimaced.

"I'm sorry," she said. "We ran out of coffee this afternoon. I had to reuse the grounds from this morning."

"We did?" He frowned.

"Yes. I did mention yesterday that I thought we might."

Paul rubbed his hand across his forehead. Now he remembered. He was supposed to stop at Hardy's this morning before he left to pick up more coffee, flour, and sugar.

"Do you have enough flour for the morning?"

Millie shook her head. "But I can make eggs, bacon, sausage, and potatoes. That should be plenty."

He groaned. Mr. Lowrey would give her no end of grief for not serving bread or biscuits of some kind.

She smiled, as if reading his thoughts. "Don't worry about Mr. Lowrey. I saved a few slices of bread from supper tonight for him."

———

When a slow smile stretched across Paul's lips, Millie knew she had impressed him with her foresight. She welcomed the warmth that spread from her middle to her heart.

His smile was short lived. "I'm sorry I forgot to get the supplies you requested. I…"

As his shoulders stiffened, she reached for his hand. "I will make do."

Her breath left her lungs in a soft puff when he curled his fingers around hers. The gentleness of his touch caught her off guard.

"I will see to it first thing in the morning. I promise. And I'll talk to Mr. Osborn to see if we can borrow some coffee from his restaurant for the morning."

The intensity in his eyes spoke more than his words. She could tell he was upset with himself. He gave her hand a light squeeze then released his hold.

"Thank you," she said once she could trust her voice not to shake like her hand was. She quickly dropped it to her lap.

She sat in silence as Paul finished his meal. Then she stood and set his dishes in the wash basin.

"Well, I'm off to Osborn's."

Millie felt a light tug on the end of her braid. When she turned to look over her shoulder, Paul smiled and winked at her.

"Unless you think you could make do without coffee in the morning."

She smiled and motioned for him to leave. "I can, but I don't think I want to see what Mr. Lowrey is like without any."

As he ducked out of the kitchen, his laughter floated down the hall. "Me either."

When his footsteps faded, she turned her attention back to the dishes. Once washed and dried, she planned the meals for the next day before retiring to her room.

Millie readied herself for bed and turned down the lamp. She stared at the darkened ceiling for some time as sleep eluded her.

She liked Paul. He was a kind man. Even though she knew he was worried about the tax debt—she wasn't supposed to know about that, but she did—he still managed to keep a friendly disposition with her and the boarders.

A smile stretched across her lips as she thought about him teasing her right before he left. He made her laugh. The way her heart turned upside down when he was near—she could see a life with him.

The thought sobered her faster than a shock of cold water on her face on a winter morning. She couldn't love him.

Just look at what happened with Cade. Her mind warned her.

It was not the same, she argued with herself. She had been fourteen. Young. Gullible. Stupid. Paul was nothing like Cade.

Oh, but there was a time when she thought the world of Cade too. He had been kind and sweet. He made her laugh and smile. He made her feel alive, amazing. Until he betrayed her.

The memories and images from decades ago trampled through her mind. His eyes. His smile. His kisses.

His lies.

What would her life have been like had she not listened to his silver tongue? Her family would never have had to leave Ohio. Perhaps she would be happily married with children by now instead of carrying around the burden of failure and regret.

Tears moistened the corners of her eyes. Spilling over like a swollen river after a heavy rain, her tears dampened her cheeks and then her pillow. She wanted a man who would look beyond her past and see the woman she was now. Someone to love her and cherish her. Someone devoted.

No matter how nice Paul was—how handsome and kind—if he knew the awful truth about her past, he wouldn't want her. No man ever had.

She needed to clear Paul out of her heart now, before it hurt even more than it did. She would not let herself hope for something beyond spinsterhood. That was her destiny. She accepted it years ago and she would remind herself of it daily if that's what it took to kill the hope that Paul could be the one man who was different from the others—different from Cade.

CHAPTER 18

Millie still felt down the next afternoon as she walked from the boardinghouse to Caroline's house.

Would she feel better if she shared her deepest secrets with Caroline? Though the two had lived apart for several years, the closeness they experienced on the journey west instantly renewed when she moved to Prescott. She talked in depth about how she lost her mother and how difficult life seemed for several years afterward. Caroline listened sympathetically then.

Yet, her secrets—what happened with Cade—she hated herself for it. She was ashamed of it. How could she share the darkest part of her heart with Caroline? She would be shocked if she even believed Millie capable of such things.

No. This was far different than sharing her grief over her mother's passing. It would involve shedding light on the ugliest parts of her being. There's no way that would help her feel better. This was a burden she would continue to carry alone. Only her dad and mom knew the truth.

She forced herself to hum a song, hoping it would improve her mood before she arrived, and Caroline questioned her.

As she stepped onto the porch Caroline threw the door open.

"Millie!" She drew her into a big embrace—well, at least as much as her belly would allow. "Come in. I've missed you so much!"

Millie laughed. "It hasn't even been a week yet."

Caroline mock-pouted. "Sunday services never seem to give me enough time to catch up with everyone. How have you been? I noticed you were humming. Any reason?"

Her friend's eyes danced with merriment. Millie avoided the question as she took a seat at the table.

"Hmm," Caroline continued without waiting for a response. "I'll bet it has something to do with Paul."

Heat burned the apples of her cheeks. He wasn't the reason for her humming, but her reaction would not convince Caroline otherwise.

"I knew it. You do like him. I thought you would. When you first wrote and said you'd be coming to Prescott, I knew I would have to introduce the two of you. I mean, you're both about the same age. Never married. I thought there might be a chance—"

"I don't think of him that way," Millie lied, remembering her resolve to push him from her heart. "I work for him. We're friends. Nothing more."

Caroline set a steaming cup of tea in front of Millie and then took a seat. She played with the handle of her teacup, her eyes narrowed. "I don't believe you."

Millie lifted the teacup to her lips and gently blew on the liquid to cool it down. She ignored Caroline's comment and shifted the conversation. "How much longer before the baby comes?"

Caroline cocked her head to one side. "Maybe another three months. I'm not sure. I'm ready for him to arrive."

"Him?"

Caroline giggled. "Thomas is convinced it's another boy. I'm almost hoping for a girl."

"Almost?"

"Yeah, almost—until I think that she might turn out to be like me or my sister, Missy!"

Millie laughed, knowing both women were rather spunky.

"Mama says it would serve me right to have a girl." Caroline sipped her tea. A frown settled on her face. "I just hope if it is a girl, she turns out wiser than me."

"Oh?"

Caroline looked over to where Drew was sitting, drawing pictures on a slate. She sighed heavily. "I flirted way too much as a young lady. It eventually got me into trouble. Only now, having Drew, I understand what I put my poor mother through. How many nights had she lain awake praying fervently that I might grow wise? Neither she nor I could have imagined the real cost of that prayer."

"Yet, look at what blessings came from it." Millie almost cringed at the words that came from her mouth. Couldn't they apply to her situation too?

No. The only blessing in her case was that she learned the value of obedience. Otherwise, the tragedies far outweighed the blessings.

Caroline's eyes misted. "When I think of how my actions could have altered the course of little Drew's life..." She cleared her throat. "Some lessons are learned but once and last a lifetime. I only wished I had learned that one earlier."

Caroline dabbed at the corners of her eyes before changing the subject. "So, are you settling in?"

Millie nodded. "I suppose so. I still miss Dad." She fingered the cookie on the saucer.

"I imagine it's hard to be far away after living with him all your life."

"I... He has someone to take care of him." She wasn't needed anymore. Her eyes burned but she blinked away the would-be tears. She still hadn't found her purpose, her place.

Caroline crossed her arms over her chest and began tapping one finger rapidly against her temple.

"Oh no." Millie groaned.

"What?"

"I know what that means."

"What *what* means?"

"The tapping."

Caroline lowered her hand to the table. She lifted her chin and wiped the emotion from her face. "It means nothing."

Millie shook her head. "I don't believe you. You're scheming something."

Caroline relaxed for a moment then waved her hands in the air excitedly. "Fine! I was just thinking that Paul really needs someone to take care of him. He's been alone for a long time. He's a little lost right now. You can see it. This whole tax thing has him all knotted up."

Millie nodded, before realizing the action served to fuel Caroline's intention.

"I knew it."

"I was just agreeing with your assessment of Paul's tenseness. Countless times over the past few weeks, he's come home from the mine dejected."

"So, you've noticed?"

Millie frowned. "I live under the same roof. It is hard not to notice when he doesn't show up for supper." Never mind that she noticed everything about him. His broad shoulders. Shining blue eyes. His calm disposition, even under stress. Her cheeks warmed again.

"Uh huh."

Millie sighed, wishing Caroline would leave off.

"Thomas and I are trying to figure out how we can help. We thought about giving him a loan, but Thomas would prefer to wait until after the baby is born. Only that will be too late to really help Paul keep the boardinghouse."

Millie's heart sank. "Could he really lose it?"

"I suppose. Thomas says that if Paul doesn't pay up, then they will put Paul's property up for auction. Depending on who wins the auction, Paul could truly lose it."

What would she do if that happened? It would be hard not to see him every day. Millie raised the teacup to her lips. She would miss that.

CHAPTER 19

After working the morning at the mine, Paul headed home and picked up the rest of his gold dust, including what he mined that morning. He needed to get it converted to money. Only then would he truly know how much more he needed to earn in the next two days. That's all the time he had left.

He opened the door of the assayer's office. The earthy aroma of dirt and dust tickled his nostrils. He tried to hold back a sneeze.

Mr. Douglas looked up. "Morning Lancaster. Figured you'd be by soon enough. I'll be with you as soon as I finish up with Talbert's man."

Paul tried not to frown. Of course, Douglas had seen the newspaper article. The whole town had. And, just like the rest of the town, they knew how he'd try to make the money to pay the debt.

He shuffled from one foot to the other as he waited for Douglas to finish up. Hopefully he had enough gold dust in his pouch to settle his debt. He was tired of the stares and sneers and snide comments from the rest of the town. For some reason they seemed to particularly rejoice in his misfortune.

It *was* misfortune. He was innocent, certain he had paid the tax debt on time all those years ago. Yet, with no record of those transactions, his only choice was to pay this debt.

Talbert's man nodded as he left the counter. Paul stepped forward and set the pouch on the scales.

Douglas quickly snatched the bag from the scales, opened it and poured the contents directly onto the scales. "You know how it works, Lancaster. Gotta be sure it ain't filled with dirt. Sides, I don't care to pay out for the weight of the cloth on your pouch."

Heat rose to his face. He did know the rules, but in his eagerness to get this whole thing behind him, he wasn't thinking. When Douglas handed him the empty pouch, he took it and stuffed it in his pocket.

"Hmm. How much do you owe, again?"

"None of your business."

"No need to get testy." Douglas scratched some notes on a piece of paper. "Looks like I can give you about three thousand one hundred and eighty-seven for the pile of dust."

His heart pounded. He was so close—only two hundred fifty dollars short. Surely, he could make that in the next two days at the mine.

"I'll take it."

"Gold or greenbacks?"

"Greenbacks." Paper notes were good enough to pay the tax collector. No worries about the value changing in the next few days.

Douglas counted the notes and handed them to Paul. "Good luck, Lancaster."

He didn't need luck. He had enough time to make up the rest. Surely the mine and the boardinghouse would remain his. He wished Douglas a good day before heading home.

———

In a good mood from the meeting at the assayer's office, Paul whistled an upbeat tune. It had been a long time since his spirits were this high. He darted up the stairs of the front porch and stopped in his room to drop off the stack of greenbacks before heading toward the kitchen.

As he suspected, Millie was singing a hymn softly as she assembled a pie. He stood just outside the entryway and watched.

Oh, how he longed to hold her in his arms. To kiss those soft lips. To feel the warmth of her breath mingle with his just before he stole a kiss.

The longing frightened him. He only met her a month ago. How had she so quickly wrapped herself around his heart, with so little effort?

What if he couldn't see her every day? What if he lost the boardinghouse and she had to leave? He would miss her terribly. Not just her beauty or the attraction he felt. He would miss her soft words and her kind heart. He would miss seeing her smile at Mr. Lowery as the man complained about his food. He would miss her singing with abandon on Sunday mornings as she stood next to Caroline. He would miss everything about her.

A thought quietly slipped into the back of his mind. *Lord, is it possible she is the woman you've made just for me?* Goodness, he hadn't even kissed her yet and he was already thinking something permanent.

He couldn't deny his feelings for her. He only hoped she might feel the same—even after the short period of time they had known each other.

Perhaps it was time to see if she felt the same way. He entered the kitchen and leaned against the counter as she slid the pie into the oven.

"Afternoon. Smells delicious," he said as he flicked one of her braids.

"Why do you do that?" she asked as she turned toward him with a half-smile on her lips.

So, she liked his teasing. "Dunno."

"I don't believe you."

He stepped closer and reached for the end of one of the braids trailing down her back. She beat him to it and slid them over her shoulder out of reach.

"That's not fair." He pouted.

"I need to clean up." She pointed at the flour-coated counter-top.

Paul reached for her arm, letting his fingers brush lightly

down it, until they rested on her hand. The act sent his heart pounding in his ears. With a slight tug, he pulled her closer, but not into his arms as he longed to do.

"Got something right here." He acted like he was going to wipe flour away from her cheek, but at the last second, he flicked one of the braids back over her shoulder. When her cheeks flushed, he almost stepped in to steal a kiss. Instead, he released her hand as a chuckle escaped his mouth.

"You, Paul Lancaster, do not play fair." Her poor attempt at a frown quickly transformed into a smile.

He leaned forward and studied the features of her face. Her soft lips captured his attention. Now would be a good time to kiss her. Just one step forward.

Someone coughed from the doorway.

Millie ducked her head and grabbed the nearest dirty bowl, scurrying to the sink. Paul frowned, annoyed at who interrupted the moment.

"Talbert." Paul spat out the name as he tore his eyes away from Millie to the man standing in the doorway. What was he doing here?

"Am I interrupting?" Simon Talbert asked.

With fist clenched at his side, Paul shook his head. "Join me in the parlor." He pushed past him leading the way.

Once in the parlor, Talbert sat down on the edge of a chair with his back as straight as a rod. He leaned his ivory-handled walking stick against the side of the chair. Everything about the man oozed wealth—from the expensive suit to the silk vest to the gold rings adorning his fingers.

Pretentious. That's how Paul always thought of him—from the very first time they met. Pushing his dislike for the man aside, he asked, "What did you want?"

Talbert's chin lifted slightly. "I believe I have a solution to your problem."

"What problem is that?" Paul glowered at him as he sat down.

"I am willing to offer you more for your mine. Would four thousand be acceptable?"

"My placer isn't for sale."

"Come now, Lancaster. The entire town knows of your issue. Surely you would be willing to sacrifice your mine to save this more lucrative business?"

Paul hesitated. He hated to admit that Talbert was making sense. But the same old arguments kept surfacing. He had most of the money he needed to pay the back taxes. Just a few more hundred and he would be set. Why give up after working so hard to keep both the boardinghouse and the mine?

"Four thousand two hundred and fifty dollars," Talbert countered.

"The mine is not for sale."

"Everything has a price. Name yours."

Paul stood and moved toward the front door. Holding it open, he said, "My placer has never been for sale. It is not currently for sale. And it never will be."

Talbert's face flushed to a deep red. He fumbled with his walking stick as he stood. "You'll regret this, Lancaster. You would really risk losing everything just to keep that stupid placer?"

"Why do you want it so badly? What's your angle?"

"I see it as a good business investment. Nothing more. This is your last chance. Name your price."

"It's not for sale."

Talbert started to argue again.

"Get out."

As Talbert stepped over the threshold, Paul slammed the door shut behind him. The front window rattled in its frame. The placer was his. He wasn't giving up his independence that easily and certainly not to Talbert, no matter how much he offered.

A little voice in the back of his mind echoed Talbert's words. *Everything has a price.*

CHAPTER 20

Friday morning Paul woke up from a fitful sleep. The last few days the placer didn't yield anything. He should have accepted Talbert's offer. Then, he would have nothing to fear as he appeared before the judge this morning.

Instead, he was risking everything. He was still a couple of hundred dollars short. But he hoped for some leniency from the judge. After all, he had made every payment for four years. The first year…

He sighed and rubbed his face with his hands. It wouldn't matter. The law was the law. The judge wouldn't look at his character. He wouldn't consider his good standing in the community. His lack of receipts for the first year would be his demise. He should have done a better job accounting for them.

As his gut twisted in a huge knot, he stepped from his room.

"Paul."

He closed his eyes and almost ran back into his room at the sound of Ma's voice. Instead, he opened his eyes and faced her.

"Ma."

"Do you have enough?" she asked.

He shook his head. He should have known she would make Ben bring her to town for the trial. It was just the way she was.

"How much do you need?"

Clenching his jaw, he debated whether to tell her. She would badger him until he did. "Two hundred fifty dollars."

She grabbed his hand and dragged him into the parlor. "Benjamin and I will cover it."

"No, Ma. I don't want your money."

When she turned toward him with pleading in her eyes, he almost lost his resolve. The boardinghouse was still important to her—even though she didn't live there anymore.

"This place. Paul, I don't want you to lose it. You sacrificed so much for me and your brother and sisters after your pa died. Let Benjamin and I do this for you."

He swallowed back the lump in his throat and walked past them. "I have to get to the courthouse." Then he strode out the door and down the street.

Prideful man. The voice in his head sounded like his father's this morning.

His father was right. He was being prideful. But for once in his life, he wanted to either succeed or fail on his own, without Ma in the background making everything right. He was thirty-eight years old for goodness's sake! It was time to be independent, make up his mind, and live with whatever happened.

He yanked open the door to the courthouse and walked in. A handful of onlookers sat on the benches at the back of the courtroom, including Simon Talbert. Ben and Ma slipped into one of the empty seats.

Paul walked towards the two tables in the middle of the courtroom. Levi Brooks and his brother Caleb, the District Attorney, sat on one side. Another man he didn't recognize sat at the other table. He stood as Paul approached.

"Mr. Lancaster, your mother asked me to represent you this morning."

Paul held back a groan of protest and shot a frown toward Ma.

"Name's Noah Gaffney."

Paul barely had time to introduce himself before the bailiff announced, "All rise!"

He remained standing.

"The honorable Judge Radcliff residing."

The judge entered the room and sat behind the large desk at the front.

"You may take your seats."

As Paul sat down, his hands grew sweaty. Prior to this very moment, the tax debt did not seem so real. He hadn't realized the seriousness of what was about to happen. He could lose his home—the one he built with his own hands. It was Millie's home too.

He glanced back at Talbert. The man sat with the same rigid posture, only this time a smug look overtly rested on his face. Why hadn't he just given Talbert what he wanted?

Caleb Brooks stood and announced the reason for the case. "Your Honor, the defendant, Paul Lancaster has been found to be in arrears of his tax payments for 1864 and part of 1865. This is the formal complaint against him for failure to pay back taxes and the assessed penalties."

"Your Honor." Mr. Gaffney stood. "Mr. Lancaster has provided the court with records showing payment for part of 1865. We request that the complaint be amended. The amount owed for back taxes and penalties should be adjusted to show February of 1864 through June of 1865, as Mr. Lancaster did not start operating the boardinghouse until such time."

"Agreed," Judge Radcliff responded. "Mr. Brooks, can you advise the court of the new amount owed?"

Paul held his breath. He and Levi Brooks already discussed the amount owed—it was the goal he had been working towards, but he still came up short. Perhaps Levi had calculated it wrong, and he would still be able to keep the boardinghouse.

"The total amount owed for back taxes for February of 1864 through June of 1865 is three thousand four hundred and thirty-seven dollars, plus fifteen percent for the cost associated with this court appearance. The total amount owed is three thousand nine hundred and fifty-six dollars."

Paul closed his eyes. He didn't know about the additional fifteen percent for the court appearance. He was over seven hundred dollars short. He was going to lose everything.

When he opened his eyes, Judge Radcliff's dark eyes pinned him to his seat. "Can you pay the amount in full today Mr. Lancaster?"

He shook his head. "No sir."

"Then be advised that the court authorizes Mr. Levi Brooks to seize the property and assets of Lancaster's Boardinghouse to be held for auction one week from today. Mr. Lancaster, you have until then to bring your tax payments current. Otherwise, the auction will proceed, and the boardinghouse will be awarded to the winner."

Paul nodded as the reality of the judgment pressed down on his stomach.

Judge Radcliff tapped his gavel closing the case. The loud noise echoed through the room, solidifying Paul's anger with himself. He was going to lose everything. Perhaps he could still accept Talbert's offer to sell the mine. It would mean the death of his dream, but at least then he wouldn't lose his home and business.

The bailiff asked the courtroom to rise again. As soon as the judge left the room, Ma approached him.

"Paul, we'll cover the rest of what you owe. Don't let them take this away."

He frowned. "Not now, Ma."

She opened her mouth to protest, but her husband grasped her hand and led her from the courthouse.

Mr. Gaffney asked, "Do you have any questions about the judgment?"

Paul snorted. "I don't suppose I can bid on my own property?"

"I'm sorry. They will start the bidding at the amount owed."

He gave a curt nod. "Thank you, Mr. Gaffney."

Then he turned on his heel and headed back to the boardinghouse.

———

When Paul entered the parlor of the boardinghouse, he groaned. Ma and Ben sat in two chairs. None of the boarders were around. Ma was not going to stay out of this.

"Take a seat," Ma said.

He did.

"With the judge's ruling, how much are you short?"

He pursed his lips.

"How much?"

"Seven hundred."

Ben said, "We'll pay it."

Paul stood to his feet. "No. I'm not taking your money."

"Sit down," Ma said.

This time he refused. "Ma, this is my problem. I will take care of it."

She stood and moved closer to him, wagging her finger in his face. "You listen to me Paul Lancaster. We spent years pouring sweat and tears into this place. I am not going to stand by and watch you throw it all away because of pride. We are going to cover what you don't have so you can keep this place."

Anger rose to the surface. "Ma, it's none of your business. If I can't make it on my own, then maybe this is God's way of saying it is time to move on."

She frowned and propped both hands on her hips. "It is not! It's time for you to stop being so doggone stubborn!"

"What difference does it make to you anyway? You're not here. You left. Remember?"

Her frown softened. "Is that what this is about?"

He rolled his eyes. "What are you talking about, Ma?"

"You're still mad that I married Ben and moved to the ranch. That was almost three years ago!"

"I'm not mad that you left."

She narrowed her eyes. "Then why won't you accept my help? Why won't you let us help you save your dream?"

Paul threw his hands up in the air. "It was never my dream, Ma. It was always yours. My dream is the placer mine. Not this." He turned around with arms spread wide to emphasize his point.

"This was all for you, Ma. Like everything always has been. The farm in Missouri. Letting you come west with me. This place. It has always been for you.

"None of it was ever my dream. I just wanted to come here by myself to this crazy wilderness. Be on my own. Give mining a try. And guess what? Over the past month, I've spent more days at that mine than I had in all the years prior. I love it."

"It's too dangerous, Paul. Too much Indian activity."

"It's my life! If I want to risk it mining that's my business, not yours."

"You're my son. You are always my business."

She reached out to touch his arm, but Paul pushed it away. Then he tilted his back and let out a long, loud growl. "I'm thirty-eight years old, Ma! At what point do I get to make decisions on my own without your interference?"

His ma backed away and sat down. Tears ran down her cheeks. "I didn't mean to stifle him," she whispered as Ben handed her a handkerchief.

Even though he knew he should smooth things over with her, he couldn't. He turned and stormed out the front door, heading to his mine.

Ma didn't understand how humiliating it was to have her constantly questioning his judgment, which seemed to happen more often since she moved to the ranch. Why wasn't he married yet? Why didn't he court such and such a gal? Why didn't he sell the placer? Why didn't he let her pay his debt?

On and on. Why couldn't she just let him be?

He was tired. Tired of her nagging. Tired of every decision and action being for her benefit. For once—just once—he wanted to decide for himself what he wanted to do. That's why he refused to sell the placer to Talbert. It was the one thing his mother had never controlled. It was the one thing that was completely his. And if he lost it, he wouldn't be able to replace it.

CHAPTER 21

Before Paul took ten steps from the boardinghouse, he saw a familiar figure approaching him. He held back a groan. On any other day, at any other time, he would have appreciated seeing Jake. But, not after this morning's humiliation or after the argument with Ma.

He kept walking briskly towards his mine. Within a few minutes, Jake fell into step beside him.

"I don't understand you, Paul."

He grunted.

"Why won't you just sell your mine to Talbert and save your boardinghouse?"

Paul ignored the question and started shoveling dirt into the sifters.

"Didn't the attack scare you at all? Aren't you afraid of being out there alone?"

"I'm not afraid."

"Well, maybe you should be."

The cold edge in Jake's voice captured Paul's attention. "Why's that?"

"You heard what happened to old miner Dodge, didn't you?"

He nodded.

"That was just two weeks ago. Them Apache aren't going to stop, you know."

Paul frowned. He still wasn't convinced that the men who attacked him were Apache. Nor was he sure of who really killed Dodge. Could have been vagrants. Could have been after his mine. Didn't matter. None of it would change his mind.

"I'm not selling."

Jake grabbed Paul's arm and jerked him around. Paul stopped the sifters and studied his friend. His face was pale, and his eyes were full of fear with dark circles resting beneath, giving him an almost haunted look. He dropped his hands to his side and nervously swayed back and forth from one foot to the other.

"I'm serious, Paul. You could be next."

Paul snorted. "Mining has never been without risk, Jake. That's never stopped me before. Look, despite the recent attacks, it's still safer than when I first started."

"It's not safe. You must stop."

Paul's ire rose. "I'm not selling. I worked hard to make this mine what it is. There's nothing that could make me give it up. Nothing. I'm not afraid to die and if it is my time, then it's my time. At least I would go out doing what I love."

Jake frowned and fisted his hands at his side. For a moment Paul thought he might take a swing at him. Then, after a moment of silence, Jake spat at the ground, turned on his heel, and stormed off to town.

"You don't understand," he called over his shoulder before disappearing out of sight.

"I could say the same," Paul said under his breath. Seemed no one understood why this mine was so important to him. Not his Ma. Not his friends.

———

Millie heard the entire argument between Paul and his mother. Mr. Lowrey probably even heard them from his room. A part of her could sympathize with Betty. She was just trying to protect her son.

Yet, she understood Paul's feelings better. Always being overshadowed by his parent. Always thinking of that parent first.

She understood because she spent so many years doing the same thing for Dad. When he wanted to move to Wickenburg, she followed him. When he wanted to give more to the poor, she figured out how to stretch their already minuscule budget. When he didn't want her to stay at the house alone because he was traveling, she went to stay with a parishioner.

From the moment her mother passed—perhaps even before then—her life revolved around her dad.

Millie pushed her feelings aside and prepared some lemonade. Then she took two glasses of the sweetened drink into the parlor.

"I smothered him," Betty cried as Ben held her close. "I didn't mean to."

"I know ya didn't. He knows it too."

Millie shuffled her feet to create just enough noise so they would notice her. "I brought some lemonade."

"Oh," Betty said, turning toward her. "Thank you, dear."

She smiled in return.

"You are such a dear girl, Millie."

Heat warmed her cheeks. "Thank you, Betty."

"Maybe you could talk to him?"

Millie blinked, not understanding the question.

"To Paul? For me? Help him understand I didn't mean to hurt him."

"Of course," Millie agreed, to help Betty feel more at ease.

"I think he went to his placer."

"Oh." She meant to talk to him now?

"Ben can walk you there, right dear?"

Ben stood and offered Millie his arm. She took it, still confused by Betty's urgency.

As they walked in silence, Millie mentally fought against Betty's request. She could see Paul's side of things and wasn't sure she wanted to convince him to think differently. It almost felt like an act of betrayal.

"There he is," Ben said. "Will ya be fine iffen I head back now?"

She nodded and watched Ben for a few seconds as he started

back towards town.

Then she turned her gaze to Paul. He hadn't seen her yet, so she watched him while she gathered her thoughts. He thrust a shovel into the dirt then he flung it into the top sifter. He repeated the action several more times. Her breath caught as she noticed for the first time how incredibly thick his arms were. Strong. Steady.

What would it feel like to have those arms wrapped around her? She was sure it would feel wonderful—like being home. For a few seconds, she let the hope linger. Maybe he would be different. Maybe she could really have a chance at love.

As she let out a shaky breath, her hope faded into the shadows.

———

In the distance Paul heard voices, soft at first, but growing louder. He glanced over his shoulder to catch a glimpse of Ben escorting Millie towards the mine. He kept his focus on working. An angry surge of energy moved from his arms to power the sifters. Ma sent it to her. He was sure of it.

As Millie stood a few feet from him in silence, he began to have his doubts.

"For the past twenty years, I have taken care of my dad," she said. "Did his laundry. Cooked for him. Made sure he didn't have any concerns."

The sifter fell out of rhythm for a moment. He worked it back into a steady pace.

"A few years ago, when he wanted to move from Santa Fe, I hadn't wanted to go. Mother was buried there. My friends, the few that I had, lived there. Things were comfortable. Safe. But he kept insisting he needed my help. I was part of his ministry. 'Partners' is what he said."

She took a few steps towards the creek. He glanced up to watch her. She stood with her profile facing him and her gaze settled over the creek.

"So, I went to Wickenburg four years ago."

Paul continued working the sifters and didn't hear her walk back from the creek to stand next to him. When she placed a hand on his shoulder he tensed and immediately stopped the sifters. Once his gaze met hers, she dropped her hand to her side.

"I understand what it is like to live under the shadow of a parent. I don't think I even realized I had been until I moved here. At first, I was angry with Dad. How could he send me away after all the years I devoted to him? But it truly was for my own good. I see that now."

Millie let out a slow breath. "It's been hard to feel comfortable, to redefine my role in life, without it involving him."

He understood what she meant more than he cared to admit. As she grew silent, he spoke. "After my pa passed, I had to step up and take care of the farm. I was the oldest. It was my responsibility. I missed out on an easy transition from childhood to adulthood. I just woke up one day and had to worry about Ma and my brother and sisters. I had to worry about the crops. I had to figure out how to make the money stretch until harvest."

Placing his hands on the edge of the sifter, he set it into motion again. "There was a time when I rebelled against the responsibility, but eventually I settled into the role of provider. Once my youngest sibling was grown and married, I started thinking about what I wanted. I told Ma I wanted to be part of the Gold Rush— to explore and live adventurously."

He frowned. "I thought I'd be moving away from her, but instead she told me the Lord was calling her to come with me. It was her turn to care for me. I could have left her behind with one of my sisters or even my brother. But I prayed on it. Prayed some more. And some more. No matter how many times I tried to reason it away, I always got the sense that she was supposed to come."

He stopped the motion of the sifters and turned to look at Millie. His heart flipped upside down as he studied her. She was so beautiful and at that moment he mentally thanked her dad for sending her here.

"But you didn't think about what it would mean to have her here, did you?" she asked.

"No. Ma is the type of person that always must be doing something. We decided the boardinghouse would be a great enterprise for her. Neither of us expected she'd fall in love and leave it behind."

Sadness coated his words before he could catch himself. Even a little jealousy. Ma had found love a second time and he was still looking. It almost didn't seem fair.

"The plan was always gonna be that I'd mine, and she'd run the boardinghouse. I was just supposed to help get it started, but most days I would be at the mine. Only from the very beginning it just didn't seem to work out that way."

Millie nodded.

They both fell into silence for a few minutes as he began gathering the gold dust from the sifters.

She asked, "What is most important to you?"

Paul swallowed hard. "I'm not sure I follow."

"Is it your placer? The boardinghouse? Your ma? Something else?"

Someone else. The thought threatened to stop his heart from beating. He finished securing the gold dust in a pouch before answering her with a whisper. "Ma. Ma is most important to me."

"That's why you keep fighting to save the boardinghouse even when you don't want to."

He frowned. Maybe there was truth in her statement.

"Then why not let her help you?"

Inhaling deeply, he let the air tighten his lungs then released it slowly. "I'm not sure. I guess 'cause I think I should be able to do this one thing on my own. If she hadn't come west, she wouldn't know if I failed or not."

Millie took a step closer. "But she is here. And she does know that you are a success no matter what happens with the boardinghouse."

A lump settled into his throat. Emotions warred. Should he take his ma's money? Or was it really time for him to succeed or fail on his own?

He cleared his throat. He wanted the boardinghouse to succeed, but without taking his ma's charity.

Silence settled over them and Millie moved to the edge of the creek again.

She let out a slow sigh. "It's so peaceful. I can see why you like to come here."

Paul followed her gaze to the sky.

"It's getting late. I need to go get supper started," Millie said.

"Shall we go, then?" he said, securing the small pouch of gold dust to his belt before offering her his arm. When she placed her hand in the crook, he realized that his answer to her earlier had been a lie. His ma wasn't the most important to him any longer. Millie Pritchett was. Sometime in the last week, she became the reason he wanted to fight to keep the boardinghouse.

CHAPTER 22

June 4, 1869

Paul's hands grew sweaty as he walked to the courthouse. He was about to lose his home. All over one hundred dollars. That's all he was short now. The last week at the mine yielded more than he expected. He had done everything he could to save it.

No doubt Talbert would win the auction. He was the wealthiest man in the area. Yet, it seemed his interest lay more with Paul's placer than the boardinghouse. Talbert stopped by last night again, with one more offer for his placer. Paul refused to sell again.

Why? Why is it so important to me to keep both?

He didn't know his own heart on the matter. Some invisible force compelled him to keep both the placer and the boardinghouse running.

Lord, I'm so close. Just one hundred dollars away. Why let me get this close only to fail?

The verse he read from Isaiah this morning came forward in his mind again. It struck him as odd then, and even more so now.

"I will give you hidden treasures, riches stored in secret places, so that you may know that I am the Lord, the God of Israel, who summons you by name."

What hidden treasures or riches stored in secret places did God have planned for him? Or was he just reading into the meaning, trying to force it into the context of his day?

He shook his head. Taking away the boardinghouse and giving it to Talbert was not giving him treasures or riches. It was taking them from him.

"Mornin'," Ben's familiar voice greeted him.

Paul looked around for his ma but didn't see her.

"I left yer ma at home. She was right angry at me for it, but I thought it was best she didn't get involved. Got a second?"

He nodded.

Ben motioned him to the alleyway between the courthouse and another building. Then he bowed his head and put a hand on Paul's shoulder. "Lord, make Paul strong where he needs to be and weak where ya want him to be. Let Yer will be done this day. Amen."

Tears burned the back of his eyes at the humble words spoken by his stepfather. Oddly he realized he wanted Ben here—needed his strength more than the fear and pain he would have seen in Ma's eyes.

"Let's go, son," Ben said. "Time to save yer home."

He frowned and followed Ben.

The noise of the crowd inside the courthouse dimmed as he entered. Somber faces of friends offered encouragement. Mr. Gaffney sat at the same table as last time. No judge was present, as this was not a legal proceeding. Instead, Levi Brooks started the meeting.

"Mr. Lancaster, do you have the full amount due?"

"No, sir. I am a hundred short."

"Very well. Let's—"

"I have the other hundred," Ben spoke up.

Levi opened and closed his mouth a few times before he said, "I'm sorry Ben, but if Paul doesn't have the funds, then we must auction off the boardinghouse."

"Four thousand!" Talbert shouted from the back of the room.

Levi's face went red as dollar amounts started volleying between the men gathered. He slammed his fist down on the table and shouted above the voices. "The bidding has not yet begun."

Paul's stomach sank to the floor along with his hopes. *I'm sorry, Millie. Sorry I couldn't save our home.* He clenched his jaw and prepared for the final death blow to Lancaster's Boardinghouse.

———

Millie hurried through the morning dishes. After she set the last few on a towel on the counter to air dry, she grabbed her reticule from her room and hurried out the front door. As she neared the courthouse, she heard the loud, chaotic hum of voices.

"We'll begin in just a minute!"

She sneaked into the back of the room. Her breath caught and a lump formed in her throat when she spotted Paul. He couldn't see her, but she had a clear view of his face. His lips turned down in disappointment and regret. Sadness shaded his blue eyes. This place meant even more to him than she realized. It was going to be hard to watch as it was handed over to some unknown man.

"Let's get started," Levi Brooks said.

Paul's shoulders slumped lower with the announcement.

Levi Brooks started the bidding at the amount owed—three-thousand nine-hundred fifty-six dollars. It quickly jumped to four thousand as two men went back and forth. One man dressed in fine clothes smirked. He obviously thought he would win.

"Four thousand one hundred!" a familiar voice shouted from behind her. It was Thomas Anderson.

"Thomas, don't," Paul said.

Thomas moved past her towards Paul. She couldn't hear his response.

The wealthy man added another hundred. Thomas countered with fifty. The wealthy man jumped two hundred more.

Millie held her breath as Thomas shook his head. She knew he couldn't really afford what he had already offered, so going any higher would have been foolish.

As Levi Brooks started the customary "going once," Ben joined the bidding.

"Five thousand five hundred seventy-five dollars!"

The crowd hushed. Millie's breath left in a rush. Paul whirled around to look at his stepfather.

"Ben, you can't do this. Just let Talbert have it."

"Five thousand six hundred!" the wealthy man shouted.

"Six thousand," Ben shot back. His glare dared the man to go further.

Millie waited as Levi Brooks counted out, "Going once, going twice. Sold!"

Thank you, Lord, for letting Paul keep it. For she had no doubt that Ben did this with every intention of giving the property back to Paul.

She turned and pushed her way through the crowd before Paul noticed her. She would still get to see him every day. The thought brought a smile and a song to her lips as she headed home.

———

Paul couldn't believe what he just witnessed. First from Thomas. Then from Ben.

He shoved his way through the crowd as Ben counted out the money and signed the papers making the boardinghouse his.

"You should have let Talbert have it," he said.

"Son, I must go home to yer ma. Ain't no way I was gonna deliver her bad news."

Paul frowned. He didn't want to owe Ben or Ma.

"Sides, I been lookin' fer a good investment. Nuthin' better'n family."

Paul shook his head. "You didn't have to. Shouldn't have."

"It's done. Now let's go look over the place," Ben said with a wink.

He followed Ben as he pushed through the crowd. Right before he made it to the door, Talbert fell into step beside him.

"You may have won this time, Lancaster, but I always get what I want. Always."

"Good day, Talbert," Paul said, ignoring the threat. For now, the boardinghouse and placer were still his—well, his and Ben's.

As he and Ben walked back to the boardinghouse, Paul asked,

"Why did you do that?"

Ben slapped him on the shoulder. "Told ya. Needed investment. This is a good place for that."

Letting out a heavy sigh, Paul held open the front door of his home. It was still his, by some miracle.

Ben entered and looked around the parlor. He moved into the dining hall then into the kitchen. After wandering around the building for a few minutes, he finally said, "Well, guess I won't be changing a thing. Looks like ya got a handle on it."

He turned and walked back toward the front of the house. "See ya, Sunday."

"Wait!" Paul shouted after him, dumbfounded. "What do you mean?"

Ben shrugged. "It's still yer place. Keep doin' what yer doin'. I gotta run. Got some deliveries before I head home."

With that, his stepfather hurried from the house.

Paul sank into the closest chair. What just happened?

I will give you hidden treasures... So, you will know I am God...

Bowing his head, he closed his eyes. Somehow during this crisis, he had forgotten that very important truth. God was in control—in control of the placer, the boardinghouse, and even whatever happened with Millie.

His heart soared. He would still get to see her every day. Still get to flick those braids and listen to her sing. Still get to sit with her in the parlor on quiet evenings. Perhaps one day soon he would even kiss her.

CHAPTER 23

Jake stalked away from the courthouse. Paul was foolish and stubborn. Didn't he know his life was in danger?

He thought back to his last conversation with Paul. He had said he wasn't afraid to die. What kind of man wasn't afraid of death? Jake sure was, especially after dealing with so much of it this year.

Still, Paul seemed confident that he would never give up his mine. Jake knew he had to convince him otherwise.

Only now it would be harder. Ben Shepherd had seen to it that Paul was going to get to keep the boardinghouse. There was no incentive for Paul to sell.

Talbert would be furious.

Jake ducked into an alleyway, aware that Talbert's anger would be directed towards him. After all, he had promised the English man that he could convince Paul to let the mine go.

He swore under his breath as he paced back and forth. He didn't know Paul had such strong feelings about that placer. How was he going to get him to sell?

His mind raced. If the "Apache attack" hadn't worked, and the potential loss of the boardinghouse, what else could he do to save Paul's life? For it was only a matter of time before Talbert grew impatient and took matters into his own hands.

Well, not really his own hands. Talbert would never stoop so low as to commit murder himself. The man was far too careful about that. But Jake knew the other men in Talbert's employ. And he knew what they had done to old miner Dodge. If Jake couldn't get Paul to sell, then Paul's fate could be similar to that of Dodge's.

Jake couldn't bear it. He could not lose one more person. It was too hard to deal with losing his ma and Sissy. He couldn't go home anymore because the memories were too painful, too consuming.

If he lost Paul too, he was afraid he would succumb to the darkness brewing deep within.

No, he had to find a way.

Just then, he saw that Indian squaw that worked for Paul as she passed by on the street, headed back towards the boardinghouse. Perhaps, if he got to her, she could help him with Paul.

His stomach churned at the thought of seeking help from an Indian. He would much rather dispose of her than ask her for help. She was part of the problem. Her presence at the boardinghouse was affecting Paul. He wasn't himself around her. She was manipulating him.

Maybe the real answer lay with turning the town against her. If she was gone, Paul would start to see things clearly again. Then Paul would understand that he had to sell the placer.

Jake continued to plot his next move as he strolled towards the rundown shack at the edge of town that served as his new home. He would make all this work. He *would* save Paul's life.

CHAPTER 24

Millie hurried to get ready for the day. Last Sunday, Pastor Page announced that the church had enough money and supplies to build the church.

A church raising. She had never been to one. When she and her parents moved to Santa Fe, they held services in a building established by another congregation that moved into a larger building. In Wickenburg, her dad still held services in a tent.

"Hello!" Caroline's voice announced her arrival before she entered the kitchen. "Aren't you excited?"

"I suppose." More like nervous. From what Pastor Page said, there would be many parishioners coming to town to help build the church. There would be the Larsons, the Colters, the Cahills, Ben, and Betty—all coming from a nearby ranch. Others lived in town, like the Andersons, Paul, and her. In all, there were about seventy-five parishioners. Most of them would be there.

"It will be fun. We've waited forever for a building."

"Forever?"

Caroline frowned at her. "It's been years. Seems like forever."

Millie had started a stew last night, which she would pair with the biscuits she made this morning. She handed Caroline the basket of biscuits and she grabbed both handles of the stew pot with the corners of her apron. They wound their way through the house to the porch.

"Here, let me carry that," Paul said, trying to take the stew pot from her.

She nodded at the saws and toolbox he had in each of his hands. "I can carry this."

He shrugged and led the way. The new church site was only a few blocks away from the boardinghouse. Millie was glad when they arrived, for the stew pot seemed to grow heavier with each step.

"Shoulda let me carry it." Paul dropped his tools on the ground and lifted the pot from her aching hands. He found the makeshift table where other food items were and set the stew pot on it.

She flexed her hands to work out the soreness.

Thomas and little Drew greeted them.

"Don't overdo it," Thomas warned his wife.

She flashed him a silly grin. "I wouldn't think of it. I'm here for moral support."

"Oh, boy! We're in trouble then."

Caroline swatted at Thomas's arm, but he jumped back. "Is Mama here yet?"

"Nope. Haven't seen anyone from the ranch yet. They'll be here soon."

Millie smiled as Drew tugged on his dad's arm. "Can I help?"

Thomas leaned down and tousled his hair. "'Course. Can you carry the nails and hammer for me?"

They didn't have to wait long for the rest of the parishioners to arrive. Once they did, Pastor Page quieted the crowd and said a blessing. "Lord, we thank you for this opportunity to build a church. May it minister to your people for many years to come."

"Amen!" the crowd echoed.

Millie stood next to Caroline and watched. She wasn't sure what she could do, besides serve food at lunchtime. Many of the women gathered near them.

Paul and Pastor Page took charge telling the men how they would begin. Then Paul started assigning tasks.

"He's a fine man," one of the widows in the congregation

said.

"Who?" another parishioner asked.

"Why Paul Lancaster, of course. Can't believe he isn't taken yet."

Millie frowned and leaned closer to hear the rest of their conversation.

"Pleasant to look at," the widow said. "What I wouldn't do to secure his courtship."

The two laughed and started to walk to the shade of a tree, out of Millie's hearing.

Emotions churned. She agreed. Paul was pleasant to look at. He heaved a massive hammer—at least that's what she supposed it was—he let it crash onto the wooden peg that would hold the joist of a beam together. Sweat quickly soaked his shirt in the unusually warm weather. Some of the men already removed their shirts and worked in their long johns and trousers. Paul left his shirt on.

Throughout the day she watched him closely. When a man approached asking what he should do next, Paul greeted him with a smile. The interruptions didn't seem to bother him.

What a smile he had. It made his blue eyes dance with excitement. She wasn't close enough to see the effect now, but she witnessed it close around the supper table at the boardinghouse on many occasions.

After a while, the men took a break and headed toward the table. It was too early for lunch. The young widow rushed forward with a pail of water and handed the ladle to Paul. Paul smiled and the young widow leaned closer to him, talking excitedly.

Millie turned her back. She would never throw herself at a man like that—not even Paul. A stab of envy pierced her heart. She wished her life was different. That she could capture Paul's undivided attention, if only for a moment.

Annoyed with the direction of her thoughts, she looked around for another pail. Empty. She walked toward the nearest town well and awkwardly pulled on the rope to lift the full bucket of water from the bottom of the well.

"Let me."

Paul startled her. She hadn't realized he followed her.

He took the rope from her hands and with little effort, pulled the full bucket up. Then he dumped the water into the bucket at her feet. When he started to repeat the process, she realized he had another empty bucket at his feet. Before she could reach down to grab the bucket, he filled his and lifted both.

"We don't expect you ladies to wait on us hand and foot."

"Really?" She fell into step beside him.

"Only for lunch." He groaned in pain.

"What's wrong?"

"Smelling that stew all night. It was torture."

She turned her head in time to see the big grin on his face. "I see you look very tortured."

Paul let out a deep laugh. "I can hardly wait for lunch to taste it."

"I hope it doesn't disappoint your high expectations."

"You could never disappoint me, Millie."

The softness of his tone, the familiarity—it broke through the shell surrounding her heart. How she had longed for a man to speak to her in such a way that brought hope and hinted of love.

Before she could dwell on the thought much longer, they arrived back at the work site. The young widow that gave him water earlier now directed a hostile scowl towards Millie. A modicum of satisfaction rose in her chest.

————

Paul brushed past the young widow and returned to the labor of building the church. He was a little annoyed at the woman—he couldn't remember her name—for flirting so openly with him. He wasn't interested and had never done anything to make her think he was.

That's why he made such a show helping Millie.

He glanced over at Millie. She stood apart from most of the

women. She seemed unsure of herself. Several times he caught her twisting her hands together. Nervous? Shy? She seemed much more comfortable around the small table of boarders at supper each night than at this large gathering today.

"Could you be more obvious?" Thomas slapped him on the shoulder, drawing his attention away from Millie.

"Huh?"

"If Miss Pritchett can't read your interest, then she's completely blind."

"Yeah." Pastor Page jumped into the conversation. "It's more than obvious to the rest of us."

Heat rose to Paul's face. He picked up the heavy sledgehammer and tried to focus on building the rest of the beam joints. Only Thomas wouldn't let it go.

"I can see why you like her. She's the tallest woman I've ever seen. At least your neck won't get sore from looking down at her all the time."

"She's pretty too, when she smiles," one of the young ranch hands commented.

"Yeah. If she weren't so old, I might try courting her," another ranch hand said.

Paul grew uncomfortable with the teasing. He walked the length of the beam and worked on the joint farthest away from the other men.

As he pounded the last peg in the last joint, he looked up and scanned the crowd for Millie. Her back was to him, but he recognized those dark braids even from this distance. When someone called her name, she turned, bringing her face into his view. So beautiful. So kind. So much a woman he wanted to get to know more. He was glad he hadn't lost the boardinghouse and his opportunity to see her daily.

When her gaze met his across the distance, he looked away.

"Let's get the frame raised and in place before we break for lunch," he shouted to the nearby men.

The hard work felt good, despite the heat of the sun beating down on his back. He put Thomas in charge of calling out the placement of each part of the frame so he wouldn't injure his weak leg. Besides, Paul was built for this sort of labor. Strong arms and back. He could lift an entire section of frame by himself and not strain under the weight. Of course, he still needed his fellow workers to help line it up correctly.

After another hour, they had the building framed. Pastor announced the lunch break and gave a blessing. Paul made a beeline for Millie and her stew.

When he arrived, he had to wait in line, though he never took his eyes off her.

"Paul, you really look too much," Thomas said from behind him. "Trying to scare off the other eligible young ladies?"

"Yup." He looked at his friend.

Thomas laughed, then shook his head. "Well, you're doing a fine job of it. 'Course, she's more your type."

"What do you mean?"

"Quiet enough so your ma can still dominate the conversation."

"Hey!"

Thomas darted away, toward his wife and son, leaving Paul alone to consider the words. The longer he knew her, the less it bothered him that she was so quiet. It seemed like she could communicate so much without words.

Like now. Her shoulders were angled slightly forward. She seemed to do that a lot in crowds—as if it diminished her height. Yet her smile invited each person to return one of their own. When someone spoke to her, she engaged in the conversation with her eyes.

He stepped forward, taking his place in front of her stew pot. Her gaze lifted to meet his. He smiled.

"Still smells as good as it did this morning."

Pink colored her cheeks. She glanced down at the pot and dumped a big ladle full into his bowl.

He didn't move. "I'll take double."

She smiled and served up a second helping. Then she handed him a biscuit.

126

"Thank you."

She nodded and focused on the next person in line.

Paul was tempted to eat a spoonful in front of her and exclaim how tasty it was just to capture her attention for a few more minutes. Instead, he found Thomas and Caroline seated on a bench with their son. He sat down facing them.

"I noticed you didn't take any of Widow Whitmore's pie," Caroline said.

Whitmore. So that was the young widow's name. "I plan on filling up on Millie's hearty stew."

"I see." Caroline's face lit with a mischievous smirk.

"'Sides, Ma's pie is the best."

Thomas chuckled. "Yeah, but she didn't bring any today."

"For you. She dropped off a few at the boardinghouse."

"You holding out on us?"

"Uh huh."

He stuffed a spoonful of the savory stew in his mouth. It tasted even better than he thought. He scarfed down the rest of it and went back for more. This time there was no line.

"Back for seconds?" Millie teased.

"I told you I thought it would be good. I was right."

She dished him up two more servings.

This time he ate a mouthful in front of her. "Mmm. Better 'n Ma's."

Millie's eyes grew wide. "Truly?"

"Truly."

When she smiled, his gaze dropped to her lips. He desperately wanted to kiss her or at the very least stay there and talk to her all day. But he had work to do. He stuffed another spoonful of stew in his mouth to dispel the idea. Then he waved to her and walked away.

He noticed the way she looked at him too. She hadn't shied away from his gaze. Instead, she returned it with more boldness than he expected. Unless he was completely off base, she liked him too. She would welcome a kiss, something he would see to very soon.

CHAPTER 25

A few days after the church raising, Millie smiled as she handed the last supper dish to Paul to dry. His fingers deliberately brushed hers. She caught his gaze, and he held it for a moment before shifting to concentrate on drying the dish. Her heart warmed as she tried to remember exactly when they fell into this pattern. Perhaps it was a week or two before the auction. One evening he stayed to help her with dishes. Then the next. Then the next.

"Any plans for the evening?" he asked.

She frowned and turned to wipe down the small table, trying to stop the memories of Cade from breaking through. Softly, she replied, "I was going to sit in the parlor and finish the blanket for Caroline's baby." Her stomach tightened.

He came and stood behind her. "Millie," he whispered her name.

Then his fingers slid down her forearm to her hand.

"I think it's clean." Paul took the rag from her hand and tossed it towards the wash basin. He turned her to face him, but her gaze darted toward the immaculate table. She both loved and hated when he treated her so sweetly. Loved it because her heart wanted more. Hated it because he would never love her once he learned of her past.

"You don't like Caroline?"

"What?" she asked, scrunching her nose as she lifted her gaze to meet his.

"You don't seem excited about the gift you're making her."

Millie took a step back before moving to reorganize one of the pantry shelves. "I am happy for her. This child is a blessing for her and Thomas. After so many losses, she deserves some happiness." She prayed he wouldn't press any further.

"I agree."

A few seconds of silence ticked by. She kept her back to him, fearful that he would be able to read the deep pain in her eyes.

"Well, guess I'll go finish my chores."

As each of his heavy footfalls grew softer, her shoulders relaxed but her heart squeezed tighter. She really wanted to love Paul. But she couldn't.

Yet another day and her heart swung like a clock pendulum between two stark truths. She was falling in love with him. And her sins would steal her joy this time too.

The more she got to know Paul, the more she became convinced that his strong character and pride would never allow him to accept her. Not once did he discover the truth about her. He would leave too.

There was only one other time where she let her heart rule. It had been with Joel.

Things started out well enough. She met him at her father's church in Santa Fe. Had it really been ten years ago? She had been more outgoing then, but even at twenty-eight she was beyond an old maid. Joel teased her. Just like Paul did. He loved her singing and told her so often.

She could still remember their first kiss on a picnic outing. Dad had gone with them, but Joel suggested a short walk. On that walk he confessed his feelings for her. She thought he might. When she shared her love for him, he smiled and asked permission to kiss her. It had been wonderful.

The relationship lasted only a few more weeks. As he began courting her, he told her about his wife's passing. She had been with child when she contracted the fever. Both passed from this world.

Before Millie realized it, she poured forth all her secrets. Hers were too much for him to bear. His hurtful words still rang in her ears. He hated her for what she had done. He told her she wasn't the woman he thought she was. He even accused her of deliberately deceiving him—even though she hadn't.

A few days later, she had received a note. He had left Santa Fe and set out for California. He did not wish to correspond with her.

Joel had been the last man she had given her heart to. She swore she would never do it again. Yet here she was with Paul. Her heart already slipping from her control. A part of it held on to the hope that Paul was so very different from Joel and from Cade.

She shook off the bad memories and retrieved her knitting from her room. *Lord, dare I even pray that my loneliness might end one day?*

———

Paul whistled as he threw the contents of the slop bucket in the pig trough. He wondered what was bothering Millie. Maybe it was as simple as a longing to have a family.

She would make a wonderful mother. So patient. So gentle-spirited.

After tossing some hay toward the milk goat, he paused and leaned against one of the stalls in the barn. Now that the boardinghouse was undeniably his again, he felt more relaxed around Millie. He found himself thinking about her often. Those beautiful deep blue eyes that changed subtly depending on the color of her frock.

Longing washed over him. She would make a wonderful wife. For him. She complemented him in every way. She challenged him when he needed it. Other times she encouraged him. Oh, and the number of ways she could communicate without words.

Like tonight. In the kitchen after supper. She was sad. No, it was more than sad. Hurt.

He shook his head. No matter how many minutes he spent trying to understand, he couldn't. Maybe in time she would trust him with her pain.

Sighing, he pushed away from the stall and finished his chores. As he walked back up to the house, a sense of pride filled him. The boardinghouse truly felt like it was his, even though Ben still owned a portion of it.

Several days after the auction, when Ben was in town making deliveries for the Colter Meat Company, Paul cornered him. He gave Ben all the money he had gathered for the tax debt. It was a hard sell, but Ben eventually took it. When Paul tried to ask him about repayment terms for the remainder, Ben brushed him off. "Yer ma don't want ya thinking you owe us a thing. It's a gift."

He didn't deserve such kindness. Not after all the things he put Ma through after Pa died. Getting thrown in jail. Beating a man nearly to death. Causing a rift in the family. Drinking. Womanizing.

It was amazing how much he had changed from those days. Not a hint of his old life remained. Jesus had delivered on his promise to change Paul from the inside out.

Now he was a respected business owner. No one in the town seemed to even remember the scandal of the tax debt of less than two weeks ago.

Yet, emptiness remained in his soul. He wanted a wife. The companionship of a woman. And that woman now had a face and a name.

Paul walked back to the boardinghouse and found Millie sitting alone in the parlor.

He plopped down in an empty chair near where she sat knitting the blanket for Caroline. He smiled at her. Pink made her high cheeks glow. When she smiled in return, her eyes still held a note of sadness.

"So, when will you give Caroline the blanket?"

"On Wednesday. Grace Talbert invited many of the women from town to her home to help celebrate. She said she still remembers when Caroline gave away all of her baby things to the Women's Aid Society to help the native women nearby."

"Ah, that's right. I remember a few of the ladies convinced Fort Whipple's commander to help the Indians. Lot of people were upset by that."

She frowned and he wished he could take the words back.

"I mean—"

"Paul." Her eyes locked on his. "I am aware of the hatred towards the Indians. I experienced it growing up. My mother's people were Shawnee."

He took in a sharp breath as his head reeled. Her father hadn't just been a missionary to Indians. He had married one. His fears were true—Millie was part Indian.

The muscles in his shoulders rippled with pent up anxiety. His love, his sweet Millie could not have dealt him a worse blow had she aimed a rifle at his chest and pulled the trigger herself.

Though he suspected the truth before, he wished it away. It was illegal for a white to marry an Indian in the Arizona Territory. If he pursued her and convinced her to marry him…

Could he really break the law just to be with her? The idea started to solidify in his mind. He already loved her. Hadn't kissed her yet. Hadn't confessed his feelings to her either. But that didn't lessen the depth of love he felt.

But he couldn't break the law. Didn't it say somewhere in the Bible that he should honor the laws of the land?

He stood to his feet and looked over at her, trying to mask his warring emotions. Her eyes brimmed with unshed tears. His silence was to blame. He knew it, yet he could not force words to his mouth, nothing to comfort her—though his heart screamed at him. His heart wanted him to ignore the law. His heart wanted to take her in his arms and show her just how much he loved her.

No, he shouldn't.

He frowned and turned on his heel without a word, headed toward his room. He shoved the door shut with too much force. Surely the Lord wouldn't let him love a woman he could not have.

———

Millie's head drooped as tears splashed onto the blanket for Caroline. No matter how many times she tried to keep herself from falling in love with Paul, she would never be successful. She did love him. Why else would his silence following her admission hurt so much? Had others not rejected her for her parentage before? Why should she be so surprised?

Did it really matter which of her secrets drove him away?

Yes, it did. Somehow, she hoped he would not care about her Shawnee blood.

But he did. She saw it in his eyes. Anger. Hurt. Gone was the tenderness she saw earlier in the evening. Gone was the kindness. A steely dark cloud covered his gaze before he walked from the room.

More tears rolled down her cheeks. It wasn't fair. She couldn't control what parents she had been born to. Even if she would not have chosen different ones. Her dad and mom loved her so much. They loved each other dearly, too. It had not mattered to Dad that Mom was Shawnee.

But that was a different time in a different place. The Shawnee were respected and no longer feared by most of their white neighbors back in Ohio. Many dressed as the whites did. They farmed. They hunted and provided meat for trade. They were accepted as a part of the community.

It wasn't the same in the West. The Apache were fierce. Tensions between them and the white settlers escalated almost daily. Hadn't she just read an article in the weekly newspaper about a raid between here and Wickenburg? The Apache left no one alive. The report didn't go into all the details, but she suspected the murders had been quite brutal. All the other stories she heard since arriving in the Arizona Territory seemed to describe horrible brutalities on both sides.

Red blood was red blood. It would matter little to the citizens of Prescott if her red blood was of the Shawnee variety. It seemed that it mattered little to Paul, as well.

A noise from the dining room drew her attention. She quickly wiped away her tears and set the blanket aside. Then she stood and followed the noise.

"Mr. Lowery, can I get you anything?"

"Oh, heavens! You startled me," he replied, whirling around to face her. He pointed toward her tear-streaked face. "What's wrong?"

She held back a sniffle. "Just missing my family." She lied.

For the first time since she met him, Mr. Lowrey seemed at a loss for words. His gaze moved towards the window, though he appeared to be looking far beyond the street outside to someplace far away. A few seconds of silence passed.

"Mr. Lowrey?"

His head snapped toward her. "Sorry."

"Were you looking for something earlier?"

He cleared his throat. "Ah, yes. I seem to have misplaced my pocket watch."

Millie searched around the dining room table and under each of the chairs. She checked the buffet along the wall. Still not finding it, she entered the parlor with Mr. Lowrey following behind her.

"You remind me of my daughter."

Her hands stilled as she turned to face him with an eyebrow arched high on her forehead.

"She was quiet too. Held her pain in, until the sadness controlled her."

Millie frowned.

"Ah, there it is!" Mr. Lowrey exclaimed, startling her with his abrupt shift.

As he walked toward the small side table next to his favorite reading chair, she puzzled over his comment about his daughter.

"Thank you for your help, Millie."

Then he headed toward the dining room. At the entryway, he turned back towards her. "Don't let the sadness control you. You're much too kind and thoughtful to waste your life pining over past mistakes. You're better than that."

She blinked in silence. How could he know about her past? Had he overheard her conversation with Paul? Just what did he know about her?

"Goodnight, Millie. Think about what I said." With that, he left the room.

She stood there for another moment trying to make sense of his words. Finally, she shrugged and retrieved the baby blanket and retired to her room.

She wished she could forget about her past as Mr. Lowrey suggested. Only it always seemed too hard to really let go.

CHAPTER 26

Wednesday morning came sooner than Millie hoped. Though she managed to finish the blanket in time, she considered sending someone to tell Grace she wouldn't be attending. She never liked large gatherings—a frustrating problem to have as a pastor's daughter. She wasn't sure she would fit in with Caroline's friends.

Millie tucked the small gift to her side and headed out the front door. Whether she felt like it or not, she needed to go. Mother would tell her it would do her good to meet other women and get her mind off the growing coldness between her and Paul.

He hardly said a word to her since she revealed her secret. Each time she saw him, rejection pierced her heart again.

She shook her head. She must stop thinking about him.

As she turned the corner onto Granite Street, she stopped suddenly. Her heart pounded within her chest. Her mouth went dry. Shock clogged her throat. He could not be here!

A young man walked away from her, his form less recognizable with each step. Perhaps she only imagined that his gait matched that of Cade. His step and the swing of his arms seemed frighteningly similar. His hair, mostly hidden by a cowboy hat, was the same golden color. The drop of his shoulders from his thick neck, everything about him reminded her of Cade.

Impossible. Cade was much older than the young man walking down the street. Why, he would be around forty years old or so. The young man looked as if he was only in his mid-twenties.

Her breath caught. Not Cade, but—

"Millie!"

Caroline's familiar voice pulled her away from the terrifying thought that she might know who the young man was. She squelched her racing thoughts and forced a smile to her face.

"I'm surprised to find you walking. Certainly, Thomas didn't send you over without a carriage."

Caroline's light laugh helped ease Millie's anxiety. "The fresh air is good for me. Besides, it wasn't that far, and he did promise to bring the wagon later."

"Of course. I doubt he would expect you to carry all the gifts home by yourself," Millie teased, her earlier fear fading.

"Oh, I don't expect many gifts. Grace said the gathering would be rather small."

Millie was going to ask why, but as they neared the walkway in front of the Talbert home, numerous buggies and conveyances lined both sides of the street.

"Graciousness!" Caroline exclaimed. "I should have known Grace would invite the entire town!"

"Caroline!" Grace called from the porch. "If I had known you needed a ride, I would have asked our driver to pick you up."

"Nonsense," Caroline answered as she accepted a hug and kiss on the cheek from Grace.

"Welcome, Miss Pritchett," Grace said, motioning for the two to enter the house.

"Please call me Millie."

"Gladly."

Millie followed behind Caroline as Grace led them into the parlor. The home was the largest she had seen in the west, except perhaps Don Salvador's home outside of Santa Fe, though the Talbert home boasted wealth in a way the Don's hadn't. It was a lovely Victorian constructed of wood versus the adobe mud brick houses she had grown to love in Santa Fe.

The parlor made the one at Paul's boardinghouse seem tiny.

Several settees and plush armchairs were arranged throughout the room. Each sat near a side table which held decor varying from elegant porcelain vases, to figurines, to ornate ivory carvings. A few of the vases held roses—perhaps from the rose gardens near the Governor's mansion. Though the government had moved from Prescott to Tucson a few years back, the roses planted by the late Mrs. McCormick were still tended by the current resident of the Governor's former mansion, or so she heard.

Grace introduced Millie to several women, including Grace's mother. Some she recognized from church. Others she had never met before.

"This is Mrs. Martha Stanton," Grace said. "She's the president of the Women's Aid Society."

Millie smiled and greeted the woman.

"I've heard that you are quite a gifted singer," Martha Stanton said. "Perhaps you would consider singing at our event later this month. We are hosting an evening dinner party and dance to raise funds for the starving Indians. It is just shameful what that terrible Indian Affairs Agent is doing. He—"

Grace interrupted. "I am sure Millie would be happy to discuss this with you later this afternoon. She has yet to meet the rest of the ladies."

"Forgive me," Martha apologized. "I tend to get carried away when I think of those who suffer."

Millie smiled as Caroline said, "I am sure that is a good trait to have as the leader of the Society."

Martha laughed. "It is. Very nice to meet you, Millie. We'll talk later."

Millie nodded, though she hoped to avoid the woman for the rest of the day. She had no intention of singing before a crowd. She wondered how Martha even knew that she sang.

After a few more introductions, Grace showed Millie and Caroline to their seats. Then she served dainty sandwiches, crackers, cheeses, and some pastries called scones. It was such a strange experience for Millie. She had never been to such a party before.

Though she sat next to Caroline, she barely had a chance to

talk to her. Woman after woman presented their gifts to her and wished her well on the upcoming birth of her child.

"There is a truly charitable woman," Martha said, sliding onto the seat next to Millie.

She held back a groan.

"Giving away all her baby things to help the Indians. Takes a big heart to do that."

"I thought everyone hated the Indians here," Millie said, her tone held an edge of fear.

Martha shook her head. "Not everyone feels that way. Hezekiah, that is my husband, believes they should be treated humanely. So do several of the other prominent men from the East that now call Arizona home. Some of those from the West don't feel the same way." She sighed heavily. "I suppose men fear and hate what they don't understand."

"I suppose so," Millie said, still surprised that there were some who held a favorable view of the Indians.

"That is why it is so important for us to help. Despite the government's treaty with many of the Indian tribes, far too many of the Indian Affairs Agents are corrupt. They should be distributing food and supplies the government allocated for the Indians. But they aren't. Some agents are forcing the Indians to barter for what they were already promised. Others give the best food to the military camps and forts, while saving rotten food for the Indians. It is wrong."

Millie's heart softened towards the woman, touched by her sincerity and concern for those less fortunate.

"It is our Christian duty to help," Martha continued. "I was hoping I could count on you."

"For what?" As soon as the question left her lips, Millie remembered their earlier conversation. She wished she could grab the words back.

"Hannah Colter tells me you have a lovely voice. Perhaps you would consider singing a few songs at our dinner party? It would mean a lot to Hezekiah and me. I am certain our guests would enjoy it."

"I… I only sing in worship to my Father in heaven."

Martha frowned, and then she touched Millie's raven locks, tightly coiled into a chignon at her neck. "Such dark hair. You almost have the look of…" Her voice trailed off.

Millie cleared her throat. "While I agree with your noble cause, Mrs. Stanton, I cannot help you with your dinner party. Perhaps I could make a few blankets or quilts for the Indians instead."

Martha slowly nodded. "Thank you. That is most kind of you. If you should change your mind, please send me word."

Millie nodded. Then Martha took her leave.

After another half hour, and no end in sight to the party, Millie finally excused herself, saying that she had to get back to the boardinghouse. In truth, the hum of ceaseless conversation coupled with frequent squeals of women gushing over the cute baby things, made her long for the quiet.

Stepping from the porch, she paused for a moment, remembering the young man she saw earlier today. Could it be him? Was it even possible? How had he ended up here of all places? Would God really grant her secret request to see him after all this time?

Millie shook her head. Perhaps she should take Mr. Lowery's advice to heart. Thinking of the past was causing her to see things—rather people—that weren't there. It was foolish.

Sighing, she walked towards home. The sun warmed the back of her best dress, which seemed rather simple compared to the ornate flounces on Grace's dress or the fancy lace on Martha's. She didn't really fit in with these women.

Yet, Martha's passion for the Indians opened her eyes and ignited her hope that not all the townsfolk would reject her should they learn that her mother was Shawnee. Dare she hope they accept her? That Paul might?

As she turned the corner onto Granite Street, a man jumped from the shadows, dragging her into the alleyway. Her lungs filled with air to scream out for help, but his hand clamped down over her mouth before a sound left it.

"You keep quiet, you half-breed."

Fear sent her heart racing. How many people knew? What did he want from her?

———

Jake's hands shook. He clenched his jaw and willed his hands to be still. He was losing his mind—had been since finding Ma and Sissy's bodies. But he had to save Paul, even if it meant doing terrible things.

He could not believe his luck the other night when he stopped by the boardinghouse. He had been about to knock on the door, but he had heard her confess that she was an Indian. He had suspected it from the first time he had seen her but hearing her admit it was the proof he needed.

Millie squirmed beneath his grip. The fear in her eyes made his stomach churn. He had never hurt a woman before—would never have imagined himself capable of this. But every time he closed his eyes, he saw Sissy's face. What if this woman had somehow helped them? What if she was feeding information to the Apache?

His grief was eating him alive, making him see enemies everywhere. He knew he was falling apart, but Paul's safety mattered more than his sanity.

An eye for an eye. Part of him wanted to end this now, to get revenge for what her people did to his family.

No. Wait. He needed her alive. That's right. He had to get her to help him convince Paul to leave that dangerous mine. Paul's life was in danger, and she was the only one close enough to Paul to make him listen.

"Listen to me real good," he said, his voice rougher than he intended. "I know you're half Indian. Heard it with my own ears. Now, unless you want me spreading it around the whole town, you'll do as I say."

He waited. When she failed to acknowledge him, desperation made him grab her shoulders firmly. "Look at me! Paul's going to get himself killed out at that mine. You must convince him to sell it. That's all I'm asking."

Slowly she nodded, terror filling her violet eyes.

"I'm sorry," he whispered, the words slipping out before he could stop them. "I'm so sorry. But I can't lose him too."

"You do that for me, and I'll keep your secret. Help me save Paul, and nobody must know what you are."

The words tasted like poison in his mouth. What had become of him?

"You gonna do it?" he asked.

She nodded, sorrow and fear filling her eyes.

"Good. And don't you go telling anyone about this conversation. Paul's life depends on it."

He released his hold on her and stepped back, his hands shaking again. Then he hurried down the alley, disgusted with himself but desperate to save the only family he had left.

CHAPTER 27

Paul returned from the mine later than he expected. He hurried to his room to clean up then joined the boarders for supper. It took him a few minutes before he realized Millie wasn't there. Turning to one of the boarders he asked about her.

"She set out the food, but said she wasn't feeling well. Then she went off to her room."

Paul frowned. Hadn't she gone to Caroline's party this afternoon?

Throughout the meal, he barely managed to keep his focus on the conversation around him, hoping the meal would speed up so he could check on her. What if she was ill? What if it was something terrible?

Stop it. He scolded himself. He had to stop thinking about her. At least that's what he kept telling himself ever since she told him her mother was Indian.

Only it hadn't worked. If he thought of her once an hour before she told him, he thought of her twice an hour now. Well, he wasn't sure how often it was. Just seemed like she was always on his mind. His heart was hopelessly gone. She owned it.

As the clatter of silverware stilled, he shook himself from his thoughts. One after the other, the boarders excused themselves from the table. He stood and began gathering the dishes.

"I'll take care of those."

Millie's soft voice sent sweet tingles down his arm. When he looked up and saw her red-rimmed eyes, he wanted to rush to her and pull her into his arms. Only he couldn't since they were full of dirty dishes.

"Evening," he said, irritated at the thick emotion punctuating the word. Get yourself under control.

She flashed a hesitant smile. Then she took the stack of dishes from his hands. He hurried to gather more and followed her to the kitchen.

"Look," he started. "I'm sorry about the other night. I didn't mean to hurt you."

She stilled only for a moment before returning to the dining room for more dishes. Again, he followed her.

"It's just… I was caught off guard. I didn't know what to say."

Millie frowned. "You could have said something. Anything would have been better than nothing."

Paul's heart constricted. He hadn't planned on apologizing for the other night, yet it seemed like the right thing to do. "I'm sorry."

She hurried back to the kitchen with another stack of dishes. By the time he joined her, she had filled the washbasin and started washing. He grabbed the towel from its peg and stood next to her.

Taking a deep breath, he caught the sweet scent of lavender. Gosh, he missed this. He missed her. Sure, it had only been one— well almost two days—since he really spoke to her last. Still, he missed her.

"Are you going to fire me?" she asked.

He nearly dropped the plate in his hand. "No. What makes you think that?"

She turned and he let his gaze connect with hers. "When the town finds out you might wish that you had."

Setting the plate and towel aside, he took her face in his hands, cradling it gently. His eyes searched hers for several seconds before his gaze dropped to her lips. He took a step closer until the length of his body touched hers. Then he lowered his lips to hers. Millie slid her arms around his neck and surrendered to his kiss, sending fire coursing through him. He slid his hands down her back and rested them near the small of her back as he deepened the kiss.

When her fingers tickled his hairline, he slowed the kiss, even though he didn't want to. He stopped and rested his forehead against hers. She slid her hands down from his neck to his chest. He dropped his hands to his side and stepped back.

"No one has to know," he whispered continuing their earlier conversation. "About your mother's people."

The pink on her cheeks shaded to red. Her arm rose until her fingers touched her lips. The shock morphed into a sweet smile that melted his heart.

Then it quickly disappeared, chased away by fear. "What if they already know?"

"How could they? Have you told anyone else?"

She shook her head.

"Caroline?"

"No. She doesn't know."

Good. Not that he didn't trust Caroline, but she tended to be a bit of a gossip at times. "Then you have nothing to fear."

She gave him a soft smile, though her eyes remained veiled.

Paul reached out to pull her braid, then noticed for the first time that she fashioned her hair differently today. There was no braid to pull. Instead, he lightly tapped her nose. "Shall we finish the dishes?"

Wordlessly, she handed him the next plate. Within a few minutes they were back in the comfortable routine he had grown to cherish.

Sweet love bubbled up in his heart. Then a moment of fear. Surely, no one knew about Millie's secret. Did it really matter if they did? He loved her. He wanted to court her then marry her. She was the right woman for him—the one he waited so long to find.

He wouldn't give her up without a fight.

———

Millie sighed as she slipped under the covers. Paul had kissed her. A smile graced her lips. It was so sweet, so endearing. If she had any doubts before about his feelings toward her, they disappeared tonight. This attraction between them was mutual.

That's why she had to quit. She could no longer work at the boardinghouse knowing the pain he would suffer because of her past. It would be easier to leave now, to run far away, than to risk betraying him. After all, that is what Jake Waters asked of her. Betrayal.

She knew how much that placer mine meant to Paul. Using his feelings for her to convince him to sell would be the same as betraying him.

If she didn't do as Jake asked, then he would surely tell the town about her heritage. How he discovered it, she didn't know. But he had.

She only had one choice. She had to leave. It was the only way to protect Paul.

A tear slid down her cheek. This time her lost love would be on her terms. No chance of facing his rejection when he learned about her other secret. Instead, she would reject him.

Pain burned through her middle. Wasn't that a different form of betrayal? Running away—rejecting him—it betrayed him in a far worse manner than if she stayed and tried to manipulate him into selling the placer. It was a lie to her heart. To his.

How had she gotten into this situation? It was dreadful. She would hurt Paul no matter what she did. Which would be the least painful? Which way might he be willing to forgive her?

Millie buried her face in the pillow as sobs wracked her body. She didn't want to betray Paul or reject him or tell him of her past. She only wanted to be held in his arms with whispered promises of love forever.

Lord, help me. I cannot bear another lost love. It is too much.

In the silence she strained her ears, hoping an answer would come.

Wait.

Wait? Was God asking her to wait? It seemed she didn't have

time to wait. Jake expected Paul to willingly give up the placer mine very soon. She had to act now.

Wait in silence.

Her pulse quickened. Only once before had she blatantly ignored the Lord's command. It had not ended well. She had to obey Him above all others. She was to say nothing and do nothing.

But how could she? How could she just stand by and watch as that man destroyed her. Was there nothing she could do?

No. The Lord said wait in silence. She had to obey. Above all else, regardless of her fear, she had to obey.

CHAPTER 28

July 1, 1869

"Walk with me?" Paul asked Millie as she set the empty wash basin back in place following supper.

She took the towel from his hands and studied his face. His gaze connected with hers. He slid his hands down her arms and took her hands in his. Then he arched one eyebrow.

Millie's stomach fluttered under his intense stare. Her mouth went dry, and she moistened her lips.

"Sure."

He released her hands and offered his arm. She slid her hand into the crook and followed as he led her outside and down the street.

The evening air cooled considerably from the afternoon heat. The sound of her boots echoed in the stillness. Only a few people milled about the streets, except for the row of saloons across the square. Paul steered her in the opposite direction.

Her heart picked up pace the longer he was silent. He had never asked her to go for a stroll before, so she wondered again about his motivation.

When they neared the site of the new church building his steps slowed. He placed his hand over hers and removed it from the crook of his arm. Then he turned to face her.

"Millie, I…"

The wind rustled the leaves of the cottonwood tree that stood tall and proud near the stairs of the church. She breathed deeply, allowing the fresh air to fill her lungs.

"I have been thinking. A lot, actually…" His voice was deep, thick with emotion.

"Yes?"

"I have waited a very long time for… For someone like you to come into my life."

He released her hands and started pacing. He ran his hand through his hair before he stopped in front of her again.

"I don't want you to ever leave."

Millie frowned. Had she done something to make him think that? "I'm not going anywhere."

"I'm making a mess of this." He reached for her hands again and his eyes locked with hers. "You know I care deeply for you."

She nodded.

"I've waited so very long for you to come into my life. I want it to last forever."

She blinked.

He shook his head. "What I'm trying to say is that I would like to court you—if you're agreeable to that—with the hopes that you would become my wife."

Her mouth went dry. Her knees felt as if they would stop supporting her any second. "You want…"

"You." He cradled her face in his hands. "I want you, Millie Pritchett, to let me court you. To be my wife."

A tear slid down her cheek and he wiped it away with his thumb. The frown on his face tugged at her heart. Did he have any idea how long she had waited to hear those words from any man?

Her eyes darted to the cottonwood tree. Could she say yes? Should she? Her heart desperately wanted to believe that things would turn out differently this time. That Paul was a different man. She knew he cared for her deeply. But what if the town learned of her heritage? What if it became impossible for them to marry?

"Millie?"

"I… What if…"

Her eyes searched his as his hands released her face.

"They won't find out."

"How can you be so certain?"

"Even if they do, Millie, it doesn't matter to me. I love you. I want you to be my wife. The intention of the law is regarding the Apache. Not you." He started pacing again. "The way I feel about you... I've never felt that way about a woman. I have prayed for you for so long."

He came to stand in front of her. "I can't imagine that God would allow me to love you so fully and so deeply if we were not meant to be together."

Millie turned her head away and watched as the last remnants of light faded from the sky. She wanted to believe him. She wanted all of this to be true.

"Yes."

"What?"

She turned to look at him again. "Yes, you may court me."

A half smile turned up a corner of his mouth. "And?"

"And, yes, I want to be your wife. With all my heart, I want to be your wife."

He pulled her into his arms and lowered his lips to hers. Searching. Teasing. Sending warmth through her abdomen and radiating all the way down her arms to her hands. She touched his strong neck, resting her hands behind it, before pressing closer. A deep moan came from his throat before he abruptly ended the kiss.

"I love you so much, Millie," he whispered, his breath warm against her neck.

"I love you, Paul."

He kissed her neck slowly, deliberately, before capturing her lips once again. His arms tightened around her as he deepened the kiss. She eagerly returned it, until a distant memory invaded her thoughts and she pulled away.

Paul's breath came in short, heavy bursts. His hands settled at the small of her back, beckoning her to move closer.

Instead, she slipped from his embrace. She took a deep breath to clear her mind. The memories of the past threatened to destroy this perfect moment. She couldn't tell him. Not now. Maybe not ever.

He captured her hand in his and placed it in the crook of his arm. She glanced at him in time to catch a roguish grin.

"Perhaps we should return to our walk, Miss Pritchett?"

She giggled. "Indeed, Mr. Lancaster."

As they retraced their earlier steps, her heart filled with more love for this man. He was right for her in every way. Strong where she was weak. Handsome. Kind. A man of good character. He would never betray her.

Millie's heartbeat skipped. Jake asked her to get him to sell the placer. It had been a few weeks. Surely, he wouldn't wait for long. She squared her shoulders as they were nearing the boardinghouse.

"Have you—" She stopped abruptly, not wanting to ruin such a perfect night.

"Have I, what?"

"Have you…" Her mind raced for ways to complete the question. "Considered what your mother might say?"

Paul laughed. "'Bout time. That's probably what she'd say."

"Really?"

"She's been after me for a while to find a wife."

Millie smiled as he opened the door of the boardinghouse. "Then she'll be happy."

"More than you know."

He walked her to her room. "Good night, Millie."

"Good night, Paul."

When she slipped inside and closed the door, she leaned against it for a moment. Her heart was torn between the fears of what could happen and the joy of what might be a blessed life with Paul. She prayed her fears would never be realized.

CHAPTER 29

"Good morning, dear!"

Millie turned slowly at the sound of Betty Shepherd's voice behind her. It was time to face Paul's mother. "Morning, Betty."

"Is Caroline here yet? I brought Hannah and Julia in with me."

"No. I'm not sure if she will be joining us. She felt a little under the weather yesterday," Millie answered, thankful that there would be other women helping prepare the massive feast for the Independence Day celebration. Maybe Betty wouldn't have time to question her about Paul.

"Ma!" Paul exclaimed as he picked up his mother in great big bear hug.

"Oh! Put me down." Betty laughed as red colored her cheeks. "You haven't hugged your ol' Ma like that since you were a teen."

Paul grinned. "Figured you were overdue." He leaned closer and placed a kiss on his mother's head.

Millie caught herself smiling at his antics. When he turned her direction, he opened his arms wide like he was about to give her a similar hug.

"Oh no you don't." She took a step backwards.

As he moved closer, he dropped his arms to his side. Then he reached for her hand a placed a kiss in her palm—right there with his mother looking on! Heat warmed her cheeks. If Betty hadn't known, she certainly knew now that he was courting her.

"What's this?" Betty asked.

Paul shifted to stand next to Millie. Then his arm settled around her shoulders. "What's what?"

Millie held back a snicker. How she loved when Paul teased his mother.

"Paul Lancaster!" Betty stood in front of them wagging a finger in his face. "You know exactly what I mean."

"Relax, Ma."

Silence stretched for several seconds.

"Well, is that all you have to say for yourself?" Betty asked.

Paul dropped his arm and took a step away. "For now."

"You rascal!" Betty snapped a towel towards Paul's retreating back.

"What did we miss?" Julia Larson asked as she entered the kitchen with Hannah Colter following behind.

"Nothing," Millie said too quickly.

Hannah's eyebrow shot up, but neither woman said anything more about it.

"What's the plan?" Julia asked.

As Betty outlined all the different dishes and desserts she wanted to make, Millie turned toward the cupboard and began gathering bowls and utensils. She had not slept well last night, knowing that Paul planned to tell his mother today.

She still didn't know what she had been thinking, agreeing to his courtship a few days ago. Though her fears about the town discovering her heritage had lessened, she feared that anything between her and Paul would only end up in pain for them both. She would eventually have to tell him about Cade, about every-thing. He would be crushed.

"Could you grab the flour, dear?" Betty asked, drawing her attention back to the gathering in the small boardinghouse kitch-en.

Millie slid the sack of flour across the counter and carried it to the table.

"Perhaps we should work in the dining hall instead," Hannah

suggested. "That way we could use some of the dining hall tables too."

"Nonsense, dear. This is fine, albeit a bit cozy."

Millie absently raised her hand to flick her braid back over her shoulder but stopped. Even after two weeks of wearing her hair in a chignon, she hadn't grown accustomed to it. How many times had she imagined her hair was braided and that one of those braids slipped over her shoulder?

She missed her braids. Her mother had never worn a chignon. Maybe that was why she chose to do so now to appear more like her father's people than her mother's.

A twinge of guilt settled over her as she began peeling and slicing apples for pies. Never had she been ashamed of her mother or the Shawnee.

Millie sighed then glanced over at Betty, Julia, and Hannah. They didn't seem to notice her inner turmoil. In fact, they barely seemed to notice she was in the room as they shared stories about their children and their life at the ranch.

"I am going to fetch more water," she announced, feeling overwhelmed by her thoughts. She hurried from the room before they could respond.

"I'm sorry, Mom," Millie whispered as she approached the town well.

There was too much at stake this time. She had to be careful. Wearing a chignon was just one small thing she could do to keep people from guessing Indian blood ran through her veins. If she wanted any chance at a life with Paul, she had to do whatever it took to keep that part of herself hidden.

Her fingertips touched the tell-tale features of her face. Her high cheekbones and angular jawline. Those things she couldn't change. She would have to settle for the things she could, like how she fashioned her hair.

"Let me get that," Paul said. Falling in step beside her, he took the bucket from her hand.

"Thank you."

"Is Ma questioning you?"

"No. She has barely said a word to me."

"Hmm." At Paul's frown her stomach tightened.

"Perhaps you should have just come right out and told her your intentions."

He smiled. "Don't worry about Ma. She loves you. She'll be fine."

When she didn't comment further, he turned to face her. Then he lowered his lips to hers for a few seconds. A light, sweet kiss from him was all it took to send her heart racing.

He smiled. "Better?"

She nodded.

"Good. I would hate for you to go back in there afraid of Ma. We'll tell her and Ben later that we're officially courting. In the meantime, my little display this morning will keep her thinking about it all day."

"You're terrible."

Paul laughed. "Naw. Just like to tease Ma as much as I can. Much better than the trouble I put her through back in Missouri."

"You haven't said much about your life before you came here."

His smile faded. Then he tweaked the end of her nose. "I will, later. Right now, you better get back in there." He handed her the full bucket of water once she stepped onto the porch. "Otherwise, Ma might become suspicious."

"Yes, dear," she said in the same tone his mother used.

"Ouch. I don't think I like that."

She giggled as he headed toward the barn. Pushing the door to the boardinghouse open, she sighed. She loved him so much. She just hoped this dream would last.

———

Later that afternoon, Paul found his ma sitting on the front porch in one of the rocking chairs.

"You've made a beautiful home here, Paul," she said as he took the seat next to her. "Can't believe you almost lost it over that placer mine."

He frowned. This wasn't how he hoped to start the conversation. "But I didn't."

She sighed. "I know. I just don't understand why you keep holding on to that placer when you hardly spend any time out there. Haven't for years."

The truth of her words stung. He didn't spend much time there, but he wasn't about to give it up. "Does it matter, Ma?"

Slowly, she shook her head. "No, I suppose it doesn't. At least not to me. But it might to Millie."

His head jerked back. "What? She's never said anything to me."

"Yet."

Paul held back a growl. Sometimes he swore Ma was purposely trying to goad him. It was almost working this time.

He took a deep breath to calm himself. "I have something to tell you."

Ma snorted. "I think you already did, in your usual indirect way."

He ignored her comment. "Millie has agreed to let me court her."

"I figured as much."

Silence settled over them, save for the creak of the rocking chair.

"I love her."

"I know."

Paul looked at Ma. Her smile stretched from ear to ear and her dark brown eyes sparkled with a knowing look.

"Don't give me that look. I know you love her. It's plain as day she fancies you too."

He closed his eyes, expecting some objection. Not that Ma would try to stop him from courting Millie. There was something in her tone that hinted at concern despite the acceptance of her words.

"Might as well say it," he said.

"Say what?"

"Whatever it is you're holding back."

"Do you think you should be living under the same roof now that you're courting?"

He hadn't expected that. "We're never alone. There's always someone around."

"Upstairs. Not downstairs. She's living on the other side of your bedroom wall."

Paul swallowed hard. More than once the same thought crossed his mind. One small, thin wall separated his room from hers. Something about it both thrilled and scared him.

"Maybe you should clean out that storeroom in the dining hall. It made for fine living quarters for you and me when we first arrived."

"I'll think about it."

Ma reached over and patted his hand. "Good."

"Ma?"

"Yeah?"

"Do you like her?"

Ma rubbed her hands along the arms of the rocking chair. "I do. She's not exactly what I pictured for you, but she's a fine woman. As long as you're happy…"

"But?"

"Nothing."

"Ma."

"Fine. How well do you know her?"

He shrugged. "Well enough."

"I just… Sometimes I wonder if she isn't hiding something. Something more than her Indian heritage."

Paul swallowed hard. "How do you know about that?"

"Oh, just a hunch I suppose. You're treading in dangerous waters, you know."

"Yeah."

Ma folded her hands in her lap. "I'm not sure if that's the only thing she's hiding."

"We have the rest of our lives to get to know each other. I can't imagine there's anything she could say or do that would scare me off."

"Be careful, Paul. Blind love can cause a great deal of pain."

He bit his tongue. Perhaps his mother was the reason he hadn't married yet. Seemed she found something wrong with Millie. Maybe it had been that way with other women. It had been so long since he'd been serious about anyone, he couldn't remember.

Ma stood and faced him. "Wipe that frown off your face. I like her. I'm happy that she loves you as much as you love her. I just don't want to see you get hurt."

Paul stood and placed a kiss on her forehead. "Thanks, Ma."

"Your pa would have liked her too."

A lump settled in the back of his throat. It meant the world to him to hear it.

CHAPTER 30

Later that afternoon, as Millie started peeling and cutting potatoes for supper, a familiar voice floated down the hall from the parlor. Her heart picked up pace and a grin spread across her face as she hurried to finish preparing the potatoes. As soon as she dropped the last one into the pot, she wiped her hands and hurried to the parlor.

"Dad!"

His back had been facing her. Slowly he turned around and rushed forward to give her a hug. "Millicent, sweetheart, you look wonderful. How have you been?"

Millie smiled again as Dad released her from the hug. Her eyes moved from the top of his head down to his toes and back up to his eyes. Those same violet eyes that she shared. She hadn't seen him since she left Wickenburg, though she wrote to him often. His hair looked grayer, but his eyes shone with love.

"Fine. I didn't know you were coming."

"Yes, well, we thought we would surprise you. Come, meet Mabel."

Mabel Cleary—well, Pritchett now she supposed—was a short woman, nearly a foot shorter than Millie. She had golden brown eyes that lit up when she smiled at Millie. Though her blonde hair was streaked with white, she still looked several years younger than Dad. Her emerald green gown was edged in black lace, giving her a sophisticated and wealthy appearance. Mabel reached for Millie's hands.

"Millicent, you're quite lovely," she said. "So much taller than I imagined."

Millie's cheeks warmed. "I'm afraid that is often the case. Tell me, was your trip to Prescott pleasant?"

Mabel squeezed Millie's hands affectionately then released them. "About what one can expect from a stage. But, enough about me. Tell me all about your life here in Prescott."

"You must be parched after the long journey. Sit and I'll bring some refreshments."

Millie waited for Mabel and Dad to take a seat before she hurried back to the kitchen. She sliced some cheese and bread. Then she poured two cups of steaming coffee and set them on a tray. She placed the sugar bowl and creamer on the tray and carried it to the parlor.

"You look radiant. Who is he?" Dad teased.

Warmth spread from the apples of her cheeks over her entire face. "I don't know what you're talking about."

"Nonsense."

It wouldn't take them long to find out that Paul was courting her. Best to tell the story now.

"Paul Lancaster and I are courting. Remember, I told you he owns this boardinghouse and a small placer mine up the road a ways."

"Oh, that's wonderful!" Mabel exclaimed. "How long have you been courting?" She accepted the coffee cup and plate of bread and cheese Millie offered.

"A few days."

Dad's smile faded. "Does he know about—?"

"He knows about mother's heritage, yes."

Dad frowned. "But, what about—"

"Oh, look at the time," Millie said as she stood. "You must be tired after your long trip, and I need to start supper. Will you come back to dine with us?"

Heat warmed her cheeks at her rude behavior. Dad and Mabel had hardly touched their refreshments and already she was hurrying them along. But Dad should know better. She couldn't, wouldn't talk about her secrets now. Not in front of a woman she just met, though she figured Dad probably already told Mabel all about her past.

Dad hesitated for a few seconds before his smile returned. "We would love to meet your man. We'll go check into our hotel room and freshen up. What time should we return?"

"Six would be fine."

Dad stood and kissed her on the cheek. "We'll see you then, sweetheart."

Millie escorted them to the door. Then she hurried to the kitchen to start the meal. Before she knew it, dinner hour was upon them.

As she laid out the food on the dining room table, she grew nervous. What would Dad think of Paul? She knew what he would think of her hiding her secrets. He already hinted at that. But she couldn't risk telling Paul everything. What did it matter anyway? Hadn't they both lived alone for so long? He probably had a few secrets of his own. None of it would matter to her. She loved him. Any secret he had could be forgiven. It was all in the past. Surely, he would say the same of her.

But, just in case, she would wait to tell him about her life before him—and about Cade—until she could be certain he would not leave her.

Voices floated through the entryway from the parlor to the dining room. She set the last item on the table and looked up. The boarders filed into the room followed by Paul and her parents. She was surprised Paul's mother and Ben hadn't joined them for supper but was glad Paul would have an opportunity to get to know her parents without his mother monopolizing the conversation.

Once the introductions were complete, they all sat down at the table. Dad led them in an eloquent prayer. She expected nothing less. Soon the conversation began.

"So, Millie tells me you pastor a small congregation in Wickenburg. How did you end up there?" Paul asked.

"Well, that's a bit of a long story," Dad said.

"We have time." Paul winked at her. The act sent a wave of warmth down her back.

"Let's see. I'm sure Millie told you that she grew up in Ohio."

At Paul's nod, Dad continued, "When she was a young woman, her mother and I decided to start a mission in Santa Fe. We left the mission among the Shawnee in the capable hands of a young pastor fresh from seminary. Good opportunity for him.

"Anyway, we made the journey from Ohio to Santa Fe. The early years were the hardest. We found more of the settlers spoke Spanish than we realized. We had to learn the language. Millie's mother seemed to learn it quickly, then she taught both Millie and me."

"A few years after the new mission started, my wife took ill and passed away a few weeks later."

Millie looked down at her plate. The old feelings of guilt and shame rushed to the forefront. If only she hadn't disobeyed her father—if only she hadn't been so foolish—they never would have left Ohio. Perhaps Mom would still be with them.

She glanced at Mabel as she reached over and took Dad's hand in hers. Such a caring woman. Perhaps she had not given Mabel a fair chance. There was something strong between Mabel and her dad. If their marriage brought him happiness, she would do her best to get to know her stepmother.

"We—that is Millicent and I—stayed on in Santa Fe, continuing to reach the lost souls there. I thought for certain that Millie would settle there, but year after year slipped by." Dad cleared his throat.

She knew he wished she had married Joel, so had she. But Joel hadn't been able to see beyond her past. The experience was enough to cause her to tread carefully now. She would not lose Paul—she loved him too much and he was her last hope for marriage.

"Anyway, before I knew it, we had been in Santa Fe for more than fifteen years. I started to feel the pull of the West. I heard about the mining towns and thought Wickenburg needed a man with my talents. So, a few years ago we headed there."

Millie smiled. "He was right. They needed a pastor. The more civilized of the townsfolk welcomed Dad immediately. The Ritters, the family that owns the stage stop—were quite eager for some regular services. Same with a few other families. It was obvious the Lord put Dad in the right place at the right time."

Paul smiled at her, but there was a hint of a question in his eyes. Hopefully he wouldn't ask her anything she couldn't answer yet.

The conversation turned away from her dad and Mabel after a few more minutes. Eventually, supper concluded, and she wished her parents a good evening as they retired back to their hotel.

Paul helped her clear the dishes. They quickly fell into their usual routine. She washed. He dried.

"Why didn't you marry?" he asked.

Millie took in a slow and deliberate breath, weighing her words carefully. "It's not that I didn't want to. There had been a few suitors in Santa Fe."

Perhaps if she told him about one of them, he wouldn't press for too many details. Risking it, she proceeded to tell him about Joel. "In the end, he decided I was not the right woman for him."

Unbidden, a tear trickled down her cheek. Paul reached up to brush it away.

"I'm so sorry, Millie."

He pulled her close, wrapping his strong arms around her. She let tears fall, soaking his shirt. For the first time, she truly let go of the loss of that relationship. It was not meant to be. She would not let those old feelings of hurt and rejection weigh her heart any longer.

After a few minutes, she composed herself and turned her attention back to the dishes.

"Paul, why did you never marry?"

"Hmm. My life in Missouri was... I was such a different man then. I held so much hurt and anger in. I was angry that Pa died. I was angry that I had to help Ma raise the girls and my brother. I didn't ask for that responsibility."

The silence stretched long enough so that she thought he might be done telling his story.

"Millie, I am not the man that I once was. I... I used to spend too much time at the saloon. I would fight any man at the slightest insult. I was reckless and wretched. At one point, my anger spilled over, and I nearly killed the man who later became my sister's husband.

"That's why it was easy to leave in '63 and head west. I spent too many years keeping the farm running. Even after Jesus saved me from my ugly past, I felt like the community never forgave me. I thought life might be different if I struck out on my own."

He snorted. "I hadn't expected that Ma would want to come along. At first, it irritated me. Later, I was glad she did. Life would have been so much lonelier without her here."

He dried the last dish and put it away. Then he led her to the small table in the corner of the kitchen. Looking directly into her eyes, he continued his story.

"I never married in Missouri because no woman would have me. They only remembered the bad thing I had done. They did not want to see the new man I had become. Once I was here—well, there were no women to marry. They were all too young or too old or grieving over a lost husband. I never found the woman I wanted to be my wife..."

Paul reached across the table and took her hands in his. He slowly rubbed his thumbs across her knuckles. "Until I met you. Millie, you are the sweetest woman I have ever met. Soft-spoken, yet determined. I want you to know that I'm not like Joel. I will not end this courtship and cast you aside. I will end it only when you've stood across from me at the altar and pledged to be my wife."

Her breath caught. Oh, how she hoped—even dreamed—that was what would really happen.

As he stood to his feet, he kept his hold on her hands and gave a little tug, until she stood face to face with him. "I love you so much, Millie."

Then, he lowered his lips to hers and kissed her until warmth pulsed through her body from her fingers to her toes. When he pulled away, she whispered, "I love you too, Paul."

He stepped back and tapped his index finger on her nose. "Good. Now, off to bed. We've got a busy day tomorrow. People from all over will be here to celebrate Independence Day."

CHAPTER 31

The next morning, Millie hurried through the breakfast dishes. There was so much to do before the town square started filling up with people for the Independence Day festivities. She needed to hang the banners, set out the food tables, enlist some to help move tables and benches from the dining hall and more.

Best start with the banners. She picked them up along with a hammer and some nails. When she opened the door and stepped out onto the porch, she stopped. Paul had already seen to setting up tables and benches.

She shook off her surprise and climbed onto the porch railing. No ladder was needed. With her height, she could easily reach the edge of the porch roof to hang the banners.

"Millie!" Paul's voice held a frantic edge. "Let me help."

She reached up and pounded a nail into one corner of the banner. "I'm almost done."

Paul's hands circled her waist as she put the last nail in place. Then he eased her off the railing.

"You could have asked for my help."

She smiled. "You were busy."

He frowned. "Well, you should be more careful."

"Paul, I haven't had the luxury of asking for help for a very long time. I'm used to doing things for myself."

"Need help with the food?"

She resisted the urge to roll her eyes. "I suppose so."

He followed her into the dining hall. The kitchen was full of pots and pans of food. Millie grabbed several items and delivered them to the tables in the yard with Paul's help.

"Are you planning on feeding the whole town?" Paul teased.

"No. Just half of it. I thought you said there would be a lot of people here."

"Yeah, but some of them should be bringing food of their own."

"Well, your ma wanted to make sure we didn't run out."

"I'll bet."

He gave her a kiss on the cheek before one of the neighboring business owners called him away to help.

"I saw that," Caroline said as she greeted Millie.

Millie's cheeks warmed. "Saw what?"

"So, is it official? Is Paul your beau now?"

She nodded as the idea grew on her. Beau for now. One day soon, maybe he would be her husband. The thought sent more heat to her cheeks.

Just as she finished her last chore, her dad and Mabel arrived. She introduced them to Caroline and Thomas. Then Adam and Julia Larson arrived with their two girls, followed by the Colters, Cahills, and the rest of the Larson clan. While she recognized many of them from church and Sunday suppers, it had been a long time since the entire group had been together. Not everyone stayed for Sunday supper every week. Then there were new births, sick children, branding season, cattle drives—for one reason or another they rarely all attended at the same time.

A stunning redhead stood nearby, circled by three cowboys. Caroline lifted a hand to wave to the young woman.

"Who's that?" Millie asked.

"You've never met my sister Missy?"

"I don't think so."

"Come on, let me introduce you."

As they approached where Missy stood, Millie's heart raced. There was that cowboy again—the one she had seen on the day of Caroline's baby shower. His back was facing her. She slowed her steps, afraid of learning the truth.

Just as Caroline started to call out to her sister, music erupted from the bandstand, drowning out anything she was going to say. One of the darker haired cowboys held out his hand for Missy. As soon as her hand was in his, he whisked her away from the group.

Millie's throat tightened.

Then, the remaining two cowboys sauntered off towards one of the games, never looking in her direction. She let out a slow breath. That was close.

"Oh well," Caroline said. "You can meet her later."

"Care to dance?" Paul's voice came from behind her.

The anxiety from moments ago still lingered. Millie forced a smile to her lips and offered her hand to him, hoping the act would calm her. His fingers wrapped around hers and within seconds, he held her in his arms on the dance floor.

The tune was a lively, upbeat one and soon she forgot her fears. She focused on Paul. His blue eyes shimmered in the sunlight and his smile warmed her from head to toe. When he twirled her around, she laughed—unable to remember the last time she had this much fun.

As the song ended, Millie tried to catch her breath. The next song was slower, and Paul drew her close, resting one hand at the small of her back. She breathed deeply of his masculine scent savoring his nearness. She longed to rest her head on his shoulder. If she tried such a thing, he would probably let her. The idea brought a smile to her lips.

"What are you thinking about?" he asked.

"Hmm. How much I'm enjoying this."

Paul placed a kiss on her forehead as the dance came to an end. "I'm enjoying this too, but I'm also hungry." He wiggled his eyebrows. "I see the mayor heading to the podium. Think he'll say blessing for us, so we can eat?"

"Breakfast wasn't big enough for you?"

"It was. But that was hours ago."

She laughed.

The mayor spoke for a few minutes, officially welcoming the

townsfolk and all the visitors from the surrounding area to the fifth annual Independence Day celebration. He briefly outlined the events of the day: lunch, pony races, mining competitions, rope tricks, music, dancing, and later in the evening, the military would come for some drills and fireworks. Then he invited Pastor Page to give the blessing.

As soon as the blessing was done, Paul grabbed Millie's hand. "Come on. Show me what all the goodies are on the table."

The line formed quicker than expected, so they had to wait a few minutes for their turn. Once they reached the front, Paul held out a plate for her and he helped dish food onto it. She smiled as he put a man-sized portion of potatoes on her plate.

"I hope you don't think I'm going to eat all of that."

"Oh, that's so I don't have to come back for seconds."

"Hey, is that Mr. Lowery? Who is the woman with him?"

Paul slapped his hand on his leg. "Well, I'll be. That's Mrs. Feldman."

"Wasn't she your previous housekeeper?"

"Yeah. And the two of them fought—always."

Millie smiled. The couple was a few spots in front of them, but she was close enough to see the loving looks passing between the two, despite their complaint-filled banter. "Looks like they are getting along fine now."

After they made their way through the line, Paul led her to the front porch of the boardinghouse. It was more secluded than some of the other areas.

Millie set her plate on the small table between the two rocking chairs. Then she took a seat in one, arranging the skirts of her lavender dress. Paul sat in the chair on the other side of the small table. She picked up her plate and began eating.

"Why did you leave Wickenburg?" he asked as he took a big bite of his lunch.

She sighed. It wasn't a question she minded answering, she just wasn't sure how to answer.

"I suppose because Dad really wanted me to. When Mabel was on her way to marry him, he asked me to come visit with

Caroline for a few days. Before I finished packing, he suggested that maybe there would be more opportunities for me here."

Paul smiled. "Have there been?"

She smiled. "I think so. There's this handsome man that wants to marry me. I probably would have had to settle for some dirty old miner in Wickenburg. At least here, there are middle aged ones that bathe every now and then."

He laughed—one of his deep bellied laughs. She loved it as much as she loved him.

"Do you think we could have children when we marry?"

His question settled over that empty place in her heart, nearly bringing tears to her eyes. She had given up the dream of raising children long ago.

Memories from that night surfaced. She could still feel the cold bite to the air as the wagon train stopped for the night. They were someplace in Kansas. For two days she had felt more tired than normal.

Then the pains began. Mom had told her what to expect, but when they had arrived, Millie still cried out in fear.

"It's time," Mom had said. "Deep breaths now, sweet one. It will be alright."

Mom's calm voice had been drowned out by Dad's fervent prayers.

"Lord, help this child come into the world safely. Keep our dear daughter safe."

Millie screamed in pain. The pains grew shorter as the night wore on. Finally, with great effort and a final loud cry, Millie brought her son into the world.

Mom had been a great help, cleaning up her son before wrapping him in the blanket Millie had spent days knitting—a precious gift for her precious son.

The first time Millie had held him in her arms her heart instantly bonded to his. "Matthew," she whispered his name for the first time. She had spent many weeks thinking about what she would name the child. Then, one morning as she had been reading through the gospel of Matthew, she decided the name fit. Her son would be rejected by society, just like the disciple Matthew had been hated for being a tax collector. Only her son would be hated because he was a bastard—a result of her sins and failures. He would suffer because of her mistakes.

"Millie?"

Paul's voice brought her mind back to the present. She pondered his question as she tried to push the memories away. Was she too old to have children now?

At last, she answered, "I don't know. I would love to have a family."

"Me, too." Paul reached over and squeezed her hand. "But I'll understand if it doesn't happen."

Tears burned her eyes. What would he think when she told him she had a son and gave him away? That she had already been a mother once. The worst of all mothers—one who let someone else take her baby from her.

She hadn't wanted to let Matthew go. But Dad had been right. She had been too young, only fourteen years old. When she had given birth to him, it was a few short days after a sweet couple on the wagon train lost their baby. They could give him a good home, Dad had said. They could love him as their own. Matthew would be better off with a mother and a father to love him. Not the bastard son of a preacher's daughter.

As much as it hurt, she had let him go. She had given away her own son willingly. A choice she had hated herself for every day since.

She blinked away the tears as she stuffed her secret back into the deep recesses of her heart. She couldn't tell Paul—not today on such a happy occasion when she was celebrating her courtship and hoping for what the future would hold.

"Hey," he said. "I mean it. If we don't have children, I will be fine."

"Thank you," she whispered, glad he hadn't suspected the real reason for her solemnness.

CHAPTER 32

Paul felt terrible about bringing up children. He would love to have some of his own—of *their* own. But Millie was older. He wasn't sure at what age women stopped having children, but he thought she might be beyond those years. Obviously, it was a sad subject for her. It would be hard to see her disappointed if they did not have children. But it was out of his control.

When they finished eating, he suggested they rejoin the rest of the group of family and friends. He helped Millie take a seat next to his ma on a blanket in the shade. Then he searched for Millie's dad. He found the pastor and his wife sitting on one of the benches near the dining hall.

"Reverend Pritchett, can I have a word with you?"

"Certainly. And please, call me Paul."

Paul cocked his head to one side. Millie hadn't mentioned that he shared the same name as her father. A few seconds ticketed by before he led the elder Paul away from the crowd.

"I…" For some reason, his throat felt dry all the sudden. Millie told him it wasn't necessary to speak to her dad, but he still felt it was the right thing to do. Now that he was face to face with him, the words weren't as easy as he thought.

"Go ahead, son."

"I wanted to ask your permission to marry Millie. She has become very important to me. The more I get to know her, the more I don't want to live without her."

Millie's dad nodded and rubbed a hand over his chin.

The silence made him uncomfortable, and he shifted from one foot to the other. He hadn't expected her dad to take so long to respond.

"How much has she told you about her youth?"

"Ah… She told me that you decided to move to Santa Fe when she was fourteen—I think she said."

Millie's dad frowned. Then he cleared his throat. "I see."

Paul's heart started to beat faster. Was he going to tell him no? He hadn't considered that could be a possibility. Now, he wasn't so sure.

"Marriage vows are very serious. I've presided over many a wedding and very much respect the covenant God sets in place when two people are joined in marriage. 'For better or for worse.' That means no matter what happened in the past or what happens in the future, you agree to be fully responsible and fully committed to my daughter. Is that something you are certain you are ready to do?"

He swallowed hard. Why did he suddenly have the feeling that he was missing something? Slowly he nodded. "Yes, sir."

"Then you have my blessing."

Paul let out a slow breath, but heaviness still pressed down on his stomach.

"Son, just remember what I said: 'For better or for worse.' The past is in the past and that's where it should stay. Whatever you do, don't break my little girl's heart."

With a curt nod, Millie's dad held out his hand.

Paul shook his hand. "I look forward to welcoming you into my family."

Millie's dad smiled—at last. "Be sure to let Mabel and I know when the wedding is planned. We wouldn't want to miss it."

His tenseness eased some.

"One last thing," Millie's dad said. "About your living quarters…"

Paul held back a frown. "Yes?"

"Is there somewhere else you or Millie could stay until you

marry? I'm not comfortable with you living, um, well, in such close quarters."

"I'll see to it."

"Good. Shall we get back to the festivities?"

Once they returned to where the rest of their friends and family were gathered, Millie's dad pulled her aside. The smile on her face reassured Paul. She was pleased with whatever her father said.

A bit annoyed with the pressure from both his ma and Millie's dad to change his living quarters, he figured he better do as they suggested. For if they were concerned, no telling what the rest of the town would say.

"Thomas!" He caught up with his friend as he escorted Caroline off the dance floor.

"Paul, what can I do for you?"

"Seems like I'll need some help clearing out a spot in the storage room."

"Why?"

Paul cleared his throat. "It seems like the right thing to do. That is, I can't keep living under the same roof as Millie until..."

Thomas's eyes lit. "Ah. When do you want to work on it?"

"Will tomorrow be fine?"

"Sure, works for me."

"Good. Hey, have you seen Jake around? I thought I'd ask him to help."

Thomas scanned the crowd. "Yeah, I think that's him over there by the bandstand."

"Thanks."

Paul wove his way through the throng until he reached the bandstand. As he neared, his old concerns about Jake resurfaced. He was too thin. The circles under his eyes seemed darker than the last time he saw him. A week's growth of beard covered his chin. His shirt and trousers were filthy.

"Paul," Jake greeted him.

"Jake, how have you been?"

"Well enough."

"I was wondering if you would help me clean out the storeroom tomorrow."

"Sure, but on one condition."

"What's that?"

"Free lunch at the dining hall?"

Paul almost frowned. The question wasn't like Jake. He knew he was welcome at any time. He shrugged off the concern and held out his hand. "Deal."

Jake shook his hand. "See ya tomorrow."

Paul returned to where his ma was sitting under a tree as the band struck up another tune.

"Wanna dance?" He asked Ma as he helped her to her feet.

"Sheriff," she said as she looked over Paul's shoulder to an approaching man. Guess there would be no dance with his ma. At least not yet.

"Have you found those Indians that shot at my boy?" Ma asked Sheriff Smith.

"No ma'am. Not entirely sure it was Indians that shot at him."

"What do you mean? He said he saw them."

"Ma, I wasn't sure what I saw. I was shot at, so I didn't get a good look. I'm sure the sheriff is doing all he can to keep the town safe."

"Humph."

"Some of the other miners reported men that looked white dressed in Indian clothes hanging around the mines that day," the sheriff said. "Anyway, we are getting closer to figuring this out."

"Sheriff! Come quick!" a young man shouted as he skidded to a stop in front of the law man. "There's been an attack outside of town. A family." He inhaled a deep breath. "Killed. By Indians."

The music stopped mid-strain as a small crowd gathered around them. One of the onlookers, shouted, "An eye for an eye!"

More murderous shouts echoed around them.

Paul felt Millie press into his side. He slid his arm around her shoulders.

"Hold on!" Sheriff Smith shouted. He turned to the young man. "What happened?"

"The men from the fort found 'em. They were all mutilated not far from their wagon. Couldn't have been more than a hundred yards from town."

The crowd began to roar for revenge again.

"Quiet!" the sheriff shouted.

"They were scalped. One of the men from the fort said the mama was still alive, screaming in agony. They had mercy on her and sent her to be with her family."

Millie gasped as did several other women. Paul pulled her closer.

"It was them Johnny Apache! Let's kill 'em all!" a man shouted from the crowd.

The sheriff lost control as several men gathered their weapons and headed toward the scene.

"I'll be back," Paul whispered in Millie's ear.

"Don't go."

"I won't do anything I'll regret. I'll be back soon."

Paul followed the crowd to the gruesome scene. His stomach lurched at the violence of it all. This time, he was certain the Apache were responsible.

———

Jake Waters hoisted his rifle up and leaned the long barrel against his shoulder. He followed the angry crowd out to the scene of the butchered family. His stomach roiled at the sight. A mother clung to her dead baby, blood drenching her dress. Her lifeless stare sent chills down his spine.

A whimper sounded off to his right. He moved closer and found a small child struggling to breathe. How had the Army missed him?

He coughed and blood trickled from his mouth. Jake's stomach lurched—the boy was dying, suffering.

Fear and pain filled the child's brown eyes as Jake approached. He glanced over his shoulder. The crowd paid him no mind. His hands shook as he checked his rifle. *Lord forgive me*, he thought, remembering his own sister's suffering.

"Shh, son," he whispered, kneeling beside the boy. "You're going to see your mama soon." He closed his eyes and pulled the trigger, tears streaming down his face.

Jake sat back on his heels, bile rising in his throat. What had he become?

"Jake!" Paul called after him. "Jake!"

"Wasn't nothing to be done!" he yelled back, before he took off running for town.

Each heavy breath tried to etch the boy's face in his mind. It had been the merciful thing to do, instead of letting him suffer for hours until he died. Now he had even more reason for revenge.

He ducked inside the nearest saloon and headed straight for the bar. Maybe after enough drinks he wouldn't remember the boy's expression anymore.

CHAPTER 33

The next morning Thomas arrived just after breakfast. Paul led him to the storage room.

"When is the last time you were in here?" Thomas asked.

"The day Millie arrived."

Thomas arched an eyebrow.

"I was looking for the tax receipts. Lost track of time."

"That explains a lot. Looks like you haven't done much with the place for a while."

"Other than a few hours on that day, I hadn't been in here for months. Maybe even a year."

Paul surveyed the large stack of crates and scrap metal and wood. It was a mess. Dust covered everything. There was no order to where things were placed. He probably had just tossed each item in an open space whenever he had something new to store.

"Maybe we should clear only enough room for a bed. I don't want to get too comfortable."

"Alright. I thought you said Jake was going to help."

"Yeah. Let's start with the area by the door. That seems to make the most sense."

Thomas nodded and lifted a crate and carried it to the far end of the room. "We can stack stuff over here."

"Sounds good." Paul paused and then mentioned what was on everyone's minds. "Did you see what happened to that family yesterday?"

"No. Just heard about it from Adam. He said Jake shot one of the kids."

"Yeah. The kid wasn't going to make it."

"It's a shame. And so close to town."

Paul grew silent. It was too close to town. Several of the townsfolk had wanted the Army to ride out after the Apache. Judging by what he had seen, they would have been long gone. He hoped tensions would settle down soon.

Where was Jake? It wasn't like him to be late, but then he really hadn't been himself for a while.

Paul picked up another crate and moved it to the other side of the room.

After an hour, they barely made a dent in clearing enough space for a bed. Still no Jake.

"Let's take a break," he suggested.

He led Thomas out to the kitchen and poured them each a cup of coffee. As he was downing the last swig, Jake stumbled through the door. The smell of stale alcohol was heavy on his breath and clothes.

"Not late, am I?" Jake asked.

Paul frowned. "You sober enough to help?"

"Sure."

Thomas frowned and shook his head but led the way back into the storeroom.

"You never said," Jake started. "Why you need to clean out the place."

"He's marrying, Millie," Thomas said.

Jake dropped the crate to the floor and shook his fist at Paul. "You can't marry her!"

"Why not?" Paul fisted his hands at his side as blood pumped fiercely through his veins.

"She's Indian! They'll—" Jake's voice cracked. "Paul, you don't understand. They kill everyone. I can't... I can't lose you too."

Thomas laughed. "That's the most ridiculous thing I've ever heard. Millie wouldn't hurt a fly. You, on the other hand—"

Jake swung wildly at Thomas but missed, stumbling backward.

"Hey! I was just teasing."

"I've already lost everyone!" Jake's voice broke. "Ma, Sissy—they're gone because I wasn't there to protect them. I won't let the same thing happen to you." The wild desperation in his eyes sent chills down Paul's spine.

"What are you saying?" he asked.

"Don't marry her. Please, Paul. She'll betray you when her people come. They all do. It's what they do."

Heat rushed to Paul's face. His muscles quivered and he stepped closer to Jake. "That is my future wife you're accusing."

"I'm trying to save your life!" Jake shouted, tears streaming down his face. "Why won't you listen to me?"

"Get out!" Paul's voice echoed in the small room.

Jake's eyes widened and he took a step back.

Paul clenched his teeth, and a low growl rose to his throat.

Jake turned and darted out of the room. "I won't let her hurt you, Paul. I won't lose anyone else!" Then he was gone.

Paul paced back and forth across the small area that he and Thomas cleared. Slowly his heartbeat returned to normal, and the tension eased from his muscles.

"What was that all about?" Thomas asked.

"I don't know." Paul shook his head. "I don't know, but he is no friend of mine. Not after talking about Millie that way."

After a minute, Thomas started moving some of the lighter objects. Paul tried to make sense of what happened as he worked. Why was Jake so angry with Millie? Even though she was part Indian, she had nothing to do with any attack. She didn't know anything about the local Apache.

And just what did Jake mean that he wouldn't let Millie hurt him?

CHAPTER 34

July 8, 1869

"A wedding. I can hardly wait!" Caroline exclaimed as she hugged Millie.

"Coffee?" Millie held up the pot as Caroline took a seat at the small table in the kitchen.

"We have a wedding to plan and all you can think about is coffee?"

She poured a cup for herself and her friend then she took a seat. "Caroline don't make a big deal out of this. Paul and I just want a quiet ceremony. Probably mid-week so Dad doesn't have to be gone away from Wickenburg for too long."

Caroline waved her hand in the air dismissing the idea. "When are you thinking about getting married?"

"August or September."

"Oh, pick August. Please, please, please. I don't want to worry about popping out this baby at your wedding."

"Don't be so dramatic."

Caroline giggled. "Don't be so serious. It's your wedding. You should be happy."

That old niggling fear whispered in Millie's ear. What if Paul cast her aside when he learned about her son?

Dad had given her an earful the day he left to return to Wickenburg. He had been pretty upset that she had not been honest with her future husband.

"You have to tell him," Dad had said. "It's not good to go into a marriage with secrets knowing it might harm him."

"It's in the past. What does it matter?" She knew fully how much it mattered as the last word slipped past her lips.

"Millicent." His tone was stern, much like when she got into trouble as a child. "Do the right thing. Talk to him."

Reluctantly, she agreed. Though, over the past two days, she had completely lost her resolve.

"You're not listening." Caroline's statement brought her back to the present.

"I'm sorry. I was just thinking I needed to get the laundry started." What was wrong with her? Since when had she become such an accomplished liar? Well, it wasn't an outright lie. She did need to start the wash.

"I can help. Then we'll get it done faster."

"Don't you need to get back?"

"No. Mama took Drew out to the ranch with her for the week. He's not due back until tonight. He just loves horses so much. Must get that from Thomas."

Millie smiled.

"Anyway, put me to work," Caroline said as she rose.

"Alright."

After a half hour, the two finally had all the laundry gathered and water heated and hauled out to the wash basin between the boardinghouse and the dining hall. Millie scrubbed and rinsed the clothes before handing them off to Caroline to wring them out and hang on the line.

"So, back to the wedding. I think an early August date would be perfect."

Millie sighed. She should have known Caroline wouldn't drop the topic.

"I don't know. Neither Paul nor I are in a hurry."

Caroline laughed. "Not in a hurry? After all this time, you would think both of you would have gotten married while your dad was still here on Independence Day."

"September isn't that far away."

"Don't you do that to me, Millie. I'm serious about fretting over this baby coming during your ceremony. I would be so embarrassed!"

As she reached for the next item from the pile of laundry, her hand encountered an unexpected obstacle. Before she knew it, her arm was twisted behind her back. The cool blade of a knife rested against her neck.

"You let go of her!" Caroline screamed. When she started to move toward Millie's captor, he pressed the knife tighter against her neck.

"Stay right there, Mrs. Anderson. Wouldn't want to spill your half-breed friend's blood just yet."

The man's voice was familiar. The blood rushed from Millie's head, sending a wave of dizziness over her. Jake Waters!

Millie's throat constricted. She had to find a way to get him to shut up. If he told the town… She would never be able to marry Paul.

"Half-breed? You don't know what you're talking about mister." Caroline put one hand on her hip. "You better let her go."

As Millie searched for a way to wriggle free from Jake's grip, she noticed more people gathering in the square. She no longer feared for her life. Only her soon-to-never-be marriage.

"Waters, you saying she's one of them Apache?" a stout man from the crowd asked.

"Just look at her. What do you think?"

"Stop it!" Caroline screamed as the stout man grabbed Millie's braid. Why, oh why hadn't she worn a chignon today?

"You leave her alone!"

"Iffen she ain't Apache, she sure is injun," said the stout man as he grabbed his knife. With several rough strokes, he cut off a portion of her braid. "Just look how dark her hair is!" He held the braid high over his head.

The man holding her loosened his grip and shoved her.

She stumbled to the ground, bracing her fall with her hands. A sharp rock sliced open her palm. She pressed her apron over it as she stared up at the crowd circling her. Rage danced in their eyes.

———

Paul pressed the blade of his axe against the grinding stone. After a few minutes of honing the blade, he stopped the grinding stone and checked the sharpness of the ax. A commotion sounded from outside. The voices were too muffled through the barn wall, but they sounded close—close enough to be on his property.

He set the ax aside and stood. As he stepped from the barn, he heard a man shout, "She's one of them. I say we kill her!"

Millie!

Fear squeezed his heart. He wasn't even her husband yet and he already failed to protect her.

More angry shouts.

He ran to the edge of the crowd. Though he could see over many of the men, he couldn't see her.

"Paul! Stop them! Please, stop them!" Caroline's frantic screams made his skin crawl.

"Where is she?"

"In there." Caroline pointed to the crowd.

Old familiar anger pushed through his fear. He grabbed one man and threw him to ground. Then the next. Then the next. "Millie!"

A faint cry reached his ears. He moved toward it, pushing, shoving, and tossing aside anything or anyone that stood in his way.

One man jumped on his back and began squeezing his arm around Paul's neck. He reached behind him and flipped the man off his back to the ground in front of him. Stepping over him, he moved forward undeterred.

"Millie!"

"Paul," came her weak reply.

A hand grasped at his leg he reached down and grabbed it. When the softness of her skin registered in his mind, he loosened his grip and hauled her to her feet. Then he folded his arms around her, hunching his shoulders over her to protect her from the blows connecting with his back.

"Didn't know you were an injun lover!"

Paul froze. "Jake?"

His eyes searched the crowd. Sure enough, Jake Waters threw accusations his way, inciting the group of men to a new frenzy.

He shook off the pain of betrayal and pushed through the crowd. He had to get Millie out of here. As soon as no one stood in his way, he gave Millie a gentle shove in the direction of the house. "Go!"

She took off, running.

The loud echoing crack of gunfire pierced his ears as he watched Millie fall to the ground.

"No! Millie!"

He started to run toward her, but several hands grabbed his shoulders and dragged him back into the angry circle of drunken, bloodthirsty men.

"Millie!"

He tried to free himself—to run to her side—but too many men held him back.

"Ain't gonna get away with consorting with the enemy, Lancaster."

A fist connected with his jaw. Another fist jabbed his ribs. Then another.

He had to shake off these men. He had to get to Millie.

Each blow to his body sent fire radiating through him. Instinctively, his body curled to protect itself. A boot delivered a pointed blow to his stomach.

The blows suddenly stopped. A man grabbed a handful of his hair and whipped his head back. The bright sunlight caused him to squint.

"You shoulda never hired that half-breed, Paul." Jake's angry words rang in his ears. "She's been telling her kind when families leave this town by themselves. She been helping them—telling them when to attack us."

"That's not true." Paul's voice sounded hoarse, and his throat scratched with each word.

"Waters! I think you done killed her."

No! Lord, please.
A rifle butt connected with Paul's skull, and everything faded.

CHAPTER 35

When she heard gunfire, Millie dropped to the ground face down. She lay as still as a placid lake, taking inventory. No searing pain from a bullet. Just the bruises from the angry crowd's blows.

"Waters, you killed her!"

The man's voice came from above her somewhere. She relaxed and closed her eyes. Hands pawed at her arms. Then, she felt her body roll over.

Stay relaxed. Stay limp. The mantra did the trick. She flopped on her back as if she were unconscious. Or dead.

From the words floating around her, she sensed the crowd was hoping for the latter.

"Millie!" Caroline's frantic scream nearly broke her resolve to play dead.

Another gunshot startled the crowd to silence.

"What's going on here!"

"Sheriff!" Caroline cried. "They killed Millie. This man said she was Indian. But she's not. She's white. As white as you or me. And they killed her."

Murmurs buzzed.

"Enough!" Sheriff Smith shouted. "Grab Waters! The rest of you, get on outta here, unless you want to spend the night in jail."

The sound of boots shuffling across the dirt dimmed. Millie

lay still, afraid to give up her guise until she was certain the sheriff had everything under control.

"Miss Pritchett?" the sheriff asked.

She opened her eyes.

"You okay?"

She nodded, despite the soreness in her body.

"Don't see no blood. You hurting?"

"Just a few bruises," she whispered. "Where's Paul?"

The sheriff frowned. "Let's get you over to the doctor." He helped her to her feet.

"I'm fine. Where's Paul?"

"Millie!" Caroline flung herself into Millie's arms. "I thought you were dead."

"I'm okay. Just a little bruised," she said as she released Caroline.

"Don't you ever scare me like that again!"

"Millie!"

She turned to the sound of Paul's voice. Tears dripped down the side of her face. She rushed to his open arms, letting the sobs shake her body.

He rubbed his hands up and down her back.

"Paul," Sheriff Smith said. "Hate to interrupt, but I'm gonna need to talk to you, Miss Pritchett, and Mrs. Anderson."

Millie leaned back just enough to look into Paul's eyes. Worry and fear were quickly replaced by a deep frown. She pulled away from his embrace and answered the sheriff.

"Please come in. We can sit in the parlor." She led the way.

The sheriff waited for her and Caroline to take a seat. "What happened?"

Millie carefully studied her hands, fearing for her future, as Caroline rushed to respond, "We were just doing the laundry when a man grabbed Millie and started calling her names."

"Jake Waters." Paul's voice sounded flat, and his gaze fixed on an empty spot on the wall.

Millie nodded, keeping her eyes locked on her hands. All her dreams were going to be ripped from her. She was going to lose

Paul. All because her father had fallen in love with a Shawnee woman, married her, and raised their mixed-blood daughter. Half-breed, Jake had called her. And this time, those who heard the accusation believed it.

Lord, haven't I paid enough for my sins? Why are you letting this happen to me? When will I have atoned for the mistakes of my past? When can I see just one dream fulfilled? Her eyes burned, but she refused to shed another tear.

"What did he say?" the sheriff asked.

"He accused Millie of being an Indian spy. What a crazy notion!" Caroline said.

It was then that Millie lifted her gaze. She thrust her chin forward and pressed her lips together in a thin line. She looked at Paul. His brow puckered in a frown. He listened intently as Caroline relayed her version of the events, repeatedly glancing her way.

"She and her father were living in Santa Fe when I met them. They aren't from around here. You met him when he was here for Independence Day," Caroline was saying to the sheriff. "She's no more Indian than I am."

A light knock sounded at the front door. Paul stood to open it. The sheriff's deputy entered with his hat in his hand. "We have Waters in jail."

Sheriff Smith nodded, and the deputy left.

Paul took the opportunity to slide onto the seat next to Millie. "Are you alright? Do you need the doctor?"

She shook her head. "I'm fine."

Another lie. Her heart was breaking into a thousand rough shards, like her mother's favorite vase had when it slipped from her fingers many years ago. There was nothing left for her here. She might as well begin plans to move back to Wickenburg. This town would never forget Jake's accusations. She would never marry Paul. There was nothing left for her here.

"Caroline?"

"Thomas!" Caroline jumped to her feet and threw herself into her husband's arms, barely giving him enough time to close the door.

"I came as soon as I heard."

Millie sat with her back rigid as she watched the couple whisper. Their tenderness was clear from the way they looked and held each other. Oh, how she wished Paul would send them all away and wrap his arms around her again.

Paul hugged her to his side with one arm around her shoulders. "Sheriff, is there anything else you need from us?"

"No, I suppose not. Stop by in a few days. I have an update for you about your mine."

The sheriff stood, which drew Thomas and Caroline's attention. As the sheriff left, Caroline stood in front of her.

"Will you be alright, Millie?"

She felt numb. Dead inside. She had to leave. Millie wiped the emotion from her face, and she lied to her friend. "I'm fine."

"You send for me if you need anything."

"I will."

Caroline reached for her hands and tugged, until she stood. Then the two women embraced for a moment. Millie didn't want her heart to soften or have hope, but for some reason, the simple act of friendship did just that.

She watched in silence as Paul closed the door behind Thomas and Caroline.

As soon as they left, Paul said, "I'm so sorry, Millie. I had no idea Jake was harboring such hatred towards you. But this doesn't change anything. I still want to marry you. Even more than before."

He couldn't be serious. Hadn't he heard the crowd?

"How can you say that? You've seen firsthand how much the townsfolk hate the Indians. You know the truth. It's only a matter of time before everyone in the town will come to hate me because of my mother's blood."

"That's not true. Didn't you hear how Caroline defended you? You have several friends here that won't believe Jake."

"He's still right."

"Maybe I should move back in for a while, until things settle down."

"That's not necessary."

"Millie, look at me. I want you to be my wife. God brought you here, to this place, at this time. I have fallen so deeply in love with you. The only way I would walk away is if you asked me to. And, even then, it wouldn't be without a fight. I don't care what the town thinks or says about you or about us."

She barely believed what he was saying. "You would risk everything?"

"Even my life."

"I can't let you do that." She looked away, trying to hold back the tears.

"That's not your choice. It's mine. Besides, I think in a few days this will blow over. No one will believe what Jake said."

Paul took a few steps and drew her into his arms. Everything within her begged her to trust him—to believe him. But it was hard.

She needed some time to think. She broke away from his embrace and darted off to her room.

Once there, she caught sight of herself in the mirror. Her hair! One braid rested on her back. The other had unraveled. It was barely longer than the top of her shoulder.

Tears came unbidden. In all her life, she had never encountered such hatred because of her race. The Shawnee were accepted and even loved by their neighbors. She rarely even thought about what her mixed heritage would mean. Until Dad moved them to Wickenburg. There was such anger against the Indians—of every kind—here.

It wasn't long before she heard stories of the terrible brutalities committed by the Apache and Navajo. If she was honest, she had heard tales even when they lived in Santa Fe, though nothing compared to the stories she had heard since arriving in Prescott.

Mr. Lowrey had relayed one of the most brutal cases of Indian cruelty. As he had described it, her stomach churned. The blood. Dismembering dead bodies. Cruel torture. Things were much worse than what had happened to that family on Independence

Day.

She and Paul had talked about the tension between the townsfolk and the Apache. He told her of equally gruesome stories of what the Indian hunters had done to any Indian that came across their path.

Now she was stuck between two worlds, both full of hatred. If she wanted a future with Paul, she would have to do whatever it took to convince the townsfolk she was whiter than Shawnee.

Millie searched around for her sewing basket and found her scissors. With a few chops, her remaining braid fell to the ground. No more braids. It was the best step she could take to change their minds.

CHAPTER 36

"Millie."

Someone was shaking her body. Her mind returned to the horrible events of the day. Jake almost killed her. The town wanted her dead. She had to lie still.

"Millie, wake up. Caroline needs you."

Millie shot up in bed, nearly bumping her head against Paul's. "What?"

"It's Caroline," Thomas said from the corner of the room.

"The baby," she whispered.

Even in the dim lamp light she could see the fear in his eyes.

"She's never lost one this late."

Oh, poor Caroline. "Give me a minute to change and I'll be right there."

"Thomas, go. Be with your wife. I'll bring Millie."

Thomas mumbled. "Doc Hank is there. I... I..."

Paul clasped Thomas's shoulder. "Go."

Thomas turned and left.

"I'll be right outside as soon as you're ready," Paul said before closing the door behind him.

Millie leapt to her feet. She quickly donned the same dress she wore earlier that day. Then she brushed her hair, reminded again of the reason for its shortened length. She stuffed it under a bonnet and hurried out the door.

As Paul walked with her, Millie's thoughts taunted her. If only Caroline hadn't been there when Jake attacked her. Maybe her baby's life would not hang in the balance now. This was all her fault.

A tear slid down her cheek. Caroline would be crushed to lose yet another child. How would she bear it?

Before they reached the porch of the Anderson's home, she heard Caroline's frightful screams. Not the normal sounds of childbirth. Something much more heartbreaking.

Millie pushed open the door and hurried to the back room. When she opened the bedroom door, she stopped. Blood soaked the sheets. Caroline's pale face sent shivers through her body. Millie quickly moved to her side.

Doc Hank shouted at Caroline, "One more big push."

"I can't." Caroline's voice was faint.

Millie found a cloth on the nearby nightstand and dipped it in some water. Then she dabbed it on Caroline's forehead. Doc Hank shot her a look of grave concern.

"Caroline, you can do it. Just one more push as the doctor said."

"Millie." Caroline grasped her hand. "I can't."

"Shh. It will be alright. Just one more."

Caroline's green eyes screamed with fear before she closed her eyes and let forth a loud, gut-wrenching wail. She leaned forward and pushed with all her might. Then her body flopped back down on the bed.

"That's it," Doc Hank said.

Millie looked at him. His eyes held the answer. The baby was free but already gone from this world.

Caroline whimpered, drawing Millie's attention again. Her own memories of childbirth warred against what she had just witnessed, her loss not nearly as great as Caroline's.

"Girl or boy?" Caroline's voice was barely audible.

"Boy," the doctor confirmed.

"Millie, what name should I put on the grave marker?"

A sob caught in Millie's throat. Only one name came to her mind, and she could not share it with Caroline.

"Shh, now. Rest." She sat on the edge of the bed and dabbed the cloth on Caroline's forehead. "Rest now."

"I must name him. He must have a name when he meets Jesus."

"Matth—"

"Michael." Thomas's voice cut through her words. "Michael Andrew."

Caroline nodded. "It's a fine name." Then a sob bubbled over. "I'm so sorry Thomas. I'm so sorry."

Tears ran down his face. "Rest now, sweet wife."

When Caroline's eyes finally closed, Thomas turned his attention to the doctor. "Will she—" His voice croaked. "Will she make it?"

"I'll know more in the morning. She lost a lot of blood."

"I... I..."

"Thomas." Millie found her voice. "I'll stay with her. Is Drew back?"

Thomas nodded.

"Why don't you see how he is doing?"

He dragged his feet slowly as he left the room. Within a few minutes, Doc Hank left as well.

Millie's heart felt heavy. "I'm so sorry, Caroline. I'm sorry about this afternoon. I should have left. I should have gone when Jake threatened me."

Caroline's soft breathing did little to calm her churning guilt.

"If I had left, maybe little Michael would still be... I'm so sorry."

———

Sunlight filtered in through the small window. Millie stirred, remembering she was at Caroline's. She glanced over at the bed. Caroline stared at the ceiling.

"Morning."

Caroline didn't respond.

"How are you feeling?"

Caroline frowned. "Horrible. I... This is all my fault."

Millie was taken aback. "How so?"

"God is punishing me for my sins. For having Drew before... Thomas and I weren't married. And now God is punishing me for that sin. That's why He won't let me have any more children. I am a wretched, wretched mother."

A sob stopped the flow of self-deprecating words.

"Caroline." Millie's heart prayed for direction. "God is not punishing you. You have been a good mother to Drew. I've seen the way you care for him. He adores you. And you and Thomas did right by him. You are married now."

"But why, Millie? Why did God take Eugene and Cathleen and Michael? Why will He not let me have another child?"

Silence settled over the room.

Millie's heart pounded forcefully against her chest. Hadn't she wondered the same thing when it came to husbands? Hadn't she blamed herself for so many years because of her mistakes? How many nights had she cried herself to sleep wondering if singleness wasn't her punishment for her own sins?

"I, too, have feared that I am at fault. That God has been punishing me for being with a man who was not my husband." Millie ignored Caroline's wide eyes. "At fourteen, I rebelled against my parents, against God. I spent many nights with the man who I thought loved me.

"Only, he betrayed me when he learned I was pregnant. My family had to leave our home."

Millie picked at a piece of lint on her skirt.

"My son, Matthew, was born on the journey west. I had to give him away."

She looked into Caroline's eyes. "I spent many, many years believing that God was keeping me from having a husband and a family because of my sins."

Millie took a deep breath, as the truth settled over her heart. "My life has not been a punishment. I enjoyed a wonderful relationship with my parents. I have worked alongside my dad in his ministry. I have learned to be a good daughter and faithful servant."

Caroline reached for her hand. "And now, God has blessed you with Paul."

"Yes. All those years of waiting… God was shaping me. He was cleansing my heart. He was preparing me for a life with Paul."

Millie stopped and let her words penetrate her own heart. It was true. She finally understood. During the waiting is where she had grown the most and where she had healed the most.

"Caroline, it is not your fault that God called Michael home with him."

A tear slid down Caroline's cheek. "Deep down I know that. But it hurts so much."

"I know. I know."

"I love Thomas and Drew so much. But I still want more children. I want our family to expand. I… I'm completely undone over the loss of yet another baby."

Millie brushed the hair from Caroline's forehead. "Let Him carry you as you wait."

Tears flowed freely from Caroline's eyes. "That's so beautiful."

"And so true."

After a few minutes of silence, Caroline dabbed at her eyes. "I'm so glad you moved here, Millie. You are such a true friend."

Millie smiled and stood warmed by the knowledge that she truly belonged here.

CHAPTER 37

Paul watched Millie closely as she cleared away the breakfast dishes. She had been quiet and withdrawn since the attack a few days ago. He couldn't blame her.

He almost lost her. His gaze studied the back of her head as she started towards the kitchen. Her hair was pinned tightly to her head, a few strands too short to stay confined. The bruises on her face and hands were fading to a light yellow, much as the ones on his stomach, neck, and face were.

Several days had passed since the attack. Life for everyone except him and Millie seemed to return to normal—well, and for Andersons, of course.

He stood and grabbed the remaining few dishes she left behind. Then he walked down the hall towards the kitchen.

"I need—"

She jumped at the sound of his voice and whirled around to face him.

He set the dishes on the table and rushed to her. "I didn't mean to frighten you."

Millie let out a long slow breath. "I know." She accepted his invitation for an embrace.

"I can stay here again today. I don't have to go out to the mine. It can wait."

She leaned back and he dropped his arms to his side. "Go. I can handle myself. Just leave me the rifle."

His breathing went shallow. "Do you know how to use it?"

A frown crinkled her forehead. "Of course, I do."

"Alright."

He studied her for another minute. Her face was expressionless. What was she thinking? Would she be safe if he left?

There was no need for him to mine today. He could stay home. The only pressing errand he had was to see Sheriff Smith. He should have gone to see him days ago.

"I have to run out to see the sheriff. Then I'll be back."

She nodded, then grabbed the dishes from the small table in the corner and set them in the wash basin. Without a word, she started washing the dishes.

He watched her for several seconds, trying to assess if she would truly be alright.

Millie didn't turn to look at him. "You don't have to babysit me. I managed on my own just fine for decades when Dad ventured out to preach to the lost."

"I'll be back shortly."

Paul turned and walked out the door.

Things were awkward between them now. Millie was quieter than before. He felt like he let her down. She would not open up about how she felt. This distance between his heart and hers bothered him. Had she changed her mind? Maybe she didn't want to marry him after all. He failed to protect her. She obviously felt she could do a better job of it herself.

He kicked a small rock out of the way as he turned down the street to the sheriff's office. He hoped he wasn't losing her.

"Afternoon," Sheriff Smith greeted him as he stepped inside the dusty jail house.

"Sheriff."

"Glad you stopped by. Got some news on several fronts. Take a seat."

Paul sat in the chair across from the sheriff's desk.

"We confirmed that Waters was behind the attack on you at your placer."

"Jake?" His mouth went dry, and his stomach dropped to the

floor. The betrayal ran even deeper than he knew.

"Seems he may have been working for someone."

"Talbert." Paul was sure of it. Talbert was the only man that wanted that placer. But why would Jake be helping him? He was supposed to be Paul's friend.

"Well, unfortunately he was bailed out before we could get anything connecting him to Talbert."

Paul frowned.

"Anyway, we did find Waters' accomplices. One dead. One alive. He talked and told us that some wealthy man was buying up all the placers so he could start digging into the ground. They wanted to make it a full-scale operation. Said there were several wealthy men that came by a few days back—same day as Waters visited your establishment."

"Did this man say who the wealthy men were?"

"Nope. That's why I ain't got nothing solid on Talbert. Sounded like he wasn't the only one involved, though."

"So, why'd they shoot at me? And why did Jake come after Millie?"

"My best guess is that they were trying to scare you off your placer or get you to sell it. Not sure what his beef is with Miss Pritchett, other than she's tied to you."

Paul's stomach tightened. He fisted his hand in his lap. "You saying it is my fault they came after Millie?"

Sheriff Smith held up his hands. "I ain't saying it's anyone's fault. Just saying that it would make sense if they were trying to get your land that they'd come after anyone important to you."

"Is my ma in danger?"

"Don't think so. Far too many men at that ranch. If anyone came by, they'd be spotted long before they could get close to Mrs. Shepherd."

Paul stood and clenched a fist at his side. He wouldn't let anyone harm Millie or Ma, least of all Simon Talbert. "What are you doing about Talbert?"

"Like I said, can't do anything about him because I don't have enough on him. But I got a few deputies out looking for Waters.

PRESCOTT PIONEERS BOOK 5

We'll find him."

He headed toward the door, slamming it behind him. He wanted to yell at the sheriff to do more, but the man was right. He couldn't arrest Talbert if he didn't have any evidence of wrongdoing. Still didn't make him feel better.

And Jake. He couldn't believe Jake had shot at him and had been plotting behind his back. How could he? After all those years Paul had helped him. Nothing made sense.

Right now, he felt helpless. Helpless to keep Millie safe. Helpless to keep Talbert from taking his mine.

————

Every day since the attack almost a week ago, Millie woke in poor spirits. Despite her realization that she belonged here; she couldn't shake the feeling that her time in Prescott was ending. She would have to leave the town and Paul behind if the townsfolk did not change their minds about her.

She couldn't leave Paul. No matter if it was the best thing for him or not, she could not do it. She loved him too much. When he had startled her in the kitchen after breakfast this morning— that's when she knew that she could never leave him. The look of love on his face. The tender way he held her in his arms. She needed him.

But she still had to tell him the whole truth—why she left Ohio, why she never married. After telling her story to Caroline, her friend encouraged her to tell Paul. She had said that secrets had no place in a marriage. Caroline was right.

The verse she read that morning in Second Corinthians came to her mind again. She spoke it aloud. "Godly sorrow brings repentance that leads to salvation and leaves no regret, but worldly sorrow brings death."

The guilt she carried around about giving up her son, about the mistakes she made that led to his conception, that guilt had followed her for too many years. She was sure she had repented for these sins long ago. If so, why did her sorrow feel so raw, so consuming? Didn't the verse say that repentance left no regret? Perhaps she had never truly repented.

Shrugging off the painful thoughts, she donned a bonnet over her too short hair and headed out the door for Hardy's Mercantile.

The hot sun beat down on her dark navy dress. A light breeze carried the light scent of pine to her nose. She breathed deeply, letting the weather lift her spirits.

"Miss Pritchett!" a familiar voice called just before she entered the mercantile. When she turned, she was greeted by Mrs. Stanton. A small child fussed in her arms. Without bidding, Millie felt her lips curve into a smile.

"Good morning, Mrs. Stanton. And who do we have here?"

"Please call me Martha. This is Nancy, our newly acquired little girl."

Millie arched a brow and studied the toddler more closely. Dark hair. Tanned skin.

"Nancy recently came to live with Hezekiah and me. One of the scouts out at Fort Whipple found her wandering alone near an Indian encampment."

Despite the tightness in her stomach, Millie's curiosity was too great. "Oh?"

"The scout is a good friend of Hezekiah's, and he knew how much we wanted to raise a child." Martha lowered her voice. "You know we aren't overly concerned with a soul's race. Anyway, Hezekiah is drawing up the paperwork so we can officially adopt her. Then she will legally be considered white."

Millie had a thousand questions, but the chief one being: why on earth would Martha adopt an Apache child—especially now with the town's temper running so hot?

Nancy squirmed in Martha's arms until Martha set her down. When she went to grasp the child's hand, Nancy turned her back.

"Nancy, stay close," Martha warned.

In the silence that followed, Millie grew uncomfortable and wished she could break away from the Stantons.

"I know what you're thinking," Martha said. "Why would we

take in an Indian?"

"Um…"

"Hezekiah and I don't share the same views as many of the Indian haters around here. We believe that every person has value, and God loves them all just as much as He loves us."

Millie shifted uncomfortably, very aware of the growing distance between her and her Creator. Other than begging him to change her circumstance, she barely spoke to Him in weeks. The loneliness of that admission nearly brought tears to her eyes.

"Just as He loves you, Millie. He sees you for the beautiful woman you are—the one with a kind heart and lovely voice. He has a purpose for your life. He always has. Even when we can't see it, God is up to something."

Millie frowned. Her life was anything but purposeful. All she had done for the last twenty-something years trying to atone for her biggest mistake. Even though she understood God was not punishing her, she could not fathom that God had a purpose for her.

"What is it that keeps you from embracing that truth?"

She cleared her throat. "I'm certain you've heard the rumors."

"Yes, but that's not what is really keeping you from believing that God can use you, is it?"

The air in Millie's lungs left in a whoosh. "How—"

"I've spent my fair share of years living in regret. When my first husband and I left for the Arizona Territory years ago, I did not leave on good terms with my father. He was angry that I had married Charles and even angrier still that we were traveling so far away. I said some awful things to him in the heat of the moment. Imagine the deep remorse and guilt I felt when the very first letter I received was news of his passing. There was no opportunity to go back and make things right. I will forever remember that I never apologized for hurting him so."

Martha reached down and picked up Nancy again.

"Millie, I can see that you've experienced your fair share of hurt. Please don't let that stop you from fully embracing your Heavenly Father. Just think of all the stories in the Bible—like

King David. He was cited as a man after God's own heart. Yet, he had his friend murdered so he could marry his friend's wife to cover up an affair. Despite all that God used him to restore His people. If God could use someone like that, surely, He can use someone like you or I."

Millie held her tongue as her heart ached over Martha's words. Were they true? Could He really use someone like her? A worthless mother who gave away her bastard son.

I can.

"It... Was nice... Talking to you." Millie hurried into the safety of the mercantile, hoping Martha would not follow. Guilt had so long been her companion; she wasn't sure she could live without it. That thought pierced her heart as much as Martha's words.

She willed her thoughts and emotions to settle as she turned her attention to her shopping list. A bag of sugar. Beef jerky for Paul. Anything to keep her mind from what was probably the truth—God really could have a purpose for her messed up life.

CHAPTER 38

July 19, 1869

"Thanks for helping me with these deliveries," Thomas said as Paul pulled the wagon around to the front of the livery.

"Of course. Though, you haven't said where we're going."

"To The Cribs."

Paul sucked in a deep breath. "Hey, I know things have been hard since Caroline lost the baby, but—"

"Hold on. It's not what you think. I only agreed to deliver the new tack and gear because of Cassandra."

"Thomas—"

"I'm sorry. I'm not explaining this well. First, I'm not... My wife is the *only* woman for me. So don't read into what I'm saying."

Paul shook his head as he loaded the last crate in the wagon. "What *are* you saying?"

Thomas blew out a loud breath. "A few weeks ago, Caroline and I spotted a young girl, not more than ten or eleven years old, with Trent Montgomery while he was shopping in the mercantile. Caroline quietly approached the girl, suspecting the worst given that she kept company with the saloon owner. When she got Cassandra talking, we learned that she had lost her parents in an Apache raid on their ranch between Prescott and Verde Valley."

"I see."

"Anyway, the ranch foreman kept her around for a while—

until he learned the price he could get for selling her to work in the brothel."

Paul's stomach churned. He heard rumor that Montgomery employed rather young girls, but this was beyond sick.

"The real reason I'm going there today is to see if we can get Cassandra away from that place. Caroline doesn't think Montgomery will let her go without some sort of payment." Thomas spat. "It just sickens me."

"Agreed. Well, I'm glad to help in whatever way I can."

Within minutes, Thomas pulled the wagon to a stop in front of the tiny hovels known as The Cribs. Doors hung crooked in door frames. The windowless buildings kept their occupants' secrets too well. Located behind the row of saloons on Montezuma Street, the cribs were something Paul avoided. It bothered him that so many women had to sell themselves to survive.

Righteous anger welled in his chest. It was completely and utterly disgusting that Montgomery would purchase a ten-year-old girl and make her work in the cribs.

Save her.

He heard the voice loud and clear. Only one problem: he didn't know how to save her.

As the morning wore on, Paul and Thomas finished delivering the crates of tack and gear, along with some items Montgomery ordered from the blacksmith. Turned out the smithy didn't want to be seen in this part of town—not with him courting a young gentlewoman.

Paul started to climb onto the wagon when Thomas stopped him.

"I want to check on Cassandra before we go."

"Alright." Uneasiness slithered down his spine. The last thing he needed was for someone to spread rumors that he was here and for Millie to hear those rumors. No telling how she would react or what conclusions she would jump to.

Thomas rapped lightly on the door to the nearest room. A scantily clad woman opened the door.

"A bit early, darling." She leaned toward Thomas. "But you're easy enough on the eyes, I could make an exception."

Thomas took a step backward out of her reach. "I'm looking for Cassandra."

"What's the matter? I'm not enough woman for you?"

"Come on." Paul grabbed Thomas's arm and pulled him away from the soiled dove.

Thomas shook off his grip. "Look, I'm not leaving without her. We can't just leave her."

Paul frowned. He doubted that the poor girl remained innocent. Especially if she'd been here for any length of time.

Save her.

"Alright. You go that way, I'll ask around here."

Thomas nodded and knocked on the next door.

After a few more discrete inquiries, they heard she was probably hiding in the kitchen.

When they entered the small room, they found her sitting on the floor in the corner away from the stove. Dark half-circles under her eyes gave her an aged appearance. She drew her knees to her chest and clutched them as if her life depended on it. Paul's heart broke.

"Hey," Thomas greeted her as he knelt to look her in the eyes.

"Mr. Thomas." The girl's stoic greeting belied the hint of a smile in her eyes.

"How are you?"

She shook her head. The answer was written in fear across her face.

"We came to get you out of here," Thomas whispered.

"What are you doing in here!" Montgomery yelled as he burst through the back door, his anger directed at Thomas. "Cassandra, get back to your room."

"I was—"

Paul jumped in. "How much?"

"How much, what?" Montgomery replied.

"How much to take the girl off your hands?"

Montgomery grinned. "Didn't figure you for the type, Lancaster."

"I'm not. How much?"

"Look, she's not leaving here. I got customers who like 'em younger than her. They pay extra if you know what I mean."

"One thousand," Paul offered, feeling queasy that he had to pay for her freedom. She should already be free and not be tied to that scoundrel.

"Hmm. Almost enough for me to give it a thought."

"Two?"

Montgomery rubbed his hand across his chin. Thomas frowned and leaned forward, as if he were ready to throw his fists at the man. Paul willed him to stay calm. Apparently, Thomas understood his look because he relaxed his fists.

"Three. Three thousand dollars and you can do what you want with the girl."

There was only one way he was going to get the money for this. He had to sell the mine. Without a clock available, he couldn't be certain he would have enough time to arrange the sale of his mine today.

"Three and you swear she doesn't work another night until I can pay you in the morning."

Thomas spoke up. "She goes home with me for the evening and Paul will pay you in the morning."

"And give up all that money she could be earning tonight?"

"I'll throw in a hundred for your trouble," Thomas said.

The silence stretched. Paul sent a prayer heavenward. *You asked me to save her. I'm doing my best here.*

"Deal. Go get her outta here."

Thomas pulled out the hundred and handed it to Montgomery.

As Paul and Thomas started to leave, Montgomery said, "Lancaster, you be sure to show up with the cash before noon. Otherwise, you might find yourself in some big trouble."

He nodded and hurried out the door with Cassandra leaning into Thomas's side.

CHAPTER 39

As Millie did her rounds, cleaning the upstairs rooms, her heart felt restless. Could God really use someone like her? Martha Stanton seemed to think God had a purpose for her. She wasn't sure if she agreed. How could God use such a disobedient, rebellious woman? An insolent teen. A poor mother who gave her only child away. A failure at love.

Well, maybe that last one wasn't true. She loved Paul dearly and things were looking promising for her long-awaited wedding day.

A pang of guilt nudged her conscience. She really should tell Paul about Cade and their son. It was only fair.

She closed her eyes and remembered her life in Ohio and the man she thought she loved. Cade Ellis had charming blue eyes. When he smiled at her, she felt like she was the only girl in the room. Things between them started out innocently enough. He walked her home after school. She enjoyed her talks with him. He seemed to know more about life than she did. He was seventeen. She was fourteen.

Then things began to change, starting with the harvest barn dance. He danced with a few girls early in the evening, but as the night wore on, he only danced with Millie.

"I could use some fresh air," he said as he took her hand.

She allowed him to lead her outside, behind the barn. The moon was a small sliver of light that lent to the heady feeling she had from dancing with Cade. Then he whispered in her ear.

"You're beautiful. I've wanted to kiss you all night."

Her heart raced. Would this be it? Her first kiss?

Then he lowered his lips to hers. The fire ignited in her as his lips pressed and searched hers. He ran his hands up and down her back. She had no idea a kiss could be so wonderful and inviting. Eventually he stopped and led her back into the barn for the final dance.

For days she thought of that kiss and craved another. It came when he suggested a few days later that she sneak out after her parents were asleep. He would meet her at their barn.

One night of kissing, turned into two. Then three. Each time she craved more of his touch, more of his love.

After several weeks, Cade took things further and she willingly let him. The first time she let him be with her she didn't quite understand the implications. Or perhaps she did, and she chose to ignore it. All she knew was that she loved him. He kept telling her that he loved her.

Several months passed by. She continued to sneak out of the house at night to meet him at least once a week. She knew what she was doing was wrong. But all Cade had to do was whisper words of love in her ear, and she would give him everything he desired. He would coax her by saying that when she was a little older, he would marry her.

"Why not now, Cade? Why do we have to wait?"

"Your father will never let you marry this young."

Each time she felt remorse the next day, until she was in his arms again.

Then she missed her monthlies. A niggling of fear settled into the back of her mind, but she ignored it. Until she missed the following monthly.

The next time she was with him, she told Cade about her fears. "Marry me now," she begged.

He didn't answer but instead coaxed her into one more night with him.

As she dressed, she begged him again. "Marry me, Cade. Give

your child a father."

His reaction still tore her heart in two. He laughed at her. "Millicent, I can't marry you."

"Why... Why not?"

"'Cause I'm marrying Evelyn Newhouse."

"I don't understand. I thought you loved me."

He pulled her into his arms, but she squirmed away. "I do love you. It's just that..."

"What?"

"Her pa is making me."

She frowned. "Why would he make you, Cade? Why?"

"'Cause, she's carrying my child."

Twenty-four years had passed since he said the worst words of betrayal ever spoken to her. She would never have let him into her bed had she thought he was seeing Evelyn or any other gal for that matter. Over the following weeks she had learned that not only had Cade Ellis fathered the baby growing in her womb, but he also was suspected of impregnating at least three other girls, including Evelyn. In the end, Evelyn's pa proved the most persuasive. Cade married her.

Millie never saw him again but still lived with the scars he had inflicted. She wiped away her tears. This was why she never married. This was the secret that always destroyed any hope of real love. It sent men running away from her.

Even though Paul might run too, she had to tell him. Yes, she would tell him tonight.

She squared her shoulders as she finished dusting the first room. She moved into the next room and began singing the first hymn that came to mind.

> *Indulgent Father, by whose care,*
> *I've passed another day,*
> *Let me this night thy mercy share,*
> *And teach me how to pray.*

> *Show me my sins, and how to mourn*

My guilt before thy face;
Direct me, Lord, to Christ alone,
And save me by thy grace.

Show me my sins. He had. Long ago. Yet, she carried this guilt for far too long. How many times had she asked for forgiveness? And how many times had God saved her by His grace? Why, then, did the guilt still linger?

Silence answered.

Perhaps it was her stubbornness that refused to let go of the guilt. It felt comfortable, normal to hang on to it. It was what kept her from getting hurt again.

No, that was not true. She loved Paul with all her heart. If anything happened to tear him away from her, she would hurt deeply for a long time. Her guilt didn't keep her from hurting. It kept her reliving the hurt and shame of her past year after year.

Forgive me. Help me let this go. Help me to live free from the sin of self-condemnation. Yes, that's what it was! Self-condemnation. Not from God. From her.

A sudden rush of peace worked its way through her heart. She was free from the chains of self-condemnation.

The rest of the hymn begged to be sung. This time she sang with abandon, not concerned if she might bother Mr. Lowrey in the room next door.

Let each returning night declare
The tokens of thy love;
And every hour thy grace prepare
My soul for joys above.

And when on earth I close mine eyes
To sleep in death's embrace,
Let me to heaven and glory rise,
To enjoy thy smiling face.

Oh, how wonderful to let that guilt fall from her shoulders!

Deep peace took firm root in her heart. A sense of belonging and love wrapped her in a warm embrace. She lingered for a moment, praying the unwarranted guilt that plagued her for so many years would truly stay away.

She sat in the small chair in the corner of the boarder's room. Might she be free? Truly free?

Taking a deep breath, she let it out slowly. With freedom came responsibility. She had listened to many sermons delivered by her dad to know that God had a purpose for those He unburdened. He used them for His glory and His will.

How would He use her? What was his plan from this point going forward? Was it as simple as being the best wife she could be for Paul? Would God grace her with a second chance to be a mother?

Lord, dare I even hope... Would he let her be reunited with Matthew?

A memory from the day of Caroline's baby shower pushed forward in her mind. The young man she spotted. His gait looked so much like Cade's. Was it even possible that Matthew lived in Prescott or on one of the nearby farms or ranches?

Hope filled her heart. She might one day see him again. She might have a chance to ask him for forgiveness and get to know him.

"That's a lovely song."

She jumped up and turned to see Mr. Lowrey standing in the doorway.

"Oh, I'm sorry I disturbed you."

"Not at all. I was on my way to find you to let you know I'm headed south for a few days. Have some business in Tucson."

"Shall I hold your room for you?"

"Yes. That would be much appreciated." He started to leave but then turned back and looked at her. "That smile looks good on you, Miss Pritchett."

Heat warmed her cheeks.

"See you in a few days."

"Safe travels, Mr. Lowrey."

When he left, she hurried to finish cleaning the rooms. She could hardly wait for Paul to come home. Even though she had some difficult secrets to share, she felt at peace. Everything would work out fine. She would share both her secrets and her hopes with him this evening.

CHAPTER 40

Once Paul escorted Cassandra to the Anderson home for the evening, he headed to the Talbert residence. The last question Cassandra asked still rang in his ears. It even softened his pride— enough that he could swallow it and ask the one man who had coveted his mine to buy it now.

"Mr. Paul." Cassandra's voice was barely audible. "Will I have to... Will I have to do bad things when I live with you?"

His stomach churned. He had told her no. That when she came to live at the boardinghouse in a day or so, he and Millie would be her new ma and pa. It would be like before all the bad things. She simply nodded.

His heart broke again. How could anyone take such a sweet child and not protect her? If he had known her when she lost her parents, nothing would have stopped him from helping her— either by taking her to a good, safe home, or by caring for her himself.

Paul stopped at the front walkway leading up to Simon Talbert's house. Ma or Millie would probably try to talk him out of selling now. The mine had been his passion. But that passion was nothing in comparison to the fire burning through his veins now. Little Cassandra's life meant thousands of times more than some piece of dirt that occasionally yielded gold.

Neither Ma nor Millie knew about his conversation with the sheriff the other day either. If they had, they might talk him into selling. He feared that Talbert's men might go too far—might leave Millie a widow if they even got to the altar first.

Didn't matter. Now, he had even more reason to sell. Millie needed him. Cassandra needed them both. Best option for all involved was for him to sell the mine.

He reached for the gate at the front of the walkway but hesitated. *Lord, am I doing the right thing here?*

Thomas and Caroline were happy to take Cassandra in. They both suggested they could even pay Paul back over time. If he hadn't heard God's voice so clearly in that saloon this morning, he might have agreed to their suggestion. But he had no doubts that God was asking him—Paul Lancaster—to rescue and care for little Cassandra. So, he told Thomas and Caroline as much.

Caroline, being her usual self, said, "Guess He wants to let Millie be a mom after all." Then she smiled and told him they were praying for him and the sale of the mine.

The lyrics to a hymn floated around in his mind. Had Millie sung it just this morning?

Take my silver and my gold,
Not a mite would I withhold.

He would gladly give up all his gold for the safety of this child. But there was another part of the song that he remembered. *Take my will and make it Thine. Yes, Lord, take my will and make it yours. The placer is no longer mine, but yours.*

Taking a deep breath, Paul pushed open the gate and walked up the lane with purpose. He knocked on the door and waited.

The butler answered. "Good evening."

"I'm here to speak with Mr. Talbert."

"He is not expecting anyone this evening."

"It's important. Trust me, he'll want to hear what I have to say."

The butler eyed him suspiciously. "Who may I say is calling?"

After Paul gave his name, the butler showed him inside to a small parlor. Several minutes passed before someone came to get him.

"I must say," Simon Talbert greeted. "This is quite the surprise. Please follow me."

Simon led him down a hallway to another room, most likely a study. The large oak desk in the center of the room reminded Paul of the man's wealth. Across from the desk were plush leather chairs.

"Please, take a seat." Simon motioned to one of the leather chairs before he rounded the corner of the desk. He took a seat in an ornately carved wooden chair. Then he propped his elbows on the top of the desk and leaned forward.

"What brings you to my door?"

Paul took another deep breath, ridding himself of the last of his pride. "I am interested in selling my placer."

Simon drummed his fingers on the desktop. "And why now?"

He hesitated. He wanted to keep the news of what he was doing for Cassandra a secret. When the time was right, he would let the town meet her—as his adopted daughter. The story of how she came to be with him and Millie would remain private. All anyone needed to know was that he and his soon-to-be wife saw a child in need and stepped in to help.

Regardless, Talbert was expecting some sort of answer. He should have expected it, but so much happened in the last eight hours he barely had time to make sense of what he said.

"As you may have heard, Miss Pritchett and I are due to wed soon."

"Indeed."

"And I would like to remain close to my bride."

"I see." A frown crossed Simon's brow. Paul could only wonder what the man was thinking. "A hasty wedding is needed, then."

His blood boiled at the unspoken implication. "I assure you that Miss Pritchett's virtue is intact."

"Well, it doesn't seem that way. I heard that she's Apache. If that were true, I could see that you might need some money to persuade a judge to ignore that fact and grant you a marriage license."

Paul clenched a fist in his lap. The man had a lot of nerve. "She's not Apache."

Silence stretched for several seconds.

"Are you interested in the mine or not?"

"Now, now. No need to get testy, Lancaster. Just curious as to your sudden change of heart."

"What of it?"

"Imagine you were in my position. I offered you a rather fair sum several months ago. You were quite adamant that you would never sell that piece of dirt to me. Now, here you sit across from me mere months later asking me to purchase it. What is your game?"

"I'm not playing any games."

"Surely you don't expect that my offer still stands."

Paul held back a growl. Talbert was intentionally goading him. "What are your terms?"

"If—and that is an integral point here—if I were interested, I would possibly offer two thousand and not a penny more."

"If I recall correctly, Talbert, you offered four thousand just a few months ago. How is it that my land and mine have lost so much value in such short a time, especially given that it is the only parcel you do not own?"

Talbert narrowed his eyes. "Two thousand is my offer."

Paul stood. "Then I won't waste any more of your time." He hoped Talbert would change his mind if he thought Paul was serious.

A few seconds ticked by, and Paul continued towards the study door.

"Wait, perhaps we might discuss this more."

He smiled. Then he quickly wiped it from his face before turning toward Talbert. "Four thousand is what I'm asking."

"I cannot pay a penny higher than three thousand."

There was the dollar amount he needed. Tempted to take it and run, he thought for a few seconds. "Three thousand five hundred."

Talbert drummed his fingers on the desktop again. Paul waited, as difficult as it was. He couldn't stand to let Talbert get the placer for a steal. But could he really walk away if they couldn't come to an agreement on the price?

"Very well." Talbert stood and held out his hand for a shake. "Three thousand five hundred dollars. I will have my attorney draw up the papers in the morning."

Paul shook Talbert's hand, keeping the elation he felt from showing. They agreed to meet again at ten in the morning before Talbert showed Paul to the door.

As he walked back to the boardinghouse, he smiled. *Thank you, Lord, for providing more than enough for Cassandra.* Now, he just had to explain everything to Millie.

———

Millie decided to go ahead and serve dinner without Paul. She waited longer than usual, and the boarders were getting restless. She wondered what kept him. Last they spoke that morning, he planned to help Thomas with some errands before he came back to the boardinghouse. She hoped he hadn't gone out to the placer.

She sighed. This was so unlike him.

When the boarders finished eating, she gathered the dishes and leftovers and took them to the kitchen. She grew more worried when Paul still wasn't back by the time she finished the dishes, which had been a slower chore without his help.

She gathered her knitting and took a seat in the front parlor. Where was he?

Lacing yarn through her fingers, she set the needles to work. She imagined how their conversation might go when he returned. First, she would be utterly relieved that he was back. Then she would get him the plate she kept warm on the stove. After he finished eating—or maybe while he was eating—she would let him know she had something important to discuss. Then she would explain that she hadn't always been such a sweet girl, and she got herself into trouble. At fourteen she found herself pregnant with a man's child. Found herself. Really?

She let out a long breath and set her knitting aside. It wasn't going to be easy baring her soul—sharing her past mistakes.

What if he got angry? What if he reacted like Joel? What if he cast her aside?

No. He was different. Paul wouldn't do that.

A noise at the front door caught her attention. Paul stepped through the door, grinning from ear to ear. She couldn't stop smiling in return, despite her nervousness that the time had come to tell him everything.

In two steps he stood in front of her. Then he reached for her hands and drew her to her feet.

"I have great news!" He twirled her around in a circle.

"Paul!"

When he set her down, she struggled to take an even breath. What had gotten into him?

"I have a wonderful surprise for you and I'm dying to tell you."

"Would you like some supper first?"

His smile dimmed some. "Sure. What time is it anyway?"

"Nearly eight o'clock."

"Wow… It's been such a strange, yet wonderful day."

"Go sit at the table—"

"I'll eat in the kitchen so we can talk."

She headed in that direction with him following behind.

"You know I was helping Thomas with some errands today."

As he sat down at the table, she grabbed his plate from the stove and set it in front of him. "Yes."

"Well, he sorta forgot to mention that some of his errands involved… Well, that's not the important part. Anyway, I found a young girl who is going to come live with us—Cassandra—our daughter."

Millie started to sit down across from him but missed the chair entirely. "Daughter?" she asked as her hind end hit the floor.

The scrape of Paul's chair sounded before she felt his hands on her arms, helping her back to her feet. "Are you alright? Here, sit down."

This time she connected with the chair like she should.

"A daughter?"

"Yes. She used to live on a nearby ranch, and she was orphaned. Thomas told me about her and when I met her, I knew we had to take her in."

"Where did you meet her?"

"Ah… In town."

Her head spun as she tried to take it all in. "We're not even married yet."

"But we will be soon. Please, Millie, she needs a good home. You and I can provide that for her. I know it's all out of order, but we must do this."

She thought about her secret. What would happen if he cast her aside when she told him? "What if you decide not to marry me?"

He laughed. "Why wouldn't I marry you?"

"Just answer the question."

His smile faded to a slight frown. "I would take care of her myself; I suppose. But that's not going to happen. I have no intention of letting you slip away." He reached across the table and squeezed her hand.

Millie smiled, hoping that it was true. "How old is she?"

"Ten or eleven years old. Her parents were attacked and killed by raiding Indians. The foreman of the ranch brought her to town."

"Where is she now?"

"Staying with Thomas and Caroline. I thought it would be best for us to talk before bringing her home. Before the wedding, I thought she could move into your room, and you could… Since I'm staying in the storage room, you could move into our room early." His face turned red.

Our room. Warmth flooded her cheeks, too. She hadn't really given much thought of what would happen after their wedding. The idea turned her stomach into jelly now. What would it be like to be held in his arms every night?

"Anyway, I have several things I need to see to in the morning, but I thought we could bring her home tomorrow evening—maybe have dinner at Thomas and Caroline's house with her so she could get to know us a little first."

"That would be fine."

"Truly?"

"Truly." Hadn't she just prayed that morning about God's purpose for her life? Perhaps this was the answer to that prayer. He was going to let her raise a daughter. She would be a mother after all this time. Oddly, she would be mother first, wife second. Well, this news didn't change that reality.

He yawned, then stood and stretched. "Thank you, Millie, for understanding."

She had to tell him the truth about her past. "Paul—"

He drew her close and captured her lips with his before she could say anything else. She surrendered to the sweet kiss resolving that she would tell him tomorrow.

CHAPTER 41

"I'm off," Paul said, giving Millie a quick peck on the cheek after breakfast the next morning. "Would you mind picking up some things for Cassandra from the mercantile? Just have Abraham put it on my account. Get whatever you think she'll need. A new dress. Some fabric for another. Maybe some hair things."

"Certainly."

"Great." He glanced at the clock. "I've really got to leave. I'll be back hopefully by this afternoon. Don't wait on me for lunch."

"Okay." She followed him to the front door.

"Oh, Millie?"

"Yeah?"

"I love you." He placed another kiss on her cheek. "See you tonight."

"Love you, too," she said as she closed the door behind him. Letting out a long breath, she stood with her back against the door for a moment.

What a whirlwind they were in for today. She could tell already. Paul barely stopped talking long enough to swallow down some biscuits and eggs. He talked about all the different plans he had—including selling the mine, something he hadn't mentioned last night.

His first order of business was to head out to the mine. He had to pack up all his things and bring them back. When she asked where he would put them, he told her he'd find a place. She supposed that meant in the barn.

Then he was going to meet with Talbert to finalize the sale. Then he had a few more errands. She wasn't sure what else he needed to do, since he asked her to go to the mercantile.

Millie hurried back to her room to fix her still too-short hair under her bonnet. A quick look in the mirror. It would have to do. She refused to worry about it and headed out the door.

Once at Hardy's mercantile, she explained to Abraham Conrad, the shopkeeper, what they were doing. "We are adopting a young girl who lost her family. She'll need a new dress, under garments, hair ribbons." Did she even have a brush? "A brush."

"Seems rather sudden," Abraham commented as he showed her some dress choices.

"It is. Paul met her yesterday. Said she was in need." Then her words tumbled to a halt when another female patron joined them in the dress aisle.

"Did I hear you right, Miss Pritchett? You and your betrothed are bringing a child into your home before your wedding?"

Millie didn't miss the snide tone. But she refused to acknowledge the implications. They were much the same as the ones she heard when she was carrying Matthew. Only this time, she had done nothing wrong.

"I think this would be about the right size for an eleven-year-old." She held up a brown dress. Well, she hoped it would. She thought about the young girls and boys at church and figured some of them around the same age were probably the same size. Hopefully, Cassandra hadn't grown faster than her peers.

"Lovely choice. I have a few matching hair ribbons and even a bonnet over here." Abraham showed her the items.

By the time she finished, she purchased almost too many parcels to carry home by herself.

As she dropped all the packages on her bed, she smiled. A daughter. At thirty-eight, she assumed she was too old to have another child. She doubted one would come after her wedding night. Yet, God was granting her one of the deepest desires of her heart, even though it seemed impossible. She would be a mother.

What had life been like for Cassandra on the ranch? Had she been born in the Arizona Territory or had her parents moved from somewhere else? What had her mother been like? These and many other questions rolled around in Millie's mind as she began unpacking all the items for her new daughter.

Another song came to mind. She smiled as the words held a newer and deeper meaning this morning.

Blest is the man whose softening heart
Feels all another's pain;
To whom the supplicating eye
Was never raised in vain:

Whose breast expands with generous warmth
A stranger's woes to feel;
And bleeds in pity o'er the wound
He wants the power to heal.

Oh, how sweet was Paul. Blessed for feeling Cassandra's pain and wanting to help. *Lord, let our new family grow and share many happy memories—ones as sweet as those I cherish of my dad and mom. May we honor you in all we do.*

She looked around the room, satisfied that she had done her best to give Cassandra something of her own. Perhaps, Caroline would get her wish for a hasty wedding after all.

———

"Her real name is Annabel," Caroline said as she welcomed Paul and Millie to supper.

Paul glanced nervously at Millie. He suspected Cassandra might have been a name given to her by Trent Montgomery, but he hadn't been completely honest with Millie about where the girl came from. He wanted to spare her the embarrassment.

"Oh?" Millie asked.

"Must have been what the foreman called her. Like a nickname." He hastily tried to explain before Caroline could say more.

"Well, let's go meet her."

"Annabel," Caroline said, "You remember Paul Lancaster?"

"Yes, ma'am."

"This is his betrothed, Miss Millie Pritchett."

Annabel responded with a brief curtsy. She looked more at ease than when he dropped her off yesterday afternoon. And much cleaner, too. Gone was the coal from her eyes and the unnatural ruddy red from her cheeks. The smudges of dirt disappeared. Now she looked like a sweet innocent little girl.

He probably should have told Millie about where he found Annabel. It was bound to come out sooner or later. Then again, any odd behavior on Annabel's part could probably be explained away as her still grieving the loss of everything she had known.

As he took a seat next to Millie, with Annabel on her right, he wondered why he was so hesitant to tell Millie the truth. The girl had been through a lot. Maybe it would be easier for her if neither Paul nor Millie talked about her time in The Cribs.

"Where was your parents' ranch?" Millie asked.

Annabel looked down at her plate. "Far away."

"Between here and Verde Valley," Paul answered.

A tear slid down Annabel's cheek and he hoped Millie would change the subject.

"I'm sorry," Millie said. "I lost my mother, too." She reached for Annabel's hand and gave it a light squeeze. When Annabel looked up at her, Millie smiled. "I'm glad you will get to stay with us now."

"You'll be safe there," Caroline said.

"No more… Men?" Annabel asked.

"No. Remember what we talked about?" Caroline asked. Annabel nodded.

Paul's heart beat a little faster as he glanced at Millie. She wore a slight frown that quickly changed to a smile when Annabel looked her way. He would tell Millie all he knew about Annabel's past, but he would give the girl a few days to settle in first.

The conversation turned to other topics as the meal wore on.

"With all of the Indian activity heating up," Thomas started, "There's been talk of stopping the express line between Prescott and Wickenburg."

"How will we get mail then?" Millie asked.

"The postmaster said they are thinking of sending the express rider along with freighters or on the stagecoach as they travel through the area. The more men traveling together, the safer everyone should be."

"Will it slow down how often we receive mail?" Millie asked.

"Probably by a few days. Nothing more."

Paul understood her concern. More than once, he'd seen her hurry off to post a letter to her father. Even after she came here on her own, she still maintained a close relationship with him. Not unlike his relationship with his mother.

What would she think of all of this? She would probably scold him for not marrying Millie first. Perhaps he should send word to the ranch and to let them know he planned to wed on Sunday?

No, that would never work. Millie would need at least a week or two to get word to her father. She wouldn't marry without him there. Perhaps the first Saturday of August would work. That was still two and a half weeks away.

Once dessert was served and devoured, Caroline sent them on their way. "You'll need some time this evening to get acquainted."

Paul escorted his betrothed and their daughter home. Strange how in the matter of a few days, his entire purpose shifted. He now had a family to protect. It filled him with a sense of pride beyond anything he felt before—so much more than what he felt when working the mine.

When they got home, Millie showed Annabel her room. Paul leaned against the doorframe. The glow on Millie's face was precious. He knew she would make a wonderful mother but seeing her in action sent waves of love and—dare he admit—desire washing over him. Giving her a daughter was the best gift he could have ever given her.

"This is your room. I'll be next door if you need me."

"It's nice," Annabel said softly as she fingered the edge of the quilt covering the bed.

"My mother made it. Now, it's yours." Millie's smile was contagious. Both he and Annabel smiled too.

"I bought you a few things," Millie said as she handed a small, wrapped bundle to Annabel.

"Really?" The uncertainty on her face reminded him that he shouldn't wait too long to tell Millie about the things she endured.

Annabel untied the twine from the package. When she opened the paper to reveal a brush with an intricately carved handle, her eyes grew wide, and a few silent tears rolled down her cheeks. He wanted to run to her and cradle her in his arms. To tell her no one would mistreat her ever again. But something held him back. He didn't want to scare her, and he knew they hadn't enough time to build trust yet.

She pulled some ribbons from the package and ran her dainty fingers over them.

"They are beautiful."

Millie pulled her close for a hug. Paul's eyes burned at the tender care Millie exuded with their new daughter. He blinked a few times, then cleared his throat.

"I need to turn in for the night. Don't stay up too late." He left the room and headed out to the storage room, wishing he could kiss Millie goodnight.

CHAPTER 42

The next morning, Millie woke and slid from the bed and snuck into the room next door. She sensed there was more to Annabel's story than either Annabel or Paul had mentioned. But she figured Paul had his reasons.

She looked down at Annabel, sleeping peacefully, now—truly relaxed.

Whatever her past, Millie was convinced she suffered some abuse. She seemed so much more at ease after Paul turned in. There were other signs, too. She stiffened whenever Millie hugged her. At dinner, her hand jerked the first time Millie touched her.

Lord, please heal Annabel's heart. Help her come to know you. Help her to feel safe and comfortable around us. Show me how to help her.

She bent over and placed a light kiss on the top of Annabel's head. Then she turned and left the room, pulling the door shut behind her.

As she entered the kitchen, she continued to pray for her new daughter as well as herself. When suddenly faced with the responsibility of motherhood, she feared she would not live up to the calling. She asked God for strength and wisdom. What more could she ask for?

Her feelings of failure over abandoning her son started to break through. That late night when she went into labor. The pain. The screams that came from her but seemed as if they were coming from some other place. Then his first cry—the one that forever bound her heart to his—made everything worth it. All the ridicule and scorn from family and friends in Ohio. All the anger and betrayal from Cade. All of it was worth holding her son in her arms.

Even giving him away had been worth it.

She never stopped loving her son. She never stopped praying for him or celebrating his birthdays. She had been so fortunate to stay in touch with the couple that adopted him, the Covingtons. They wrote to her all the way up to his fourteenth birthday when she pressed them to tell him about her. Mrs. Covington's response was clear. They would not. He was their son now. Mrs. Covington was the only mother he had known.

The letters stopped after that. She didn't know what sort of man he had become. He would be twenty-four by now. Had he followed in Mr. Covington's shoes and continued farming? Had he struck out on his own? Was he married? Did he have children?

"Millie?"

She turned towards Annabel as she hovered in the doorway. "Yes, sweetheart?"

"Would you… Walk with me to the outhouse?"

Struck by the oddity, Millie pushed aside her confusion and honored Annabel's request. She walked with her and then stood right outside the door as Annabel asked. The poor thing was frightened of being alone. Not surprising, considering how brutally her parents were murdered.

When Annabel was finished, they returned inside and prepared breakfast together. She wondered if Annabel had helped her mother in the kitchen, but she kept the question to herself.

The introductions at breakfast were awkward at best. Annabel glanced warily from one male border to the next. Only Mr. Lowrey seemed to make a positive impression, which Millie found amusing.

Following breakfast, Paul dried dishes as always. Then he convinced Annabel to come to help him with the barn animals, with the promise of a chance to pet the barn cat.

Millie watched from the front porch as Annabel walked alongside Paul. The conversation was one-sided, with Paul doing most of the talking. Give them time. She already witnessed Annabel softening some.

"Morning."

Ben Shepherd's welcome drew her gaze away from father and daughter just before they disappeared into the barn.

"Morning. It totally slipped my mind that today is Wednesday."

"Who's the young-un?" he asked.

"That's Annabel. She was an orphan, but Paul and I took her in—just last night."

"Well, ya might let him know I brought his ma into town with me today. She's over at Hardy's giving Abraham what-for about not buying any of her pies yet."

"Ah." She heard the warning in his tone. She knew that Betty would be surprised to learn she was a grandmother. Perhaps it would be best to warn Paul. She stepped off the porch. "I'll go tell him now."

"Sure thing. Don't worry that none of the crates are set out. Matthew and I will just swap 'em out for ya."

She stopped and turned, her heart beating ferociously against her chest. Her hands shook and her palms grew sweaty. "Matthew?"

For the first time, she noticed the young man at the back of the wagon. When he stood full height, her breath stopped, and she feared her heart would follow suit.

"Ya ain't met Matthew Covington, yet? Hmm. He's one of our cowboys that came West with us. Guess he ain't been delivering much, but I coulda swore ya met him at church."

Covington. Matthew Covington. With his violet eyes and broad shoulders. Everything about him, except for those eyes, looked like the spitting image of Cade. Those eyes—matched hers perfectly.

The moment she never expected to come was here. She stood

face to face with her son.

"Ma'am."

As he set the crate on the wagon seat, he held out a hand. She flung herself into his arms and began sobbing. No words would come. Her joy was complete.

———

"You like kitties?" Paul asked as he opened the barn door wide.

"Yes."

"She usually hangs out on my work bench when I'm not there. You might see if you can find her while I feed Gerdie, our goat."

Annabel darted off in the direction he pointed.

He sighed. He could tell she wasn't comfortable being alone with him. In time, he hoped that it would change. He hoped she would let him hug her and pull her braids and that she would laugh at his jokes. He pictured life as fun and carefree with his wife—well, she would be soon—and daughter at his side. Who knows, maybe God would even grace them with a second child.

"I found her." Annabel emerged from the workroom with the cat in her arms. "What's her name?"

He scratched his chin and tilted his head to one side. "Don't think I ever named her."

"What?"

"Yeah. I just always called her 'Cat'. Why don't you give her a name?"

"How about Kitty?"

Paul chuckled. "How's that any different than 'Cat'?"

Annabel smiled as the cat started purring in her arms. "I like Kitty."

He shook his head. "Kitty it is."

He tried to hurry through the rest of his chores in the barn but found himself slowed down as he constantly checked on Annabel. Each time he did, he found her smiling down at Kitty as she purred up a storm in her lap.

"All done," he announced when he finished his chores. "Shall we go see what Millie is up to?"

Annabel nodded her head and stood, without loosening her hold on Kitty.

"Uh, Kitty stays here."

When Annabel's smile faded, his heart nearly broke.

"She's a barn cat. That means she stays in the barn. But you can come visit her this evening."

"Promise?"

"Yes, ma'am."

Annabel set Kitty down and followed him out the door.

When he looked toward the boardinghouse, his blood started to boil. Millie stood in the arms of a young man; her face buried against his chest. Paul ran towards them, reminding himself not to deck the man without giving him a chance to explain.

"What's going on here?" he asked once he was within earshot.

"Dunno," Ben said. "Just introduced them and she... Um..."

Matthew shrugged and tried to peel Millie from his arms.

"Millie," Paul said her name with determination. "What is going on?"

She turned her red-rimmed violet eyes towards him. His heart sank as he looked from Matthew to Millie. Those violet eyes. They both had them.

"I... Matthew is my son."

"Your son?!" Both he and Matthew asked at the same time.

She sniffled. "Yes. Matthew is my son. I gave him away on the wagon train to Santa Fe twenty-four years ago to a couple. The Covingtons."

Matthew staggered back and fell onto one of the porch steps.

Paul's heart sank to his feet—no, to the center of the earth. What was his betrothed saying?

"How?" It was a stupid question. He knew how it happened. But words and thoughts weren't cohesive now.

Millie looked him straight in the eye. "I was the reason we had to leave Ohio. I was pregnant with Matthew, and my shame caused us to leave for Santa Fe."

She reached out to touch his arm, but he brushed it away. "Who is his father?"

"Cade. Cade Ellis. He went to school with me. He was a little older. One day he offered to walk me home."

Paul couldn't stomach the thought of this Cade touching her—taking advantage of her. He clenched his fist at his side, wishing he had somewhere to direct the anger flowing through his veins.

"He was so sweet."

Sweet? Bull.

"I thought I was in love with him."

What was she saying? That she willingly gave herself to this man? That wasn't the Millie he knew.

"It was innocent at first. Just kissing. Nothing more. Then he told me to meet him in the barn that night."

His anger burned deeper as the truth unfolded. His sweet Millie was anything but.

"He told me he would marry me. That it was alright if we..." She glanced towards Annabel.

He snorted. "So, you gave yourself to him?"

Millie nodded.

"Just once?"

When she made no move, he had his answer.

"How could you!"

"I thought he loved me."

"So, he bedded you but wouldn't marry you?" He was having a hard time believing all of this. If he had gotten an innocent girl pregnant, Ma would have made him marry her. Honestly, Ma would have made him marry her if she even got wind of a dalliance.

"No. I learned later that he... He had been with several girls. He was forced to marry one of the others."

Paul started pacing back and forth. The fire in his veins wouldn't quell. He had trusted her. He had believed she was innocent. It was just so sad that she hadn't married before.

Realization dawned. "This is why that Joel fellow cast you aside, isn't it?"

"Please, Paul—"

"Isn't it?"

"Yes."

He didn't want to be around her for one second longer. She had betrayed him. She lied to him. He stormed into the storage room and grabbed a few personal items.

Where was he going to go? He didn't own the placer anymore. He couldn't go there.

Ma. He needed to talk to his ma. He would go to the ranch for a few days. Cool off there.

With things in hand, he stormed back outside. Millie stood there listlessly, tears streaming down her face. Annabel leaned into her side. Matthew remained on the stairs, head in his hands. Ben stood next to Ma. He hadn't noticed her there before. She must have heard the entire exchange.

"Where do you think you are going?" Ma asked.

"With you. I need some time away."

Millie reached for his arm. "What about the boardinghouse?"

"I'll ask Thomas to check on things while I'm gone."

"When will you be back?"

"Dunno."

He tossed his things in the back of the wagon and headed towards the livery to talk to Thomas. Millie called his name a few times. He refused to turn around. How could she lie to him like that? How could she pretend to be so innocent and sweet when she knew all along that she had a son?

His visions of a happy family started to slip away.

———

Millie watched as Paul stalked away. Numb. Fearful that he would come back and cast her aside too. Hadn't the Lord forgiven her? Why then, did the mistakes of her past threaten to undo her future?

243

"Ma'am." Matthew stood and faced her. "I don't know exactly what to do with what you've told me."

He studied her eyes. Looking into his eyes was like looking into a mirror.

"My pa told me once that I came to live with him, and Mama differently than most kids come to live with their parents. I had asked him why I didn't look like them. Anyway, I've always suspected something. But what you've just told me, well, I just ain't sure what to do with it."

Her earlier joy started to shrivel. "I understand."

Matthew reached out and touched her arm. "No, ma'am, I don't think you do. I ain't saying I disagree with what you're saying. I'm saying I need some time to think it all through. Maybe I could come out on the deliveries next week and we could talk some more."

Hope. Refreshing, purifying hope filled her heart—well, only part of it—the part that held such love for her son.

"I'd like that."

"If you'll excuse me, I need to finish the deliveries now."

"See you next week, then." The words she wanted to say stayed in the recess of her heart. *I love you, son.*

Ben cleared his throat. "We best be on our way, too." He steered Betty back toward the wagon.

"But who is that girl?" Betty put up a fuss.

"Never ya mind that right now." Ben's words were firm, but not sharp.

Millie appreciated his help. She wasn't sure what she would have said to Betty with Paul in such a mood. How could she claim Annabel as hers if Paul decided to cast her aside? He made it clear a few days ago that Annabel would be his daughter alone, should they not be wed.

Why had she insisted on knowing the answer to that question? Would she be better off now if she had reason to believe he would come back to her because of Annabel?

No. It didn't matter. All of this was her fault. She should have told him the other night. No, she should have told him weeks ago. Perhaps he would have taken it better. Could she really blame him for being upset?

Then there was Matthew. The son she longed to see again. She never would have envisioned their reunion would happen this way.

As Ben pulled the wagon away, Matthew followed on his horse. She was certain Paul would meet up with them before they left town.

"Can I go see Kitty again?" Annabel asked.

Millie smiled down at the young girl. "Later. We need to get lunch started or Mr. Lowrey might miss his meal."

She led the way back into the house to the kitchen, letting out a huge sigh. She gained a daughter and a son in a few short days, but had she lost her only hope for a husband?

Tears threatened, but she willed them away. *Lord, be with Paul. Help him to see that I didn't mean to hurt him. I love him so. Please…*

Not her will, but God's be done. If He took Paul from her—and even Annabel and Matthew—He would still guide her steps and be with her every day. She would survive. Maybe.

CHAPTER 43

The ride out to Colter Ranch seemed to take an eternity. Paul wanted to press the horse from Thomas's livery hard. Riding at a gallop would at least take more concentration than the slow walk next to the wagon.

His mind pictured a younger Millie acting out the scene she described to him. Her words made it clear. Her time with this Cade fellow had been deliberate. She knew full well what she did was wrong, but she kept inviting the man into her bed. She was anything but innocent.

A low growl settled in the back of his throat. He stifled it before it erupted. His muscles twitched with pent up anger that had no place to vent.

This could not be happening to him. Hadn't he lived a good life? Well, at least the last fifteen years or so. Didn't he deserve some happiness? Why couldn't Millie have turned out to be the sweet woman he thought she was?

As they crested the last hill, he pushed the horse to a gallop down into the valley that nestled Colter Ranch. In a matter of seconds, he stopped the lathered horse in front of the stables. Adam Larson greeted him and offered to see to the horse. He accepted the offer and pulled the saddlebags and bedroll from the horse's back.

With the anger partially satiated, he took deliberate strides towards his mother's cabin. He let himself in and dumped his things in a corner. Then he paced the short length of the one room cabin.

"Just what do you think you are doing?" Ma said as she entered the cabin.

Paul should have known she wouldn't stay quiet for long.

"She lied to me."

"Did she? I supposed in the few short months since you've known her that you've covered all thirty-eight years of *your* history."

He clamped his mouth shut. He knew better. When Ma's got something in her mind, he had two choices. Listen or pretend to listen. And, if she thought he was doing the second—well, there'd be trouble for him.

"I understand her having a son came as a shock to you. Did to me too. But that doesn't change her character. She is still a godly woman. She's still the sweet gal you fell in love with."

His anger burned again. "How much of our conversation did you hear?"

"Enough to know—"

"She willingly gave herself to that—that man. More than once. And she wasn't married."

"And she's paid the price for that for twenty-four years. Don't you think that's long enough?"

"What price do you think she's paid, Ma?"

Ma squared her shoulders and took a deep breath. "She paid the price of lost love. She had to wake up every morning of every day knowing she gave her son away. Did you see the look in her eyes? She loves that boy. Never a day went by where she didn't. You could tell."

"So, you're taking her side?" Paul threw his arms up in the air and headed toward the door. The cabin felt too small. Too stuffy.

Ma grabbed his arm. "I am not taking sides." She tugged his arm. "Come, sit."

"Let go." He had to breathe. He had to get out of there.

"Fine. I'm just trying to keep you from destroying your last chance for happiness."

"Last chance?" He whirled around to look at her.

"Yes. Have you forgotten?"

What was she talking about?

Her voice softened. "You have."

Paul narrowed his eyes. Ma never did fight fair.

"Go." She waved her hand towards the door. "Cool off while I get supper started."

He hesitated. If he left, she'd win. If he stayed, she'd win. Letting out a low growl, he flung the door open and stormed out.

Last chance? Just what was she getting at?

Then a memory from long ago started to form a fuzzy image in his mind. He headed toward the pond at a brisk pace, hoping it would stay buried.

There had been a girl. Once. A long time ago. He had forgotten about her. Now he struggled to find her name.

Back then, it had been painful—as if she had cut his heart out of his chest. He had been twenty. Still hot-tempered, but not as bad as he once had been.

Nora. It had been a good decade since he thought of her. She was as sweet on him as he had been of her. Until he caught her kissing another man—the one she ended up marrying.

Suddenly, the agony of betrayal felt as hot as the day it happened. Or perhaps it was the betrayal he felt from Millie that sent fire through him now.

What hurt the most about the time with Nora was that he had finally gotten his life straightened out. He stopped carousing and drinking. He was turning into a responsible man. Yet, Nora took his heart and tore it in two as if it meant nothing to her.

He didn't need to go back inside the cabin and ask Ma what she was getting at. She felt that he was overreacting to Millie's secret because of what happened with Nora.

Paul kicked a rock into the pond. Ma always did have a way of getting to the heart of a matter.

He shook his head, ashamed of how he reacted. He shouldn't have treated Millie so unfairly. This was something from her past. Something she couldn't take back. She probably wished she could. It was done and it had irreversible consequences. He knew other women who had been shamed by a poor choice or who suffered the results of a forceful man. The scorn of others as they looked upon them.

Goodness, even Thomas and Caroline could be counted among their number. Hadn't their first child nearly been out of wedlock? Yet, he didn't look on them with disdain for past mistakes. He didn't judge them harshly.

So, why was he being so bullish towards Millie?

Because this time his heart was involved. He was angry at himself for assuming she was some perfect innocent woman instead of getting to know her.

Had she tried to tell him before? He mentally walked through several of their conversations—especially the ones about children. He assumed her quiet sadness was because she longed to have children, not because she had one that she was separated from. He could have pressed her about her feelings. He could have asked more questions.

Foolish. So foolish to think that a woman could spend thirty-eight years on this earth and not have some secrets.

He sank to his knees by the edge of the pond. He loved her. If he was honest with himself, he believed God orchestrated the timing of their meeting. Had he met her years ago, he would not have been ready to marry her. Had he met her later… Well, that was too hard to speculate.

In his mind he could hear her sweet voice lifted in worship. He closed his eyes, imagining she stood next to him in the pew at the church they helped build. Such true worship could only come from a heart centered on God.

He opened his eyes to see the sun dip below the horizon. He would return to Millie in the morning—too late to do so now.

"Forgive me," he whispered, unsure if it was to his beloved or to his Heavenly Father, for he sought forgiveness from both.

———

As she cleaned up after breakfast the next morning, Millie fought against the feelings of failure and guilt. Annabel had asked her at least a dozen times between last night and this morning when Paul would be coming home. Her response was the same each time. Soon.

She hoped it was true—that he would come home soon and that he would forgive her. That he would still love her and not cast her aside.

Perhaps a hymn would lift her spirit.

How much the drooping hearts revive
Of those who fear the Lord;
When sinners dead are made alive
By his reviving word!

The ministers of Christ rejoice,
When souls receive the word--
When ransomed sinners hear his voice,
Return and love the Lord.

Return and love the Lord. She did. She loved the Lord more today than when she first came to Prescott. She learned to let go of the pain and guilt that plagued her for decades about what she did with Cade and for giving Matthew away. She received His forgiveness.

Yet, she still longed for Paul's forgiveness. Was it wrong to be so restless until she knew he would accept her again?

I love him so. He is the other part of me—the part I've been miss-ing for so long. I could not bear it if he turned his back on me.

A commotion at the front of the house caught her attention. She set aside the last of the dishes and wound her way through the house to the porch. Paul stood there, twirling Annabel around in his arms.

She exhaled as if she held her breath for the last day.

"Mr. Paul! You came back!"

How selfish she suddenly felt. Poor Annabel had lost so much.

She should have heard the fear in her voice each time she asked where Paul was. Her daughter had much more cause to fear being abandoned than she did. Yet, she focused on her own pain instead of Annabel's.

Annabel giggled as Paul spun her around one more time, then set her gently on the top stairs of the porch.

"I promised you I would be back."

Had he? Perhaps, he had promised the girl, but not her—his betrothed.

"Kitty and I were playing."

Paul smiled. "Go take her back to the barn. I'll be there in a few minutes."

Annabel scooped up Kitty into her arms and ran to the barn.

Millie's breath slowed as Paul looked up into her eyes. He grabbed his hat and worked it in his hands. She waited.

"I'm sorry." Paul let out a heavy breath. "I… It was wrong of me to react the way I did. I was shocked that you had a son. More so that you never mentioned him before now. And I was angry. Angry at the man who… Angry that Cade had lied to you."

He looked down at the ground and kicked at some dirt. "I suppose we've both had our share of secrets. Nearly four decades is certainly more than enough time to build up a few."

Her hands shook and she clasped them in front of her, hoping her nerves would settle. She wasn't sure what to say, so she waited for him to speak again.

"I'm so sorry. I shouldn't have run away. I shouldn't have gotten angry."

He looked up at her again. Then he took all three stairs in one step and was at her side. His hands slid down her arms and took her hands in his.

"I love you more than anything on this earth. Even though I sold the mine for Annabel, you—dear, sweet Millie—you are precious to me. Nothing is more important than you. I loved you the first time I met you and I've just been bungling my way through each day since.

"Your past—well, that's in the past. I'm happy that you found your son. But none of it changes how I feel about you."

She swallowed hard, hoping she understood his meaning. "You… You still want to marry me?"

"Yes! More than anything else."

"Thank you, Lord," she whispered.

Then he lowered his lips to hers, searching for forgiveness, for love. She returned the kiss with a passion that equaled his, hoping he would hear the message of her heart loud and clear. She loved him. Only him. Always him. He deepened the kiss revealing all the promise of a future husband. When he ended the glorious kiss, she leaned into his strength, breathless, but with heart joined to his.

"I hope your father is still coming by the seventh." His voice was husky as he looked into her eyes.

"I sent the letter early yesterday so we should know next week."

"Good."

Millie smiled at him. "Why?"

"Because I don't think I can wait much longer."

Tingles traveled up and down her arms at the look in his eyes. She didn't think she wanted to wait much longer to be his wife.

Then Paul took a step back and pointed toward one of the rockers on the porch. "I just have a few more things to tell you."

What else could he possibly say?

CHAPTER 44

Paul waited for Millie to take a seat. Just how much should he tell her about his past? Still deciding on that question, he figured the safest place to start was to tell her about Annabel.

"Has Annabel said anything to you?"

"About what?" Her forehead puckered in confusion.

He cleared his throat. "What I told you about her family is all true, but I may have led you to believe that it happened more recently than it did."

"When did it happen? Where has she been since then? And what did you mean earlier about selling the mine for her?"

Fool. It was going to break Millie's heart. He should have told her from the beginning. The fear in her eyes spurred him forward.

"The attack that killed her parents happened nearly a year ago. Since then, the ranch foreman—the sole survivor besides her—was keeping her at the ranch. I'm not sure if he mistreated her or not. But a few months ago, maybe more, he sold her to Trent Montgomery."

He gave her a few seconds for the meaning of his words to sink in. Her face lost some color, and she gripped the arms of the chair tighter, until her knuckles turned white.

"You mean she… She worked for him?"

He nodded.

"But she's so young."

Paul swallowed away the lump in his throat. "I know. Thomas and Caroline first met her at the mercantile. When they found out about where she was, um, living, Thomas asked for my help. When I met Annabel, I clearly heard the Lord ask me to save her. I didn't know exactly how at first."

He watched as tears started to pool in Millie's eyes. "I had no idea."

He reached over and took her hand in his. "I asked how much it would cost to buy her from Montgomery."

"You bought her?" Her hand flew to her heart, and her face grew paler.

"I sold the placer to come up with the money. It was the only way to save her."

"But couldn't you have just taken her away from there? Or asked Sheriff Smith for help?"

"I don't think Sheriff Smith could have helped. If Montgomery got word of the law getting involved, he would have shipped her off to another brothel in another town. She would have been gone before we got back."

Millie withdrew her hand. "I... I don't know what to say. The whole thing... I'm horrified."

He swallowed hard. For Annabel's sake, he hoped she wasn't going to back out.

"I can't begin to understand how such a thing happens. That a little girl—Paul, she's just a girl!"

"I know."

"How can she be sold? And to do... No girl should..."

He felt Millie's anguish. He had reacted the same way when he met little Annabel.

"Will she be alright? Do you think she can have a good life, now, with us?"

Paul let out a long breath. "Yes. With God all things are possible. He can heal her heart. I know He called us to be there for her. I know He fully intended that she would come live with us."

She closed her eyes for a full minute. He waited and watched as her hands relaxed in her lap and the color returned to her face.

"I pray God will guide us in how to best help her. For now, you should go check on her. You promised."

He stood. "We still have more to talk about."

"It's fine. We can talk this evening."

He pulled Millie to her feet and kissed her cheek. "It will be alright. She'll be alright."

"I know."

Releasing her from his arms, he turned and headed toward the barn to check on their daughter.

———

Millie sat back down as she watched Paul walk toward the barn.

Her heart rejoiced when he came back, but now it was breaking for poor Annabel. What had she endured? Dare she even ask such questions? Or was it better to let Annabel speak of things if she desired?

What had they gotten into? An orphan was one thing. Grief over losing a parent she could understand. But this? She was ill-equipped for such a task.

Yet hadn't she learned that God had a purpose for her life. If it was to be a mother to Annabel, would He not give her all she needed to do what He called her to do?

She sighed, hoping it would lighten her heart.

When Paul returned with Annabel a few minutes later, he sent Annabel inside. "Why don't you and I have a picnic lunch in the square? We can ask Caroline to look after Annabel, and we can send the boarders to the dining hall for their meal."

"Alright."

Millie walked over to the dining hall to let the Pengs know they might expect a few more people for the midday meal. Then she made the rounds for any borders still in the house while Paul took Annabel over to Caroline's.

In a few minutes, she gathered some leftover roast beef and bread for sandwiches. Paul returned and carried the basket as he led them to a shady spot under a tree.

It was warmer than she would have liked for an outing but sitting in the shade wasn't so bad.

Once they were seated, Paul took her hands in his. "Lord, bless this food and bless this time for Millie and me to learn more about each other."

"Amen."

She waited patiently as they ate, wondering what else he had to say. Hadn't she already forgiven him and he her?

"So, I know your deepest secret?" Paul asked.

She nodded.

"Then I suppose it is only fair to tell you mine."

The last bite of her sandwich tasted dull and sticky as she swallowed it. She wasn't sure she wanted to know. "You don't have to tell me if you don't want to."

His eyes were tender. "I want to. I want you to know all about me and the things that shaped the man I am today."

She nodded again to let him know he should continue.

"My father passed when I was a young man—barely even a man. From the day of his death until just a few years ago, I cared for my ma. Back then, that meant acting like a pa to my sisters and brother. I grew to resent the responsibility.

"A few years later, I started drinking and… I got into fight after fight. By then, I was done growing, and I knew my size gave me an advantage over just about everyone. And I used it to my advantage. 'Bout drove Ma insane with the number of times I didn't come home until the next morning after sleeping off a night of drinking and fighting.

"The worst encounter was when I came home drunk and nearly beat my sister's beau to death. Ma had to level the shotgun at me to get me to stop.

"Anyway, not too long after that, I came to the Lord. Things were pretty good for a while. I met this girl, Nora. She was sweet and pretty. She was one of the few women that knew about my bad days, but she still seemed to care.

"Until I caught her kissing on another man."

Poor Paul. He knew as much about rejection as she did.

"I suppose it was for the best that we hadn't gotten married. She ended up marrying the other fella. I focused on raising my youngest two siblings and helping my ma. Eventually I forgot all about her, until Ma mentioned her yesterday."

Millie reached for his hand. When he took it, he looked directly at her. A soft smile graced his lips. His blue eyes sparkled.

"Guess God thought both you and I could stand to wait awhile before we found each other. I honestly gave up hope of marrying a long time ago. Didn't expect to find love in the wild Arizona Territory."

"Me either." She never thought she would find love at all. But love him she did. With all her heart. "None of what you've said changes how I feel about you. I know the man you are. The one you were—well, that doesn't matter."

He scooted over next to her and put his arm around her shoulders.

"Thank you, sweet Millie." He placed a kiss on the top of her head. "Now, what do you say we get hitched real soon?"

She smiled as she looked out over the town. Her eyes rested on the spot where she first met him as she got off that stagecoach. "Just waiting for Dad to get here."

He laughed. "Yeah, I suppose we can wait a few more days."

CHAPTER 45

The memory of the Apache camp haunted him, even as he tried to convince himself it was justice. He'd finally worked up the courage to act, but now...

Jake shook his head, trying to push away the images. The faces of the women and children looked nothing like the savage warriors who'd killed his family. But it was too late for regrets now. What was done was done. He took another drink, hoping to wash away the taste of ash and the sound of screaming that echoed in his mind.

They started this war, he told himself. *Ma and Sissy deserved justice.* But the justification felt hollow, even to him.

He watched the camp for a few nights. From the activity, it was clear the men were getting ready to set off for another hunting trip. They would be gone for days, maybe even weeks.

After the men departed, he rode out to Fort Whipple. Most of the time he wouldn't bother with the Army. But he heard rumor that their orders were clear. They were to hunt down any hostile Indian that threatened the settlers or the town of Prescott.

With a few words to the major at the fort, he convinced the Army to ride with him. He had an easy target—one that was sure to hit home to those savage Apache and avenge his ma and Sissy.

So, under the cover of night, Jake, along with the Army, swooped down on the unsuspecting camp full of women and children. They had nothing but bows and arrows and rocks to defend themselves. They stood no chance against the carbines and Dragoon revolvers of the Army. In less than half an hour, they killed them all.

The major took his plan one step further. They burned down the entire camp, including the storehouse of grain and grass seed the Indians gathered throughout the spring. The small crop of maize and squash were ripped from the soil and left to rot and die. Instead of burying the dead women and children, the major piled up their dead bodies and burned them.

For a brief second, Jake considered his actions. No need to feel guilt over spilling injun blood—not after what they did to his ma and sister.

He took a long drink from his whiskey bottle before tossing it aside, empty. There was one more Indian that needed his attention. That woman who passed herself off as white. He could not let Paul marry her. She would ruin his life.

He spat at the ground. He still couldn't believe the sheriff sided with her. Sheriff Smith told him if he had harmed her, he would have made sure Jake faced trial. Imagine that. A white man being tried for ridding the town of an Indian.

Oh, he would make Sheriff Smith eat those words. He wouldn't kill her. Didn't want to risk calling the sheriff's bluff. No, this time he would use the law to his advantage.

He stood and brushed the dirt from his trousers. Then he mounted his horse and rode into town, stopping in front of the courthouse.

Once inside, he gave his name to the clerk. "Judge Radcliff is expecting me."

Another great idea.

"Waters. To what do I owe this visit?"

Jake followed the judge into a private room.

"Iffen' you heard of an illegal wedding being planned, would you stop it from happening?"

Judge Radcliff frowned. "I suppose so."

"Good. Then you must stop Miss Pritchett from marrying Paul Lancaster."

The judge cleared his throat. "And why's that?"

"'Cause Miss Pritchett is an Indian."

Judge Radcliff considered his words. "Just what did you have in mind?"

Jake told the judge of his plans. For once, it was nice to have the law on his side. He left the courthouse, his plan in motion.

CHAPTER 46

August 7, 1869

There was a time when she thought her wedding day would never arrive. And there was a time when Millie thought it would arrive too soon—when she was pregnant with Matthew. Never had she pictured a wedding in the town square surrounded by tall pines and stark clapboard buildings. Nor had she pictured standing in front of her chosen man with her adult son standing just a few feet away.

In her dreams, she pictured the day years ago in Santa Fe—before Mom passed on. Dad giving her away. The man that stood waiting for her never had a face, never had a name.

The man had a name now—Paul Lancaster—and quite a handsome face. Instead of Santa Fe, the wedding was in Prescott. Instead of her mother pinning her hair, it was Mabel. And her two children, Matthew, and Annabel, would be among the guests. Yes, the long-awaited day arrived at last, even if it looked far different from what she imagined.

When Matthew stopped by for the afternoon late last week, she still felt very nervous about seeing him. She couldn't believe he was here, in the same town as her. To think of how far away and how long ago she left him. It was solely God's doing that she was blessed to see her son face to face.

He had been cautious at first. He told her he always had this restless streak—this longing he couldn't understand. When he gave his life to Christ, he thought that feeling would go away.

But it hadn't. Not until that very moment when he was talking to her, his birth mother.

She cried for sorrow over the years they missed and for joy for the years they had in front of them. Then she told him more about his father and how he came to be. It was hard admitting her mistakes again, yet she felt such peace over the release of all her secrets. There was no more condemnation.

Matthew left that day with the promise to return soon.

"There," Mabel said. "You look lovely. Your mother would be so proud of you."

Tears threatened. She never envisioned this day without her mom. It was hard not to think of her now. How she missed meeting her grandson and granddaughter. How she missed meeting the most important man in Millie's life. The emptiness was real, no matter how much Mabel tried to make it seem less so.

"There, there." Mabel drew her close for a hug.

"Thank you." She took a deep breath and let it out slowly, calming her sorrow and her nerves.

"It was my pleasure. Now, let's see if we can't get this wedding started."

Millie smiled and followed Mabel out of the room. She looked around one last time before closing the door on that chapter of her life.

"Oh! So pretty!" Annabel rushed forward to hug her.

A moment of sadness clouded this joyous moment. Annabel had yet to call her by name or call her "mother". She longed to have that close connection with the girl. From the first moment they met, Millie had completely opened her heart to her. How could she do anything less? She was a precious child and already thriving under their love. Still, she wished Annabel would let her in.

"Give it time, dear." Betty patted her arm. "She's been through much."

Millie smiled, not surprised that Paul told his mother the entire story of Annabel's past.

"You look beautiful. My son is lucky to have you."

Caroline gave her a hug. "I just hope he knows how lucky he is. Do you know how hard it is to find a housekeeper in this town?"

Millie laughed. "I think I do."

"Does he know he's losing his housekeeper today?" Mabel asked.

"I think so. But he's gaining so much more," Betty said. Then she placed a kiss on her cheek. "I'm so proud to call you daughter today."

"Oh, the quilt!" Millie ran back to her room and opened the trunk at the foot of her bed. After all this time, the quilt she made for her wedding day would finally have a new home.

"It's beautiful," Betty said. The other ladies murmured similar compliments.

"I'll take care of it," Caroline said, holding out her hands.

Millie slowly relinquished the quilt. She hoped Paul would love it as much as she did. Tears burned her eyes, but she blinked them away. It was finally her time.

As she stepped into the parlor, her dad stood to his feet, tears in his eyes. She rushed to his side.

"What's wrong?"

"Nothing, sweetheart. Nothing at all. I'm so glad you finally get to celebrate your wedding day. You've picked a fine man."

"The only one for me."

Dad laughed. "Don't I know it! Ready?"

She nodded as the emotion clogged her throat, making it impossible to say what she really meant. She was more than ready to become Paul's wife. She was more than ready to raise Annabel with him. She was happy her dad was here. Sad that her mom wasn't. Excited about the future. Hopeful for tomorrow. Thankful for the past.

She would no longer be Miss Millie Pritchett. She would finally become Mrs. Paul Lancaster.

The thought brought a rush of warmth to her stomach. How she loved him so.

"I'm ready," she said, letting her dad lead her out the door of the boardinghouse toward the crowd gathered to witness her biggest dream come true.

CHAPTER 47

"Stop pacing. You're going to kill that patch of grass before the ceremony starts," Thomas said.

Paul returned to his designated spot in front of the preacher. He let out a long, slow breath. He was too nervous and excited to stand still, but he tried his best.

A moment of disappointment distracted him. Jake should have stood up for him beside Thomas. He wanted to shake his head, still not understanding what happened to his friend or why he had betrayed him so.

"Here she comes," some of the crowd whispered.

Paul pushed aside those regrets and turned. He stared at his bride as she walked toward him. A huge grin lit her face. His gaze settled on those violet eyes. So deep. So beautiful.

Never had he imagined himself married to such a quiet, shy woman. So different from his ma. Yet, they shared a similar strength, one born out of faith and perseverance.

He glanced over at Annabel as she stood in the front row next to his ma. He gave them a wink and Annabel waved back. What an honor it was to be trusted to raise and love such a dear child. He hoped one day she would call him "pa".

His gaze returned to Millie, his lovely bride. Until that moment he didn't realize just how much he longed for a wife of his own, one that complemented him in every way. Patient, kind, gentle, loving. How wonderful it would be to share the rest of his life with her.

Millie took the last step to stand beside him. As soon as her father stepped back, she looped her hand into the crook of his arm. Pastor Page began the ceremony by speaking words of blessing over them.

As they started saying their vows, a commotion off behind the pastor in the square caught his attention.

"Stop! You can't marry a half-breed Indian!"

Paul tensed as he recognized the voice. Jake Waters.

Pastor Page stopped in mid-sentence and turned toward Jake. "Move along Jake."

"Ain't right. You can't marry that—"

"Careful, Jake, that's my wife you're about to slander." Paul leaned toward the man ready to spring into action should he do anything other than turn and walk away.

"Paul, please do something," Millie pleaded with him.

"Stay where you are." Judge Radcliff joined Jake, now only a few feet from Paul.

"What's the meaning of this?" Reverend Pritchett asked.

"Jake says this young lady is Indian. Is that true?" The judge looked at Paul.

He hesitated. It was true that she was part Indian, but he didn't trust the judge's motives, and he wasn't about to hand over his wife.

"If it is," Judge Radcliff said, "Then this proceeding is illegal, and the sheriff will have to take you in."

"Wait a second," protested the sheriff. "Don't drag me into this."

Blood boiled in Paul's veins. He fisted a hand at his side and stepped closer to Jake. "What are you doing?"

"I'm stopping this Apache-loving whore from marrying you."

Paul swung and his fist connected Jake's jaw. It had been years since he touched another man, but he felt no restraint now. "That's my wife you're talking about!"

Jake staggered back, rubbing his jaw. "No, she ain't. She's as red as them Johnny Apache that killed that family on Independence Day. And she is going to ruin your life!"

Paul surged forward again. This time Thomas grabbed one arm and Ben the other. He growled in protest.

———

Millie's eyes burned with tears as she fought against the wave of emotion stirring. *Lord, please!*

Though her vision blurred, she could see the muscles beneath Paul's shirt ripple and jump as Ben and Thomas held him back.

"Ma'am, I'm going to have to ask you again. Are you Indian?" the judge asked.

Her heart pounded—torn between her love for Paul and love for her mother's people. How could she truly deny either? Yet, she could not just walk away from Paul. She loved him too much. *Don't ask this of me.*

"Her mother and I would like you to leave." Dad stepped forward with Mabel on his arm.

Shock registered on the judge's face. "Is this woman your mother?" He pointed at Mabel, confusion crinkling his brow.

Millie nodded. *Please forgive me.*

Judge Radcliff took a step back. "Very well. I'm sorry for the mistake. It appears I was given some incorrect information."

Jake Waters began yelling hysterically as the judge walked away. "She's Indian. I know she is. Just look at—"

"Leave!" Paul's voice thundered, bringing a rush of quiet to the assembly.

As the sheriff led him away, Jake's shouts turned to sobs. "I just... I couldn't lose him too," he wept, the fight finally leaving him completely. Sheriff Smith's grip on his arm gentled. He'd seen too many men broken by loss in this territory.

Millie's heart ached as she watched Jake's broken form disappear down the street. Despite everything he'd done to her, she recognized the raw grief in his voice--the same desperate pain she'd felt when giving up Matthew.

She squeezed Paul's hand. "We should pray for him," she

whispered. "And maybe... maybe we could ask Sheriff Smith to let us know how he's doing."

Paul nodded, his own anger softening as he saw his friend's true condition. "That's not the Jake I knew. Grief has stolen him away, but maybe we can help him find his way back."

She sighed, letting the fear and tension leave her. A few seconds passed in silence. Then Pastor Page started again with their vows.

Paul took her hands in his as he turned to face her. He met her gaze, and he repeated the vows with determination, his eyes echoing the promise of his words.

Then Pastor Page introduced them as Mr. and Mrs. Lancaster.

"Mrs. Lancaster," she whispered. It all seemed so surreal. Hadn't moments before, her father convinced a judge that Mabel was her mother. Now she was a wife. Paul's wife.

"You may kiss the bride."

Paul pulled her to him. His arms circled around her, and he lowered his head. Then he whispered, "Illegal or not, you're mine." Then he kissed her, stirring her heart and her emotions.

She was his. At last, she had a husband.

The whirlwind of the afternoon faded into the evening. Friends and family departed. Thomas and Caroline took Annabel for the evening, leaving them alone as a newly married couple.

Millie grew nervous after the sun set and the evening turned to night. She sat with Paul in the parlor, but she knew what was coming next. Part of her old guilt threatened her. She shouldn't know, but she did. That was not a gift she saved for Paul and now, she wished she had.

He stood and blew out one lamp, then another. "Come." He held out his hand for her.

When she hesitated, he moved closer and pulled her to her feet. Then his lips lowered to hers. He tasted sweet. As his hands roamed over her back, she kissed him with more fervor. A deep longing rose in her chest. She wanted to be with him, her husband, no matter what her mistakes had been. She was his now. And she would cherish every moment with him.

Epilogue

July 4, 1870

"Come on, Millie!" Paul yanked on one of her braids. "Everyone is waiting for you."

She smiled. "Not everyone. You're not."

He sighed. "I'm trying to, but you're being too slow."

She looked down at her extended belly. In a few more months, it would be flat again.

"Don't even think of blaming Paul Junior."

She stopped. "How do you know the baby will be a he?"

Paul laughed. "I know. Besides, Ma said you're carrying him like he's a boy."

"And you've named him already too."

He smiled. "Of course. With a grandpa named Paul and papa named Paul, does he really have a choice?"

She shook her head.

"There you are!" Caroline exclaimed. "They're waiting."

"I know, I know."

"Then come on!"

"I don't know why I ever let you talk me into this."

"Because, if I didn't, Martha Stanton or Grace Talbert would have," Caroline said. "Better if it comes from your best friend."

As she neared the podium, her heart raced twice as fast. Why had she let Caroline talk her into this?

"Ladies and gentlemen," the mayor started. "It's my pleasure to welcome, Mrs. Lancaster to the stage."

She swallowed hard and leaned against Paul's supportive arms as he led her up the stairs and onto the stage. The band began playing once she stood at the center of the stage.

On cue, she began singing. "My country 'tis of thee. Sweet land of liberty. Of thee I sing. Land where my fathers died. Land of the pilgrims' pride. From ev'ry mountainside. Let freedom ring!"

The remaining verses of the song flowed from her lips. As she started the fourth verse, the crowd joined in.

Our fathers' God to Thee,
Author of liberty,
To Thee we sing.
Long may our land be bright,
With freedom's holy light,
Protect us by Thy might,
Great God our King.

Amen. God was her great King. So much freedom she had come to know over the last year. Blessed under her Heavenly Father's love. Blessed with her husband and daughter—with the unexpected blessing of one more child on the way.

Paul waited for her at the stairs. "You were wonderful."

"Thank you," she said as she descended the stairs.

"Mama, that was beautiful!" Annabel exclaimed as she wrapped her arms around Millie's waist.

Mama. She glanced at Paul. He smiled, knowing just how long she waited for Annabel to call her that. As Annabel ran off to play with some of the Colter and Larson kids her age, Paul slipped an arm around her shoulders.

"What riches we have. Liberty. Freedom. Love."

"But you, dear husband, Matthew, Annabel, and this baby are my greatest riches. You mean so much to me."

"And you to me."

They walked towards the rest of their family. Her heart was full, reveling in the riches she found in such unexpected places.

The son she gave away and found again. A husband to love at last. A daughter to care for. So much more than she could have ever hoped for stepping off that stage on her first day in Prescott, Arizona, over a year ago.

Her heart sang praise to her God who made her new—who makes all things new.

Author's Note

I hope you enjoyed the long-awaited story of Paul and Millie. Parts of this story have been running around in my head for years. Sometime between books 3 and 4 of the Prescott Pioneers Series, the idea of Paul and Millie began to take shape for me. Yet, I didn't feel like it was time to tell their story yet.

As in real life, their story needed time to mature and develop. There were certain things I knew—like their story had to be different. They were both single for a long time. What would cause them to wait so long to marry? How did they feel about it? These questions and more helped shape their story.

There were several other things I knew I wanted to include. One was making Millie part Indian. During the late 1860s and 1870s, the conflict between whites and Indians in the Arizona Territory escalated. This story picks up some of the early rumblings that led to General Crook's first campaign against the Apache in 1872.

I also wanted to capture something special about singing. When I was growing up, my mom and I both sang in church choir. We even sang a few duets together. I sang a few solos. Mind you, I am not trained in voice and, these days, I limit my singing to being one of the many voices singing in worship. But there was an element of that experience that I wanted to bring to you through Millie.

In preparation for Millie's singing, I was fortunate to find a mini-hymnal published in 1840. It only has the lyrics, but that was all I needed to find authentic songs from the era. Most of the songs quoted in this book come from that hymnal.

Paul's interaction with his mother might have caught some of you off guard. After all, in the Prescott Pioneers Series, they seemed to get along well. But we never got to see his point of view in that series. It got me thinking. What would a thirty-eight-year-old mama's boy really think about his ma?

Thank you, dear reader, for joining me on another western tale. I hope you enjoyed *Hidden Prospects*. Keep an eye out for the Arizona Frontier Series that will take you deeper into the Indian Wars.

May God bless you as learn to see the hidden prospects in your own lives.

Blessings,

Karen Baney

SONG REFERENCES

Chapter 3
Nettleton, Asahel (1840). *Village Hymns for Social Worship: Hymn 184.* New York: E. Sands.

Chapter 13
Elliott, Charlotte (1835). Just As I Am (verses 2-3). Retrieved from: http://library.timelesstruths.org/music/Just_as_I_Am/

Chapter 14
Nettleton, Asahel (1840). *Village Hymns for Social Worship: Hymn 426 (verse 4).* New York: E. Sands.

Chapter 39
Nettleton, Asahel (1840). *Village Hymns for Social Worship: Hymn 510.* New York: E. Sands.

Chapter 40
Havergal, Frances R. (1874). Take My Life and Let It Be (verses 4-5). Retrieved from: http://library.timelesstruths.org/music/Take_My_Life_ and_Let_It_Be/

Chapter 41
Nettleton, Asahel (1840). *Village Hymns for Social Worship: Hymn 184 (verses 1-2).* New York: E. Sands.

Chapter 43
Nettleton, Asahel (1840). *Village Hymns for Social Worship: Hymn 426 (verses 1-2).* New York: E. Sands.

Epilogue
Smith, Samuel Francis (1831). My Country Tis of Thee. Retrieved from: http://library.timelesstruths.org/music/Take_My_Life_and_Let_It_Be/

ABOUT THE AUTHOR

Karen Baney is passionate about writing stories full of flawed characters. She enjoys weaving together stories of second chances, redemption, and overcoming personal trials. As a transplant to Arizona, she loves researching the state's history and finding ways to seamlessly incorporate real history and real settings into her novels. In addition to writing and speaking, Karen works as a Software Development Manager for a Christian ministry.

Her faith plays an important role both in her life and in her writing. Karen and her husband, Jim, make their home in Gilbert, Arizona, with their two dogs, Bella and Daisy. Both Jim and Karen are active at Rock Point Church in Queen Creek, Arizona.

Discover faith-laced stories with characters who feel like lifelong friends.

Visit www.karenbaney.com to discover more historical romance series set in the American West. Follow Karen's writing journey and get behind-the-scenes glimpses of her research adventures on social media.

Facebook:	@AuthorKarenBaney
X:	@karen_baney
Instagram:	@AuthorKarenBaney
BookBub:	Follow Karen Baney for new release alerts

———

Want More Arizona Territory Romance?

Get a FREE book featuring characters connected to the Pioneers series! Plus exclusive updates on new releases, special offers, and historical insights from the frontier.

Subscribe at: books.karenbaney.com/perry-quinn-story

BOOKS BY KAREN BANEY

HISTORICAL WESTERN ROMANCE

Prescott Pioneers Series:
Step back in time to the wild, untamed Arizona Territory where survival depends on grit, faith, and the courage to start over. Follow three pioneer families—the Andersons, Colters, and Larsons—as they risk everything for the promise of a new life in a land that demands both strength and hope.

A Dream Unfolding
A Heart Renewed
A Life Restored
A Hope Revealed
Hidden Prospects

Desert Manna Series:
Sometimes the most beautiful love stories bloom in the desert. Set in the growing frontier town of Prescott during the early 1870s, these tender romances follow women rebuilding their lives after heartbreak and the unexpected men who help them discover that second chances at love are worth the risk. Set in Prescott, Arizona between 1871 - 1873.

Beauty for Ashes
Joy for Mourning
Oaks of Justice

Colter Sons Series:
Power, legacy, and forbidden love collide in this sweeping family saga set in the Arizona Territory. The Colter ranch empire has weathered decades of frontier life, but now family secrets and buried betrayals threaten to destroy everything. As five brothers—

and one resilient sister—navigate the treacherous waters of love, loss, and redemption, they must decide what's worth fighting for. Set in Prescott and other locations within the Arizona Territory in 1887 - 1906.

The Reluctant Cattleman
The Roaming Adventurer
The Railroad Magnate
The Resourceful Stockman
The Restless Wrangler
The Resilient Bride

Larson Sisters Series
Meet the next generation! These delightful novellas follow the three daughters of Adam and Julia Larson from the *Prescott Pioneers Series* as they navigate love, courtship, and finding their own happily ever afters in territorial Arizona in 1886 – 1894.

In Love at Christmas
In Love with the Rancher
In Love with the Horse Trainer

CONTEMPORARY ROMANCE

Vargas Ranch Series:
Love is in the air at the Vargas Guest Ranch & Resort near Wickenburg, Arizona. Meet the Vargas family—five swoon-worthy brothers and their cousins who live by their family motto: "We do not deviate from the Lord's plan." These rugged cowboys run a successful working ranch and luxury resort while navigating the rollercoaster of finding true love.

Falling for a Fake Cowboy

Falling for a Real Cowboy
Honeymoon with a Real Cowboy
Falling for a Shy Cowboy
Falling for a Bossy Cowboy
Falling for a Smart Cowboy
Falling for a Humbug Cowboy
Falling for a Devoted Cowgirl
Falling for a Pregnant Cowgirl
Falling for a Cowboy's Legacy

<u>Steadfast Love Series:</u>
The *Steadfast Love* series follows a close-knit group of friends as they navigate the beautiful mess of modern life in the Phoenix area—workplace drama, complicated families, and love that shows up when they least expect it. These contemporary romances blend emotional depth with authentic faith, reminding us that even when life unravels, God's love never does.

The Heart I Rescue (prequel)
The Air I Breathe

Will one interview change my life forever?

Mama knew a secret about me...

My name is Sam Colter, and I am the misfit of my family.

Papa wants me to take over the family ranch. I don't think I'm the right son. Will I disappoint him or figure out how to run it successfully?

Then my life turned upside down when a journalist showed up.

The journalist dug into my parents' past. Found a secret about me that rocked me to the core.

Can I get over the shocking family secret and what it means about me?

It was my job to protect the ranch, and I failed. Worse yet, I find myself falling for the woman who betrayed me.

Is she the one? Can I forgive her?

Only the good Lord, and maybe Mama, knows for certain. 1887 is gonna leave a mark.

Set near Prescott, Arizona Territory in 1887.

DESERT LIFE MEDIA

Desert Life Media: *There Is Life in The Desert*

Entertainment-first Christian fiction set in the Southwest, featuring redemption, family, and faith

Publishing clean, wholesome, and uplifting fiction since 2010

If you enjoyed Karen's storytelling and crave more action-packed western adventure, discover R.J. Sloane's *The Rustler Hunter* at desertlifemedia.com

www.ingramcontent.com/pod-product-compliance
Lightning Source LLC
Chambersburg PA
CBHW020541020726
47494CB00006B/1862